MONSTERS

The Complete 4104 Serial Novel

by
PHIL ELMORE

IRE Press
Tampa, FL

Published by IRE Press

An Imprint of League Entertainment, LLC.

Tampa, FL

This is a work of fiction. Names, characters, places and incidents are either the product of the author's imagination or are used fictitiously. Any resemblance to actual persons, living or dead, events or locales is entirely coincidental.

Created by Phil Elmore

Cover Art by Johnny Atomic

Edited by Deanna Hoak

ISBN: 978-1-940139-95-1

Printed in the United States of America

For

M.A.E.

A Kind Heart

"You have to share," said Annika. "Sharing means you have a kind heart."

Harlan "Pedro" Willis smiled with his mouth closed. His teeth were stained and rotten and he knew she would notice. They always noticed. It wasn't so bad once you got a few drinks into them. But they always noticed.

He shifted on the plastic edge of the sandbox. Wiping sweat from his palms on the fabric of his jeans, he took up the plastic shovel. This he gave to her. She plucked it eagerly from his hands. It was bright and yellow and had a character's face painted on its plastic blade.

"Thank you," she said. "My name is Annika. What's yours?"

"Pedro," he said. He smiled again. "Are you here all alone?"

"You don't look like a 'Pedro,'" said Annika. "I'm twelve. I like this park. I was on the swings before, but I decided I wanted to play in thc sand."

The little playground was quiet, screened from the adjacent motorways by double stands of trees and a fence that was used to secure it at night. The dampening effect rendered the nearby traffic almost silent. There were surveillance poles at either end, but these had been repeatedly vandalized. They were currently inoperative. Willis checked the sky for drones. It was a beautiful day.

"Are you all alone, Annika?" Pedro asked again. His lips felt dry. He ran his tongue along them. He could feel his fingers, feel the tingling in his fingertips, as he looked at her.

She wore colorful leggings and an oversized sweater bearing knitted flowers. Her hair was gold and reached her shoulders. A purple ribbon held it back. Annika hummed as she dug a trench in the sandbox.

"Daddy said I could play here," she told him. "He said I could play as long as I want."

Willis looked around. The swings, the climbing wall, the gravity well—they were all empty. He scanned the trees around the park but saw no one. The parking lot was empty except for his own truck.

"I have lots of toys," said Willis. "You could come to my house. We could play there."

"I'm hungry," said Annika. "Can I have breakfast?"

"Of course!" Willis said, too quickly, not caring. "All the breakfast you want. Let's go." He held out his hand. She took it.

"Your hand is sweaty," she complained. But she went with him. He hurried her to the truck, feeling his heart hammer in his chest, worried that at any moment her father or some other park-goer would appear and ruin it. He did not start to believe his good fortune until she was seated at his kitchen table, happily eating waffles printed in his dining nook.

His back was to her. The cooler door was open. He held the dropper of benzodiazepine.

He was trying to decide how much to give her, how many drops to put in her orange juice, when she spoke up. "It's warm," she said. "You keep it warm here. Can I play video games?"

"Of course you can, honey," said Willis. "The wessdeck is in the bedroom."

"Okay," said Annika. "But it's so warm. Can you open the

windows in the living room? The big ones? I like big windows."

"Sure, honey," said Willis. He hurried to do it, pocketing the dropper. When he came back to the kitchen she was already drinking the juice. He frowned. "Finish your juice, beautiful," he said. "And I'll fix you some more." His voice cracked. He didn't care.

Annika got up and went to the cooler. She began rummaging through it, making a pile of vacuum-sealed steaks. Then she examined the printer menu. Whatever she saw pleased her. Willis thought she had a beautiful smile.

"Let me show you the games, honey," he said. He could hear his own pleading. Every part of him ached. "Right after you have your—"

"No," said Annika. "I'll play them by myself. Good-bye, Mister Pedro."

The floor creaked. Willis turned, looking for the noise, head down. A very large pair of boots was waiting. The boots were worn by a man. The man was also very large.

Willis looked up and opened his mouth to scream.

The big man folded heavy hands over Willis' face.

And squeezed.

Peyton woke on the living room sofa. It was almost big enough. Sunlight streamed through the open windows. The early breeze was cool. He had slept in his boots, and his feet would be swollen. His joints ached.

He stood and went to the kitchen. Annika had made him steaks and Neggs in the night, leaving them on a plastic-covered plate in the dining nook. He stepped over the dead man on the floor and, plate in hand, ate the steaks with his fingers. He did not eat the Neggs. They had served Neggs in prison.

Annika was in the shower. He would need one as well. He estimated they had a day, perhaps two, before the pedophile's employer or parole officer sent a drone to check on him. Peyton and Annika would need to be gone well before that.

The shower noise stopped. He checked the bedroom down the hall from it. The wireless gaming deck was still powered on. Its game was suspended or paused. Peyton did not understand games, but he had seen them played. He was glad they made Annika happy.

He felt the ambient moisture increase. Annika appeared at his flank wearing several towels, one of which was wound on her head. She paused to hug him. He kissed the top of her head through her towel.

She retrieved her clothes from the cleanser on the bedstand. He turned away while she dressed.

"You're so smart, Daddy," she told him. "He said almost exactly the things you said he would. And he had good games. Do all the men who visit the park so much have good games?"

"Only some of them," said Peyton.

"He must have had a kind heart, to share with us the things we need."

"I don't think so."

"Then you gave him a kind heart," she said, convinced. "He had better food than I thought he would." She looked up at him, briefly concerned. "Did you find your lunch?"

"I didn't eat the Neggs," he told her, nodding. "I don't like them."

"Nobody does," she said.

He waited for her to finish dressing. "When you're ready,"

he said, "it's time for us to go. We'll have to find a new place to stay tonight."

"There are other parks," said Annika.

All Frowny

Peyton reached up and plucked the sensor leads from his chest. The steel table groaned when he turned to sit up. Gorsky looked anxious. The little man had been fretting over his furniture from the moment Peyton arrived.

"Well?" Peyton asked.

"Your implanted glands are operating as they were designed to do," Gorsky said. He wiped his hands, which were reasonably clean, across the front of his coat, which was not. "The growth hormones that maintain your mass are stable, so you shouldn't see any more height or girth. Barring a radical change in diet."

"That isn't what I asked about."

"No," said Gorsky. "The pains you are feeling are due to the build-up of by-product crystals in your joints. Your artificial glands are inefficient. They produce wastes as your body breaks down the hormones they feed it. Was this not explained to you?"

"No," said Peyton.

Gorsky took a step back. "I can prescribe a cleansing agent," he said. "Its effects are . . . unpleasant. I don't carry it here, but I can order it."

"Then order it."

"I'll need quite a bit of money," said Gorsky. He hesitated, then said, "Quite a bit of money *up front*, I mean."

Peyton pushed himself from the table. He landed on his boots so heavily that he rattled the glass-fronted cabinets full of medical paraphernalia. Gorsky was against the wall in heartbeats.

Peyton sighed. He took his ragged shirt from the hook on the wall. He was going to need a new one. Annika would need an entire wardrobe. Peyton had no idea how to shop for clothes.

"How much?" Peyton asked, pulling his shirt across his massive chest. Gorsky cited a figure, practically whispering. Peyton nodded.

He turned sideways and let himself out of the examination room, past the beaded curtains. Annika was watching one of her mysterious computer-generated entertainment programs on the wall screen. There were toys and books in the waiting area as well. There were no patients waiting.

"Are you all done, Daddy?" she asked. She nodded her head at the screen, causing it to switch off, and stood to take his hand. Peyton held out his own and let her grab the edge of his palm. His fist would have enveloped her hand entirely.

"Almost," he said. As they exited into the alley behind the medical shop, the smell of Hongkongtown assailed them. Annika skipped while they walked, deftly leaping over trash and other debris.

"What's wrong, Daddy?" she asked. "You're all frowny."

Peyton paused and looked down at her. The mouth of the alleyway waited, and beyond it, a city nearly as busy at night as it was in the day. He shook his head, started to speak, and stopped. It took him two more tries before he could explain. Honesty was his only option. He lacked imagination.

"I don't know what to do," he said. "As long as we stay in places like this, the police won't find us. But we need things. And I'm not sure if everything we need is here."

"Places like what?" she said.

"This is a privateer zone. Hongkongtown and the sectors around it are free market. Police are paid for here. Subscribing, they call it."

"Subscribing," Annika repeated.

"Nobody here is going to pay to have us brought in. It's too expensive and they don't have reason to care."

"They don't?" said Annika. "I would care if I thought somebody bad was nearby."

"Yes," said Peyton. "But you're special." He offered her a smile before sobering. "I need medicine from Dr. Gorsky." It occurred to Peyton that Gorsky probably had no medical license. Not a valid one, anyway. But his back-alley surgery was the best they could do. And he did seem to understand Peyton's composition.

"I didn't like Dr. Gorsky," said Annika. "He seems nervous. He seems like he would tell people where to find us."

Peyton eyed her curiously. "What makes you say that?"

"I don't know. He just seems that way."

"Well, let's hope not," he said. "But I need money. And we'll need to buy you clothes. And clothes for me. But if we have money we can get those things."

"And your medicine," said Annika. She let go of his hand, skipped to the end of the alley, and looked both ways. Before Peyton realized what she was doing, she was beckoning to him to follow. He lumbered to her and crouched behind, staring out of the alley. She looked up and down the street for a long time.

"What is it?" Peyton asked. There were strips of shops on either side of the street. Many were porn huts and drug dens. There were several whose purpose he could not identify. Most had bars over their windows. One that did not had a picture of an analog clock face painted on its window.

"I want a watch, Daddy," Annika said.

"You . . . want a watch?"

"Yes. May I have one?"

Peyton shrugged. "Sure. Stay close to me."

They crossed the street. Traffic was light at this hour, but there was still plenty of it. Annika had to run to keep up with Peyton's long, heavy strides. She stayed glued to his hip as he pushed open the locked door of the shop. The lock plate came away in fragments.

"We're . . . closed," said the old man behind the counter. His eyes turned wide. Peyton dropped the broken door handle on the floor.

"You don't have to be nice to him," said Annika. Something in her tone was oddly stern. Peyton looked at her, confused. She pointed to the plastic sign adhered to the front window, beneath the hand-painted watch face. The sign bore a code that Peyton did not understand.

"What is that?" he asked.

"He can't have bars on his windows because the police won't let him," Annika said. "He's on the Registry. It's why nobody comes into his store. They see he has no bars and they stay away. He lives on government allowance, I bet."

Peyton glanced around. The glass cases were full of timepieces, some expensive, some cheap. But the glass was smudged and dusty. He looked back the way they had come. Their feet had left tracks in the carpet, which was also laden with dust.

When he looked back, the old man's expression had hardened. He was holding an antique shotgun above the countertop.

"I don't need your trouble," said the man. He gestured with the cut-down muzzles. "Just get out. Get out or I'll blow you in half—"

Peyton reached across the counter and snatched the weapon.

He grabbed it so hard that the old man's hands crashed against the glass of the counter. The man yelped.

"You're very fast, Daddy," said Annika.

Peyton took another step and grabbed the proprietor by the throat. His fist completely encircled the man's neck. Annika skipped around them both, behind the counter, and plucked the disc of the man's phone from his pocket. She let it sit in her palm and tapped a few buttons.

"This says his name is Marachuck," she told him. "It's a nice phone. I would love to have a phone like this."

"Not a good idea," said Peyton. "We'll get you another. Police can track that one. And probably do."

"Oh," said Annika. "That makes sense."

"Please," wheezed Marachuck.

"What was your crime?" Peyton asked. He asked again, and shook Marachuck for emphasis. Something cracked inside the old man.

Annika was already using the phone. Her fingers danced across its screen with practiced ease. "I found some news from two years ago, Daddy. It says he's a wrap-ist."

"A what?" Peyton turned from where Marachuck was quickly becoming a darker red. Annika held up the phone so he could see it. "Rapist. That's pronounced *rapist*."

"What's a rapist?" Annika asked.

"A bad man," said Peyton.

"Why would a bad man have his own store?"

"The privateer zones are full of predators," said Peyton. "These are among the last places they can go, legally. There are more criminals here, as a percentage of the population, than anywhere else. I guess that's why they make them put up window signs. It probably makes somebody feel better." He let go of

Marachuck. The old man made a meaty heap on the floor.

"You dropped him," said Annika.

"He was done telling us things," said Peyton. "Do you need so many watches?" Annika had somehow divined the function of the latches securing the display case panels and had opened two of them. She was scooping watches into a black velour bag the size of a pillowcase, something that had been inside the display.

Annika laughed. "They're not all for *me*, silly."

"How did you know about that card on the window?"

"School," said Annika.

Peyton blinked. "What are you doing with those?"

"Dr. Gorsky had a whole box of these under his sofa," she said. "Watches and phones and metal pens. Pens! Can you imagine? And some other things. Some junk. Some jewelry. Some knifes."

"Knives," Peyton corrected.

"Knives," Annika repeated. "We can pay Dr. Gorsky with the watches. He must like them so much." She stopped and took a gold pocket watch on a chain from the bag. "I like this one," she said. "May I keep this one?"

"It's yours," said Peyton.

She beamed all the way back to Gorsky's. Peyton looked down at her before he knocked on the surgeon's door. "You're very smart," he told her.

"I know," she said.

Nightmares

"Watch your programs, Annika. Keep the door locked."

Annika stood in the doorway to the hourly flat's single bedroom. She looked unconvinced.

"Is it time?" she asked.

"Yes," said Peyton. "I'm going to take the medicine. It will make me feel worse before it makes me feel better. I'm going to need to stay in bed."

"I can stay with you," said Annika. "You need someone to look after you."

Peyton felt himself smile.

"You're a good daughter. But Dr. Gorsky warned me that the medicine has very serious side effects. You may hear me thrash around and yell a lot."

"Why?"

Peyton thought for a moment. "Nightmares," he said finally. "It might give me nightmares. No matter what, Annika, I want you to stay out here and watch the screen, all right? Download anything you want with the prepaid." He handed her the plastic chit with its embedded circuit. "Don't come in. I'll come out."

Annika looked at her shoes, which had faded considerably. "Okay, Daddy," she said.

"Good girl," said Peyton. "And Annika?"

"What, Daddy?"

"If you fall asleep out here, that's okay. I put a blanket on the table. If you wake up and the sun is out again, and I don't come out, don't check on me. Go to the transit station on Harper and wait there. Okay?"

Annika nodded, sullen. She turned and trudged to the wall screen in the living area, switching it on with a jerk of her chin. Peyton waited to make sure she was engrossed in something he could not grasp—he understood none of the programs she enjoyed—and then closed and locked the bedroom door.

The bed groaned when he sat on it. He waited to see if it would collapse. He had snapped two flophouse beds already. This one had a metal frame, however. It held. He took the ampule from the bedstand, removed it from its plastic wrapper, and placed the sharp tip against his neck.

He pressed.

Warmth flooded him. It was not bad at first. Gorsky had warned him that there were many side effects of the cleansing procedure. To rid his joints of the waste crystals produced by his implanted glands required an extremely powerful solvent. Muscle spasms, pain, and hallucinations were all possible results.

Peyton was terrified that he might strike Annika while in the throes of the cleanser. He could easily kill her if he lost control. Each of his fists was larger than her head. But she would be safe in the next room. He would not leave the bed. Not until the drugs had done their work. He reached down and gripped the mattress with his fingers, making the springs squeal.

His limbs grew heavier. He began to sweat. He started to reach up, to pull his shirt off, but thought better of it. Instead he gripped the mattress harder.

Don't let go, he told himself. *Don't leave the bed. Stay on the bed no matter what.*

Pain. It came slowly, building in waves that crashed into him and through him. Soon the waves were pinpoints. The pinpoints became knife wounds. The knife wounds were soon gunshots.

He held out as long as he could before he started screaming.

Knocking. Tapping. "Daddy." Pounding.

Peyton felt his heart hammering in his chest. His face felt tight and cold. His sweat had evaporated. The sheet beneath his neck was stiff with salt.

Knocking. "Daddy." Knocking.

He hadn't thought to turn on a light. It must still be dark outside. That was good. He ran one hand over his face. His skin tingled.

Pounding.

He turned to look at the clock on the bedstand. He couldn't see the display. Had the power gone off?

"DADDY!" screamed Annika through the door.

Peyton threw himself from the bed and crashed into the bedstand. He tossed this aside and heard the clock shatter on the floor. Turning, he stepped again, only to collide with the wall.

Blind. He was *blind.*

Something about the cleanser. A side effect.

Annika was pounding on the bedroom door, screaming his name. With difficulty, he found the handle and threw the latch. He felt her collide with him.

"Police, Daddy! Police! At the front door!"

Peyton knew a moment of complete panic. He couldn't fight the police like this. He couldn't protect her. He could hear them now, pounding on the door outside, announcing their intent to break it in.

"I can't see," he whispered. "I can't *see* anything."

Annika was tugging at his shirt. He started to fold his arms around her, to comfort her, but she wriggled out and up, climbing him, using his shirt for handholds. Then he felt her arms around his neck. She had almost no weight as she hung there, riding on his back, her face inches from his right ear.

"Annika," said Peyton. "The clock. Where?"

"Kneel down, Daddy," she told him. "Left. More. There."

Peyton picked up the shattered clock. Pieces of plastic fell off in his hand, but the heavy rear housing felt intact. The police took their time, but when they were finally ready, the door collapsed under the pneumatic arm of what sounded like a tracked breaching drone.

"They're coming!" Annika said.

Peyton waited half a beat more for the first of the police to clear the drone. The robot would be off-center, near the lock plate. They would have to climb around it. He visualized the square of the door.

And threw.

The clock struck flesh and fouled the first cop's shot. The whine of a projectile skimmed past on his left. He bladed his body to put himself between Annika and the police.

Peyton charged. "The door!" he shouted. "Out through the door!"

Something struck his chest, hard. It burned.

"Left," Annika said. "No, right. Right, Daddy! Hit with your right hand!"

Peyton balled his fist and punched as hard as he could. He felt ballistic armor under his knuckles, heard ribs crack, heard the cop scream. He tried to draw his hand back, felt something cold and hard. His fists came together and he was holding a weapon of some kind. His finger found the trigger. He swung the barrel out and away.

"How many?" he asked.

"One two three!" Annika said. "Three!"

Three men. Armed, ready to shoot. Would the gun he held have a safety switch? ID coding? He held it at waist level and started pulling the trigger. Twice more he felt impacts, felt his flesh tear, felt his own blood leaking from his body. They were shooting him. They were shooting him and he could not see them.

Annika shouted in his ear, crying now. The weapon Peyton held was a flechette launcher, a riot piece. He fanned the barrel from left to right, hosing the room. The gun was deafening in the little flat. He felt warm liquid spatter his face.

This blood was not his.

"Left!" shouted Annika. "Hurry! Shoot!"

Peyton rotated left, fired, and did so again, shifting his point of aim each time. Was that a flash of light? He thought he could see the muzzle blast. The dark was no longer black, but gray. Something burned along his ribs on the right side.

A body hit the floor. The gun no longer fired when he pulled the trigger. He dropped it.

"How many?" he demanded again. He was panting, breathing heavily. His wounds hurt, but not too badly. He would live. He would heal quickly.

"No more," Annika said. She was sobbing into his ear. "No more in here. Turn. Turn more. Go straight."

He listened and obeyed. When the outside air hit his face, the sunlight overpowered him. He fell to his hands and knees, eyes watering. Tears streamed down to splash his hands. He groaned.

"Hurry, Daddy," Annika said. "I see a parked police car." He turned to her voice and now he could see shapes. The shapes were becoming a face.

He grabbed her, held her, hugged her. "Guide me down the street," he told her. "Find the first alley and we'll turn. We need distance from this place."

"Can you see now, Daddy? You're all bloody. Are you hurt?"

"I'm okay. Don't worry. I can't see well, but I think it's getting better." He hoisted her up and carried her under one arm. Tears were still streaming down his cheeks, but he didn't care. His vision was returning. Annika had saved both of them. She had been incredibly brave. He did not know how to explain it to her. He did not try.

She did not speak for a long while, and when she did, he could not hear her.

"What was that?" he asked.

"I told you, Daddy," she said again. "You need someone to look after you."

Hongkongtown

Neiring had to pause at the doorway and put his hands on his thighs. His sudden pallor betrayed him; he was close to being sick.

"I told you," said Mox.

"I should have believed you," said Neiring. He took a moment to compose himself, pulled a coffee-stained handkerchief from his pocket, and put it over his face. Then he stuck his head back through the doorway. Mox gave him a shove and sent him in the rest of the way. Neiring speared the private detective with a baleful glance.

"Don't," said Neiring.

"Touchy," said Mox. The private detective was squat, bald, hairy everywhere a man should not be. His bare scalp was pocked. His overcoat and his skin were wrinkled and worn.

Neiring cared about appearances; Neiring knew that his height, at his slender weight, would look awkward if he did not dress well. His uniform was pressed. It was tailored to fit him. The white lettering declaring him a Governmental Inspector was crisp and defined against the blue-black fabric.

"You nearly pushed me into the crime scene, you idiot."

"Look around you," Mox said. "You think there's anywhere you can step that's not in your precious crime scene?"

Neiring had to admit that the unctuous little man was correct. "Where . . . Where is the rest?"

"Kitchen," said Mox. "The head, anyway."

Neiring pressed the handkerchief more tightly against his face. The walls, the floors, even the ceilings were coated in whorls of blood. At least where it was thin it appeared to be dry. Whoever . . . *whatever* had done this was long gone.

"How is there this much? Does one man even *have* this much blood in him?"

"Anybody'd think you'd never seen a man turned inside out," said Mox. "What are you even *doing* here, Neiring? This isn't a government case. We're still in Hongkongtown, unless they've moved the border again."

"Across the street," said Neiring. "There was a Seven-A. The death of anybody on the dole requires government oversight."

"So?"

"So *he* was murdered, too." said Neiring.

"This is Hongkongtown," said Mox. "People get murdered on the hour. You honestly think there's a connection?"

"Yes, people here kill each other like it's free," Neiring managed a nod through his handkerchief. "But I don't believe in coincidence. Not when both men were killed like *this*."

"Like what?" Mox said. He grinned. It made his round face look fatter.

"The Seven-A practically had his head ripped off," said Neiring. "I don't want to believe there are two people walking around strong enough to do that." Mox followed him into the kitchenette. A lumpen, bloody mass waited in the sink. "What the hell?" said Neiring.

"Crushed it," said Mox. "He ripped it off, crushed it, and dumped it in the sink. There's a couple of legs in the next room. We're still looking for the arms."

Neiring coughed so badly into his handkerchief that he saw

stars. When he looked up again, Mox was looking smug. "What do you get out of this, Moxley?" said Neiring. "You've never lifted a finger that wasn't financed."

Mox shrugged. "The victim had a confidential insurance policy. That's paying for an investigation."

"Which I'm sure will bear fruit," Neiring said.

Mox rolled his shoulders once more. "The dead man's a number on an anonymous policy. It cashes out when his heart chip says he's dead. They pay me up front. I give great due diligence."

"So I've heard in the Redlight," said Neiring. Mox made a rude noise. Neiring pushed past the beaded curtains, checked the . . . legs . . . and then backed out into the main room again. "This place has been stripped," he said.

"Door was open," said Mox. "Security system smashed. Whatever happened, when it was over, the local scavengers came in, took anything that wasn't nailed down. Happens all the time. You leave your car out there overnight, government tags or no, they'll have it gnawed down to the frame by sun-up."

"Hongkongtown," said Neiring quietly. "Mox, there's a local assistance rider in it for you if you give me some departmental cooperation."

"How much?" Mox put his hand on his nearly invisible chin.

"Standard expenses per day," said Neiring. "And I'll buy you lunch when we're done."

"Sold."

Mox was cheaply bought. Neiring would probably get his money's worth. "So," he said. "Do we know who this man was?"

"How would you like to identify him?" Mox asked. "His DNA's unregistered. You won't check what's left of his head against any dental records unless you like puzzles. And you've got to have arms to check prints. Arms with fingers attached, which

I'm not gonna take for granted if we find them."

The inspector had to remind himself that Detective Moxley, despite his cultivated dishevelment, was not stupid. Neiring made a slow circuit of the mostly bare room. Even the furniture had been taken, leaving odd silhouettes in the blood coating the room. Only a broken-down sofa had been left behind. It was crusted with dried blood and gobbets of flesh.

Neiring knelt and peered under the sofa. Taking a canister of glove spray from his pocket, he doused his left hand. Then he reached under the sofa and removed a half-crushed pasteboard box.

"What have you got?" asked Mox.

Neiring shook the box, half expecting to find an ear or an eyeball inside. Instead he found three broken phones and a cheap analog watch. There was nothing else. The face of the watch was cracked.

"Not much, as clues go," said Mox.

"No," said Neiring. "It isn't." He lifted out the watch with his gloved hand. It had a metallic wristband of the type that contracted on springs. From the seams in this he lifted a single blonde hair, long enough to be shoulder-length.

"Could be from one of the locals. Whoever cleaned this place out," said Mox. "Think it might be on record?"

"Maybe," said Neiring, holding the hair up to the light. "If it isn't, this just got a lot more interesting."

Three of the Clock

"One of the clock," said Annika. "Two of the clock. Three of the clock." With each stanza of her little poem, she swung the gold pocket watch on its chain, twirling it around her finger. Peyton smiled down at her.

"'Of the clock?'" he asked. "Why do you say it like that?"

"That's what *o'clock* means, Daddy," said Annika. "Clock towers used to ring the hour. Sometimes they didn't even have hands. People didn't always care about minutes. Things were slower then."

"I guess they were," Peyton said, nodding.

"'Clock' comes from Latin. The original word meant 'bell.'"

"Where did you learn that?" Peyton asked.

"School," she said.

They found the correct alley. Peyton led the way to the trash receptacles at its midpoint. Annika made a face and stayed several steps behind him, covering her mouth and nose. He knelt by the metal bin, reached underneath, and removed the rag-covered bundle he had stashed there previously.

"Do you want this now?" Annika asked. She had tucked her watch back into the pocket of her sweater and produced a slim length of saw. He had been hoping for a diamond blade when, early that morning, he had sent her into the little tool shop three blocks over. This carbide was the best they could do. He would manage.

"Let's wait until we get a little farther down," Peyton told her. "Where it's darkest."

The streets beyond the alley buzzed with ground traffic and pedestrians. At the opposite end of the alley, an enormous gray Sweeper collected trash in its compactor maw. It was fed by a pair of ancient hook-armed robots, machines with no intelligence. A thin figure shrouded by a rain slicker hurried past, dodging puddles in his metal-shod boots. He was followed by a second cloaked man, small enough to be only a boy, chasing after.

Everyone in Hongkongtown was in a hurry. That was good. People who hurried didn't see things.

"Smell better?" Peyton asked.

Annika nodded. She watched, eyes solemn, as he unwrapped the ancient shotgun they had taken from the sex offender's timepiece shop. Peyton broke the double-barreled weapon, removed its shells, and closed it again. Then he sawed through the wooden stock. The carbide moved quickly.

"Is it broken?" Annika asked.

"No," said Peyton. "I'm making it shorter. So I can hide it." He did not tell her why he had changed his mind about the gun. His metabolism, processing the steady stream of hormones and other chemicals fed his body by his implanted organs, had mostly healed his gunshot wounds. But the encounter with the police had shaken him. He needed an edge. He needed a weapon.

He had not needed weapons in prison. Big as he had become, he could kill with his hands more easily than most men could kill with a homemade knife. But this was different. He was back in the world now. He had Annika to think of.

"I'll need friction tape," he said. "For the grip. And it's going to take a while to trim these barrels. I don't know where to get more shells. The two we have look new. I hope they don't blow up the gun."

Annika looked worried. "Should I stay?" she asked.

"No," he said. "Do like we talked about. Between these buildings and on the other side is the entrance to the shopping plaza." He handed her a stack of plastic chits. "We have more cash if you need it."

"We got a lot for all the watches and phones," Annika said, smiling.

"Yes," said Peyton. The chits had come from a robot pawnshop. "Do just like we said this morning. I'll be right here."

"Okay, Daddy," she said.

Annika walked through the gleaming aisles of the shopping plaza. She was carefully counting in her head—not the poem she sang, which was easy to remember—but the running tally of the merchandise she was buying. She did not want to have to put anything back. That would be rude.

She had selected what seemed a reasonable amount of clothing, as well as a pair of bags to put it in. One was pink and small enough for her to carry. The other was an enormous black duffel, which she could barely manage empty. Daddy would be able to lift that easily.

Clothes for him had been harder. She had checked the size of his boots while he slept, and had managed to find a new pair large enough. His clothing size was another matter. She had nearly given up on finding pants or shirts that could fit him until she stumbled across Exercity.

Exercity was an indoor gym, open to the plaza concourse. Gravity equipment at its entrance was in active use by extraordinarily developed men and women. The women had muscles larger than most of the Hongkongtown men she had seen. They wore very little, to show them off. The men, however, wore form-fitting pants and shirts with special logos on them. None of them were as big as Daddy, but a few were close. She watched for a few minutes until she realized: The clothing stretched. It must be of special fabric meant for exercising.

"Can I help you, princess?" asked a man. His voice was very deep, but cheerful. He smiled through thick, white teeth. His skin was the color of pavement. He looked sweaty. An Exercity badge was pinned to his sleeveless shirt, which was stretched over enormous chest muscles.

"I want to get some of those clothes for my daddy," she told him. "For his, uh, for his birthday. He's very large, like you. Do you know where I could get some?"

"We sell them right here in our gift shop, in fact," he said, smiling more broadly. "Follow me."

After that, things had been easy. She worked her way through the plaza, mindful of the time, singing her song. "One of the clock, two of the clock, three of the clock," she whispered. Her watch was safe in her pocket. She checked it now and then.

The robot cart that followed her was a delight. It was like a happy dog, content to stay two paces behind her, waiting patiently while she filled it with nice clothes. The plaza had a crafts-and-repairs nook that even sold a few tools. She paused there and fixed the salesman with her most adult expression.

"Do you have friction tape?"

The man's eyebrows went up. "Why, yes, young lady, we do," he said. "That will be four, please." He handed her the roll of tape, which was rough like sandpaper. Annika handed him four chits.

"Do you have . . . Do you have shells?" she asked.

Something changed in the man's expression. "That would be at the other end of the concourse," he said. "But there are no sales to minors. Do you have identification? They'll want to see some."

She had made a mistake. "No," she said. "I mean, never mind. Thank you." She hurried away. She could see him reaching for a phone on the counter of his little shop window.

She walked quickly, forcing the robot to hurry after her. She still had money left, but Daddy hadn't said she needed to spend it all. They had plenty of clothes now. She would have to forget about the shells, but at least she had gotten him his tape. She took out her watch and pressed the button to release the cover. It was less than ten to three.

"Three of the clock," she told herself. She would need to circle back and take a side corridor in order to leave by the entrance nearest Daddy's hiding spot. She had taken no more than two steps when a firm hand clamped down on her shoulder.

"Excuse me," said a woman's voice. "I'm going to need to read your chip, miss."

Annika turned and found herself staring into the eyes of a woman in a beige uniform who had a gun on her hip and a pair of radio glasses on her face. Annika watched her own face in the reflection of the lenses.

"Privateer law," said Annika, reflexively. Daddy had taught her to say it. "You can't detain me unless I've committed a crime. I'm a free citizen."

"The shopping plaza is private property," insisted the security woman. She was younger than she had seemed at first. Close to her, Annika could see how smooth her skin was. She smelled of soap and moisturizer, but not perfume. Annika supposed that if she were a security guard, she would not wear perfume either.

"I'm shopping," said Annika, pointing to the cart.

"There's a policy posted at the entrance," said the guard. "No unsupervised minors. I'm going to need to take you to the office, miss, until we can get hold of your mother or father."

"No," said Annika. "Don't do that."

The guard's grip tightened on her shoulder. Annika looked down at the woman's hand. The guard's knuckles were white. It made Annika angry. There was no reason to be mean like that.

"You're coming with me," said the guard.

Annika looked back up at the guard until the two locked eyes. With her free hand she held out her pocket watch. "Do you see what time it is?" she said.

"So?" the guard asked.

"If I don't leave here by three of . . . by three o'clock, my daddy is going to come in here looking for me."

"That's what I want," said the guard.

"No," said Annika. "It's not what you want. Nobody wants that. You're mean. You don't have a kind heart. But my daddy can give you one. You won't like it."

The guard stared into Annika's face. Her grip began to ease. She said, "Look, miss, if you've run away from home—"

"You don't understand," said Annika emphatically. She looked at the face of the watch, then back to the guard. "In seven minutes my daddy is going to come here. He's the largest man you have ever seen. He's bigger than the people at Exercity. He's stronger than all of them. And if you make him angry he'll pull all your arms and legs off."

The guard started to laugh. As she stared at Annika, the laugh died in her throat. "I don't—" she started.

"Your arms," said Annika. "Your legs. Your head." She

reached into the cart, took out the roll of friction tape, and ripped off a piece. "As easily as that. And then when all your blood is on the floor and the ceiling and your head is flat and your teeth are in a pile and your arms are in the disposer, we'll take what's in your pockets, anything valuable you have, and you'll never be mean to anybody else again. Just like Dr. Gorsky."

With that, Annika wrenched her shoulder free, slapped the robot cart's override, and nearly ran for the exit with the cart close behind. The guard watched her go, her mouth open, making no attempt to interfere.

Peyton had just finished cutting the barrels from the gun when Annika reappeared. He helped her take the bags from the cart. She was unusually quiet, even for her. Finally, he pushed the return button on the robot. It trundled off in the direction of the plaza.

"Did you get everything, Annika?" Peyton asked.

"I couldn't get your shells," she said. "But I got the tape."

Peyton looked surprised. "You don't need to worry about those things," he told her. "I was just talking out loud. That was, you know, Daddy stuff. Not something for you to worry about."

She looked up at him. He met her gaze and could not interpret her expression. Love? Pride?

"I don't," she said.

"Don't what?" he asked.

"I don't worry about *anything*, Daddy."

Baycon and Neggs

"Daddy?" Annika asked.

Peyton was hunched over the kitchenette table. He was too big to sit on a chair and fit under the table itself, so he sat cross-legged on the floor, his elbows and his chin touching the vinyl overlay of the tabletop. He looked up at her. Annika was standing before the printer, waiting for the warmer to open.

"What is it, Annika?"

"I've been thinking," she said.

"You do that a lot."

She smiled and frowned at him at the same time. He would not have thought it possible had he not seen her do it before. It was as close to exasperation as she got.

"I'm a liability."

That froze him. He stared at her as she brought her plate from the warmer, placed it on the table, and shoved her chair as close to him as she could. When she climbed into her spot, she poked at her Baycon discs and then dug into the Neggs with her spoon. Peyton opened his mouth.

"I—" he began.

"You didn't eat your Neggs," she said.

"I keep telling you. I don't like them."

"Nobody likes Neggs," said Annika, her tone one of long-suffering tolerance. "Neggs are good for you. Neggs have a full complement of thyroid-proactives that help mitigate background rays from the solar flares."

"You read that off the box."

"School," she said.

Peyton sighed. He wondered how many thyroids he actually had. Turning once more to Annika, he made sure she saw him spear a slippery chunk of Neggs with his fork. He chewed deliberately. She nodded.

"Annika," he began again.

She knew. His tone told her. He was not going to let it drop.

"I'm serious, Daddy," she said. "I'm not fast or strong like you. And I saw on the news. The police patrol these flophouses. They're the first places they look during Sweeps weeks."

Peyton frowned. He put his hand on hers. His palm was the size of her breakfast plate. "Then we'll find someplace else. I've been thinking about that."

"I should go back to school," said Annika.

That paralyzed him again. He managed to swallow another tasteless hunk of his breakfast. "Do you *want* to go back to school?" he asked.

She stared at the table. "No," she said. "I want to stay with you. But I make you less safe."

Peyton took a deep breath. She did not want to leave him. She was not *going* to leave him. "I've been thinking about the man from the park," said Peyton. "The man who shared his home with us."

Annika nodded. "You fixed him," she said. "Something was wrong with him. Something bad enough that he was on the Registry list."

She had figured it out, somehow. She knew what he was thinking. "There are lots of people on those lists, Annika," he said. "All of them very bad people. Very bad people who can't ever again be trusted. That's why they're registered. And that's why there are lists of exactly where they live."

"We'll make them share?"

"Yes," said Peyton. "If we use the list randomly, if we don't follow it in order, there will be no way to predict where we might be."

"But the *list* makes a pattern," said Annika. "They could figure it out. Or somebody like Dr. Gorsky could tell again."

"Annika," said Peyton, "I spent last night using the wall screen, searching the list. When I told you how many predators the privateer zone has . . . Even I didn't realize how many there truly are. The police will never have the resources to stake them all out. And they won't want to try. They might even look the other way, if someone figures out what we're doing."

"It's still a pattern."

"We'll alternate with the paid flops, as we've been doing," he said. "Just less. This can work, Annika."

"Can I have a set of jeweler's tools?"

Peyton's jaw fell open. "What on Earth for?"

"So I can take my watch apart," she said. "I saw a tutorial last night while I was watching screen. It looked easy."

Peyton rubbed one huge thumb on this chin. "You can have any tools that you want," he told her. "But if you break the watch, it will be, uh, broken."

"I'm not worried about that," said Annika. "I can take a computer apart and put it back like it was."

"You can?"

"School," she said.

"Oh," said Peyton.

She pushed her plate away, climbed down, and walked over

to sit in his lap. He leaned back so that she would not bang her head on the edge of the table. Before he knew it, she was asleep against his chest. He was not surprised. She had been sleeping strangely, almost without a distinct cycle.

With some difficulty, he managed to push away from the table and stand. Annika, supported under his left arm, weighed nothing. He carried her into the bedroom, put her in the flop's bed, and arranged the blanket around her. Then he went out. He shut the door carefully.

Without realizing he was doing it, he picked up his plate from the kitchenette. Then he sat in the living area, on the floor in front of the sofa. Nibbling absentmindedly at the cold, rubbery Neggs, he started searching the sex offender registry.

He might go out later if he thought she was sleeping deeply enough. He had taken to walking the alleys of Hongkongtown, trying to clear his head, trying to figure out what to do next. He was not smart like Annika clearly was. His plan was not a brilliant one. It would not sustain them for long.

From his pocket, he pulled the crumpled handbill he had ripped from a utility pole the previous night. It was a plastic sheet bearing his printed image and a lurid list of crimes. "WANTED: REWARD," it read. "IAN W. PEYTON."

Annika was no liability.

He was.

Authority

"Just leave it in the bin," said the clerk. "Everybody's been in a state since the Warden was killed."

Neiring did not know what to say to that. He let the clerk check his sidearm and his stun baton. The administrative wing was close to bedlam. Investigators from the Office of Government Oversight were tearing the place apart, cataloging individual circuits in the computer network and sifting through the internal database. At least, that was what Neiring assumed they were doing, based on the equipment he saw. Not one of the workers stood still long enough for him to get a good look.

Past the administrative hub, he took the lift to the lower level, where the wall panels told him the archives were located. There was less chaos here, but he saw several OGO personnel moving in and out of the digital stacks. A knot began to form in Neiring's stomach.

"Chip," said the attendant behind the archives desk.

Neiring offered his right wrist. The attendant wanded him and read his pertinents.

"Neiring," said the inspector. "I'm here to—"

"So it says here," the attendant said. He yawned silently into his hand. "Please be quick, Inspector. We're in the midst of an audit."

"I need the files on Peyton, Ian W., serial number 0341674."

That got the clerk's attention. He looked up. "I suppose you'll want all the ancillaries, too."

"You suppose correctly," said Neiring. The clerk's attitude was beginning to grate. Before the man behind the counter could speak again, however, footfalls rang on the poured stone floor. The man who approached was wearing polished, silver-tipped boots.

Neiring checked the urge to bolt. The man before him looked like a corporate headhunter. He was all angles and hollows, wrapped in a black leather suit that seemed a size too large in the shoulders. A silver gun belt was strapped across his belly, the grip of the weapon close to the buckle.

"VanClef," said the man in black leather. "Intelligence."

"Neiring," said the inspector. "I'm—"

"I know," said VanClef. He wore black leather gloves over long, slender digits. One index finger now hovered above Neiring's chest. "And you, Inspector Neiring, are a bit far afield for a truancy report."

Neiring felt his jaw drop. "I . . ." he tried again.

"You were assigned erroneously," said VanClef. "The truancy report your office received for Peyton, Annika M., should have been shunted to *my* office. Ms. Peyton is next of kin to a dangerous death-row fugitive. But you know that. I pulled your travel records. You've been all over Hongkongtown, following leads on the Peyton case, trying to connect our escapee to murders in the privateer fringe. Yes?"

"Yes," Neiring said. "But—"

VanClef waved a gloved hand. "Don't think your efforts are not appreciated," he said. His tone was greasy. "Would that all government employees had your initiative. Assigned to locate the truant Ms. Peyton, you tracked her here . . . . I assume through her use of public transit?"

"Yes," said Neiring. He did not try to say more.

"Then, of course, you learned of her father's escape. Clearly, you are not stupid, Inspector; you see the connection. We are working on the theory that the elder Peyton, who has been cooperative for more than a decade while awaiting execution, lost his nerve when he considered that his daughter might be watching."

"Respectfully, Agent VanClef," Neiring said, more loudly than he would have liked, "none of that makes any sense. I've watched the logs. Warden Richards and Peyton had some kind of agreement between them. I'm trying to learn what that was. I'm also trying to determine exactly *what* Peyton is. His file indicates no synthetics."

"Ian Peyton is not an Augment," said VanClef. "Not in the traditional sense. He is certifiably human . . . although, on paper, that description does not do him justice. It's what the criminal syndicates call a bag-job. He's loaded with extra adrenal glands, a few hormone regulators. Enough to bulk him up and inure him to pain. It's nothing special. A biological parlor trick."

"That's not what it looks like on the logs," said Neiring. "After leaving the gallows chamber he fought his way through another dozen armed guards to escape this prison. That escape includes *punching* his way through two interior fences and the exterior wall. The robot guards at the tramway never stood a chance. He smashed them to pieces."

"That's all very colorful," said VanClef. "I imagine the distraction must be a desirable one. Why else would you be trying to find this pair in Hongkongtown?"

"They're in the privateer zone," said Neiring. "I'm certain of it. And Peyton has killed several times since escaping. I recovered a strand of Annika Peyton's hair at one of the crime scenes."

VanClef reached out and put a hand on Neiring's shoulder.

His grip was cold. "No," he said. "You didn't."

"Excuse me?"

"Effective immediately, Inspector," said VanClef, "this case does not concern you. The Peytons are the subject of a Government Intelligence operation. You will immediately cease and desist in any actions relative to the identification, location, or attempted apprehension of Ian and Annika Peyton. They were never here. You were never assigned. You have never heard of either of them."

Neiring flushed. "You don't have the unilateral authority to—"

VanClef's grip became a vise. Neiring felt air escape his lips. Pain shot through his shoulder, and he fought to keep his feet. "But I do," VanClef said. "Don't doubt me, Neiring. People get killed in Hongkongtown all the time." He released the inspector, causing Neiring to bleat in relief.

Without another word, VanClef turned on his heel and walked away. Neiring looked over his shoulder to the archives desk. The clerk had disappeared.

Shaken, Neiring left the archives. He reclaimed his weapons and made his way to the prison's motor dock. Moxley sat behind the driver's seat of Neiring's "For Official Use" vehicle. The detective was sucking on a flavored vapor tube. When he saw Neiring approach, he made as if to move to the passenger side, but Neiring waved him off. Moxley watched as Neiring climbed into the passenger seat.

"Jeez. You okay?" Mox asked him. "You look like somebody punched your grandmother." He blew a cloud of water vapor.

"Just drive, Mox," said Neiring. "Get us out of here before I change my mind."

"About what?"

"About the very stupid things I'm going to do next."

"I like where this is going," said Mox.

Goldilocks

Peyton sat in the lee of carefully tended acoustic trees. The growths were genetically engineered to dampen sound and screen the playground from view. This was an upscale, gated neighborhood, accessible to Peyton and Annika only because the perimeter wall sensors required maintenance. Scaling the wall had become a pastime in itself, for Annika, who giggled and clapped whenever he hoisted them both over the barrier.

He had suggested that he wait beyond the wall while she played, knowing how out of place he would look. But Annika would not hear of it.

"That's why I bought you your clothes, Daddy," she told him. "So we can go out and do things together."

Staring down at the exercise shirt with its trendy logo, he had been dubious. "This won't fit."

"It stretches, silly," she told him. "To show people your muscles. That's why people wear them. You're just a big exerciser, that's all. Tell people you're a personal trainer. There were lots of personal trainers at the exercise place on the concourse. Some of them were almost as big as you."

"Really?"

"Almost."

That had ended the argument as far as his daughter was concerned. And now Peyton sat in the shadows of genetically engineered privacy trees, cross-legged and hunched to disguise his mass. There were a few other parents milling about the park, but not many. There were several robot minders, one of which someone had dressed in a hooded rain poncho. There was also a pair of camera drones floating overhead in lazy circles, drifting on carbon-fiber turbofans. Peyton recognized the brand, if not the model. The drones had been everywhere in the prison yard, watching from above, missing nothing.

The children of the wealthy wore brightly colored clothes of resilient, often reflective fabric. Annika had chosen her wardrobe well. At a distance, except for the flash of her blonde hair, she was indistinguishable from the other boys and girls. The age range seemed to run from three or four years to roughly Annika's twelve. There was one boy who seemed a year or two older, but it was hard to tell. He was very large compared to the others, a stevedore among grazing goats.

Peyton chuckled, despite himself, surprised by his own small joke. Goats. Kids.

Annika looked to him periodically, as if to reassure herself that he was still there. Apart from that, she left him alone. He had never had to explain to her the danger in calling attention to him. His presence in any open space was vulnerability enough.

The sky was very blue. Birds sang in the acoustic growths. The breeze cooled his skin. For no reason at all, he experienced the urge to close his eyes. To smile.

It was a feeling utterly alien to him. He shook it off.

Playground equipment had not changed since his own childhood. There were swings. There were slides. There was a pit of crystalline grit, carefully sanitized, in which the children dug holes with small entrenching tools, or built spires using a heavy electric wand that temporarily hardened the outer layer of "sand."

He watched for a long time, feeling ill at ease. Annika, in the pit, built towers on top of towers, then smashed them, smiling all the while. The crystal grit did not stick to her clothes.

One of the parents drifted toward Peyton's spot. He was middle-aged, of decent mass and height. His hair was brown and thinning. Peyton tensed. Was this a trap? An attack?

The man nodded. "Hey," he said. From his glossy windbreaker he produced a vapor tube. The end of the tube glowed blue when he drew on it. He extended the oblong plastic pack to Peyton.

"No thank you," said Peyton.

"I almost didn't see you there," said the man. "Anybody'd think you were dressed to hide." Peyton's shirt and workout pants were dark blue. "Sorry for the offer. I wasn't thinking," said the man, wagging his vapor tube. "Obviously a healthy guy like you wouldn't want one."

Peyton wasn't sure what response to make. He offered none. When his visitor began to eye him strangely, perhaps finally picking out Peyton's true size in the shadows, he said, "I'm . . . a personal trainer."

"Right," the man said brightly. "That makes sense. You must have a lot of clients. I'm Jim, by the way."

Peyton grunted something that was not a name. Jim nodded again as if he'd heard.

"Which one is yours?" said Jim.

Too many questions. Peyton jerked his chin vaguely in the direction of the playground. Jim was not paying attention. He pointed to the large boy, the one Peyton had noticed before. "That's my Jim Junior," he said. "He's all-district for laneball this year."

Peyton grunted once more.

Jim Senior, proud father of Jim Junior, finished his vapor tube and dropped it casually in the grass. He took a second tube from the pack and ignited it with his thumb.

Jim Junior was now talking to Annika. Peyton's daughter was digging a trench around her latest crystal spire.

Annika said something, gestured toward the spire. Jim Junior walked to her, snatched the shovel from her hand, and cut the spire in two. His laughter drifted to Peyton's vantage. Annika shook her finger at him furiously. Peyton could imagine the scolding. Satisfied, Annika walked away, toward the nearest slide.

"Boys," said Jim Senior. "Full of energy."

Jim Junior pursued Annika. When she climbed the slide, he followed. When they were both at the top, he shoved her.

Peyton surged to his feet. Annika rolled down the slide, landing in a heap at the bottom. Peyton checked himself. She was already getting up.

Jim Senior chuckled. He did not turn; he had not seen Peyton stand. "I think maybe Junior is sweet on Goldilocks there," he said.

Annika walked back to the sandbox. Her pace was deliberate. When she got to it, she turned and fixed Peyton with a look. He met it. When Jim Junior arrived, the boy shoved Annika again, knocking her into the grit. She very deliberately reached out, grabbed the electric spire wand, and clouted Jim Junior across the face with it. He went down. She continued to hit him with the wand.

"Hey!" Jim Senior shouted. He took a step as if he would join his son, but Peyton was behind him now. A heavy hand the size of a cycling helmet grabbed him around the neck. He sputtered.

"You move," whispered Peyton, "and I'll change your life forever."

Jim Junior was squalling now. Annika looked to Peyton again

and then resumed her methodical beating. Her blows were not particularly hard, but the wand was heavy and she was persistent. It only took a few minutes for Jim Junior to curl into a ball, sobbing. Deliberately, Annika placed the wand in its receptacle in the enclosure wall.

"Take your son," said Peyton to Jim Senior. "Say nothing to the girl. If I ever see you again, you will spend the rest of your life drinking your meals." He shoved Jim Senior forward, releasing him. The man wasted no time. He did not even look at Annika as he hurried to flee the playground with his boy.

Annika walked over, slowly, unsure. He nodded to her. "We'll have to go," he said. "It will be a little while before we can come back."

"I know," said Annika. Peyton stood and she took the edge of his hand. As they walked from the playground, she said, "Daddy?"

"Yes, Annika?"

"Did I do okay?"

Peyton stopped walking and looked at her. "Were you angry?"

She thought about it. "No," she said. "Not really."

"Did you *want* to hit him?"

"No."

"But you did," he said. "A lot."

"I had to," said Annika. "I had to make it so it was no fun for him."

Peyton smiled at her. He knelt and, very carefully, hugged her. She disappeared within his arm.

"Then you did right," he told her. "You did exactly right."

Daddy's Home

The smell was very bad. Peyton nearly gagged. He put out his hand, blocking the doorway. Annika was already covering her mouth and nose with her palm.

"Gross," she said.

"Wait right here," said Peyton. "Don't come inside. I'm going to check it. We won't stay here."

Annika nodded. She slipped her pocket watch from her sweater and snapped it open. She would stare at it intently for the next few minutes. The watch had become a kind of worry stone for her. He was not sure if that should concern him. It did.

It was dark inside the flat. This dwelling sat at the end of a sprawl of similar units at the edge of Hongkongtown's freight yards. He had selected the address specifically because it was isolated. He had not anticipated anything this foul. He should have.

He wished for a torch. There was a lot of simple equipment he did not have—things he'd stopped wishing for, things that would have been confiscated in prison. It rarely occurred to him that he could accumulate these items now. As big as he was, and given the "wanted" bills he had seen posted for him, it was hard for him to visit public markets. Annika did most of their shopping. He would have to ask her about it. She would probably be able to suggest things he did not know existed. There were many gaps in his knowledge.

Glowing task lights beneath the kitchen counters cast shadows on rotting garbage. A mountain of dirty dishes waited in the sink. A plastic garbage bin next to this bulged with half-filled takeout containers. Crumpled soy-dog wrappers rustled as he walked through them. Unseen insects crunched beneath his heels.

The kitchenette table was piled high in dirty laundry, some of this stained black with what looked like machine oil. He looked at these closely but did not touch them. He smelled no blood.

The living room was mostly bare. The wall screen had been badly damaged long ago. Thick dust covered the crater that spiderwebbed across its blank expanse. The crater was the size of a fist. It was at the right height for a normal man. There was a plastiform chair in the center of the room. Next to this was a stack of empty pizza cartons. The stack was as tall as the chair.

Peyton's boot brushed an empty cylinder of spun sugar. He picked this up. *Zyrup*, the bottle proclaimed. Processed, sweetened mango liquor, 100 proof. Not a significant source of vitamins or minerals. A network address for complete nutritional information. Fat free. Vegan. *Eat the bottle when you're done!*

The bedroom door was locked. He pushed it open with his palm, popping the deadbolt and breaking the cheap plaster frame bearing the lock receptacle.

An inflatable bed. Bare walls. A portable screen connected to an auxiliary battery pack and a network transceiver. Filthy carpets. A grimy nightstand. Another bottle of *Zyrup*, half full, on the nightstand.

A large butcher knife, its blade rusty, also on the nightstand.

A cage containing a small boy.

The cage sat at the foot of the bed. It was a dog's kennel, Peyton realized. These had not changed greatly while he went to prison. Connected to the kennel's simple lock was a control panel of some kind. Wires ran from this to the lock.

"Hello," said Peyton.

The boy pressed his face to the slats in the kennel. His eyes were bloodshot. There were deep bags beneath them.

"I'm hungry," he said.

"Who put you in there?" Peyton asked. He dropped to one knee and bent to put his head near the cage. "Are you hurt?"

"Mr. Alan," said the boy. "No."

Alan, Jeremy. The registered occupant of the flat. "How long have you been in there?" Peyton asked.

"I don't know," said the boy. "Since yesterday. Mr. Alan said he had to go to work."

Oil-stained clothes. The freight yards nearby. It made sense. "What's your name?" he said.

"Gabriel," said the boy. "I miss my mom. I want to go home."

"I'll take you," said Peyton. "Do you know your address?"

"Yes," said Gabriel. "But I can't tell you. I can't tell strangers."

Peyton nodded. He pointed to the control panel. "Is this anything?"

"Mister Alan said not to touch it," said Gabriel. "He said it would 'splode."

Peyton considered that. In any city but this one, a sniffer drone could pass at any moment, detect bomb-making materials, and assign a special tactics squad to raid the address. There were fewer laws in Hongkongtown, but explosives were still a public hazard. Keeping a bomb here would be a risk.

"I'll be right back," said Peyton. "I'm not leaving you. I'm going to the front door and coming right back."

Gabriel started crying.

Peyton stood and went to the door. Annika looked up at him. "Daddy?" she said.

"I need you to look at something," he said.

She followed him to the bedroom, covering her mouth and nose with her hand. She paused when she saw the boy in his cage. Peyton pointed to the control panel.

"I don't know what this is," he said. "You told me you can take apart a computer. I know you take your watch apart. Can you help?"

"It's a squawk-box," said Annika. She sounded relieved, as if she'd been given a quiz and learned it was easy. "They sell them on the 'nets. If you unlock it without the code it sends you a message."

"A warning device," said Peyton. Annika nodded.

"Mr. Alan said that I wouldn't like it when he got home," said Gabriel.

"I'm Annika," said Peyton's daughter. "I'm twelve."

"I'm eight," said Gabriel.

"I want this off, but I don't want it to tell anyone," said Peyton. "Do you know if that can be done, Annika?"

"That's easy," said Annika. She removed the carbon-fiber card of jeweler's tools from her pocket. "Can we be best friends, Gabriel? Just for now, I mean. I don't have a best friend right now."

"Okay," said the boy.

"Tell your best friend your address," said Peyton. "We'll take you home."

"Okay," said the boy.

Jeremy Alan, thirty-six, leasing for eighteen months, let

himself into his flat with a great deal of noise. He was juggling a plastic sack full of groceries, a six-slot of *Zyrup*, and his heavy coat. He kicked the door shut behind him and dropped the groceries amid the laundry on his kitchenette table.

“Daddy’s home,” he called out, his voice pitched high.

“No,” rumbled a voice behind him.

Alan turned. The shadows of the living room grew by a meter. The biggest man he had ever seen stood before him.

“Daddy—”

This was the last word Jeremy Alan would speak. Peyton wrapped one enormous palm around the back of Alan’s head. He took the thumb and index finger of his other hand, curled them into a “C,” and stabbed them into Alan’s eye sockets. Then he touched his thumb to his fingertip inside Alan’s brain.

“That’s not a word for you,” Peyton said to no one.

Fourth and Dragon

"So Gorsky sees one of your handbills," said Detective Moxley. "Or he's just smart. He figures, hey, double payday. So he performs whatever medical service Peyton visits him to get, then turns around and rats Peyton out to the cops."

"According to the informant log I tracked down, yes," said Neiring. "The prison is offering cash for Peyton's retrieval. The freelance uniforms who responded to the call were looking to get paid, just like Gorsky, and they ended up with the same reward he did." Neiring looked dubiously at his bowl of dumplings. "The log is how we eventually identified Gorsky's remains."

"Never did find the arms," said Moxley. "So Peyton figures out what must have happened and he puts a hole in the local shadow economy. That fits." He paused to sip from his drink, which was red and viscous and bore a trio of colorful paper umbrellas. He had already devoured his crab wontons. Neiring had learned not to look at the man when he was actually chewing or swallowing. "If you're curious, Gorsky's customers migrated over to a robot bodega at Fourth and Dragon. There's a rumor they even do Augment conversions. Not just the cosmetic mods stuff, either. Real full-body transplants."

"That needs to get shut down, then," said Neiring.

"Shame," said Mox. "Getting so a guy can't find good unlicensed surgical attention in this town."

"I thought your interest in Gorsky ended where the insurance policy did," said Neiring.

"I like to keep an eye on things," said Mox. He reached out and grabbed Neiring's hand in his own. Then he shoved a pair of plastic chopsticks into Neiring's grip, carefully arranged Neiring's fingers around them, and made a pincers gesture. "Eat, already. You're killing me, Neiring. You know the prices are only going to go up again. Rice crop failures for the next three years, they're saying."

Neiring tried the chopsticks. To his surprise, he managed to grab a dumpling. He popped it in his mouth.

"You're right," he said, chewing. "The food *is* good here."

"Just avoid it from the middle of the month until after the first," said Mox. "They run out of UV pellets about two weeks in until the rents clear."

Neiring stopped chewing. He eyed Moxley, wondering if the man was joking. It was impossible to tell.

They sat in a plastic booth on the street outside the eatery. Hongkongtown roiled around them, thick with sounds and smells. Their waiter was a corroded robot the size of a trashcan. Three times it had tried to deliver rice, only to drop the bowls in transit.

"I don't get you, Neiring," said Mox. "Why try so hard? They've already warned you off. Ian and Annika Peyton are somebody else's problem."

"It doesn't *feel* right," said Neiring. "Something *wrong* is happening. Something I can't identify because I don't have enough data. I can't just let it go, Mox. I can't shake the feeling that if I don't pursue it, something big will have slipped past me."

"Have you considered what happens if you do find him?" Moxley said. "Maybe you didn't hear me when I said *we still can't find Gorsky's arms*. This is a guy who could crush you like a tube of Graple until your guts squeezed out your eyes, Neiring. We've already seen how he deals with people who get on his bad side."

"Peyton's a monster," said Neiring. "A monster who appeared fully formed from behind a maximum-security prison complex where he's been patiently awaiting the mandatory appeals process to run its course. Mox, Peyton was on Death Row for *years*. Twelve, to be exact. He'd made no trouble since the incident that pulled him from general population. And he had no major discipline actions in his file for the three years before *that*. Just some medical notes. He got hazed pretty hard when he was incarcerated."

"What a fun bunch of guys that must be."

"The day they're to hang him from a steel cable," Neiring went on, "a computer error and a Warden with a big mouth alert Peyton to the presence of a daughter in the gallery. He breaks out and takes her with him. How does that work?"

"The guy's still human," said Mox. "Sort of. Maybe he got cold feet. It's standard procedure to invite next of kin to an execution. Closure."

"But where did *Annika* come from?" said Neiring. "Ian Peyton was behind the walls for fifteen years. Annika Peyton is supposed to be twelve years old. There are absolutely no public records of her existence prior to the weeks before Peyton's execution date. No birth certificate. No standardized test scores. No vaccination certs. I can't find anybody who'll take responsibility for locating her or transporting her to the prison and through prison security, either."

Moxley finished his drink and slapped it down on the table. He burped loudly. "So what?" he said. "So there are holes. So something doesn't add up. Maybe the reason it doesn't make sense is the same reason Intelligence told you to lay off. It's above your pay grade, Neiring, and that means it sure as hell is above mine."

"It doesn't bother you that this little girl and her pet monster are running around Hongkongtown murdering people?"

Moxley's eyes bulged. "Honestly?" he said. "No. And I can't figure how it would weigh too hard on you, either. Yeah, Peyton killed some freecops. You know what they say. 'You takes your chances, you rolls your dice.' But Gorsky was a pill-head who had sex with several of his female patients before he lost his license. Marachuck, your Seven-A across the street, was a damned rapist flagged so high on the recidivism index that he had three separate tracking chips installed. Two of those he had managed to chew out of his skin. You don't want to know where they were."

"What about that rich idiot, Jim-something? He wasn't a sex offender. He was a guy at the park with his kid."

"That kid of his is a douchelamp," Mox said. "I'd stake real chits on it. And Peyton didn't kill that guy. Just scared his shorts full. I gotta tell you, Neiring, I'm not seeing a downside to leaving this alone. Those cops wouldn't have died if they'd just let Peyton be."

"You're out, then?" Neiring asked. He put his chopsticks on the table.

"I didn't say that," said Mox. "You think I became a detective for the glamorous lifestyle?"

"So you'll help."

"Yes, dammit," said Moxley. "I want to *know*. Just like you do. I just want it clear up front, while we're pouring hour after hour into something that might get us both sanctioned or killed, that we're both morons."

"I already knew that about *you*," said Neiring.

"That's why I like you, Neiring," said Mox. He stuck a vapor tube in his mouth. "You class up the joint."

Twelve Years Ago

At two hundred scratches, the grooves in the wall thicken.

They become deeper.

They are more defined.

Of the 1,090 scratches arrayed in blocks of seven on the stone wall of the cell, only the first 199 were made with a contraband nail.

It was on the two hundredth day that the occupant of the cell first used his finger alone to scratch that day's mark.

Since his body first hardened, he has gained 145 kilos. He has grown more than half a meter in height. His upper body has distended. His arms have swollen. His hands have tripled in size.

He is not indestructible, but if indestructible has a next-door neighbor, he lives at this address. Since he began gaining weight he has been stabbed thirty times and shot twice. The wounds have healed. There are scars.

He has permanently injured nineteen men, all of them fellow inmates. For a period of eighteen months he has harmed no one. The attempts on his life have ceased.

He moves through the yard and across his prison tier silently, inevitably. He is a drifting iceberg. He speaks to no one and no one speaks to him. If he thinks, if he dreams, if anything at all happens inside his thickened skull, he shares nothing.

The other inmates now call him "the Monster." It is

unimaginative, but it is accurate. No one says it to his face, but he knows. He does not disagree.

Left alone, he has become a model prisoner. He is very nearly ignored. Many take him for granted.

One thousand and ninety scratches after his first night in prison, he will murder a man who has never threatened him.

Richards is florid, very nearly panicked. It has been years since the prison logged a fatality. He tries to calm himself; he succeeds only in sounding more peevish.

"Tell me again," he says. "Remember that we're recording this."

The guard is a man named Lemmet. He opens his mouth, closes it. Opens it again. Richards thinks he looks like a fish. "I think he—"

"No!" says Richards. "Don't *think*. I want the *facts*. I want your eyewitness account without editorials. Sit there with your mouth closed and think about what you'll say." He erases the official record for the second time. The heat in his office is not working properly. His fingers are cold.

For the third time in as many hours he calls up the file on the dead man. The inmate's name was Fiorino. He had been processed into the facility only six hours before. His first hour in the prison yard had been spent sitting quietly against the south wall, where the sun made the tiles warm.

Fiorino has a reputation. Fiorino has killed eighteen women on the mainland, most of them prostitutes. He is the closest thing to a celebrity the prison has seen. His trial was a media circus.

His defense was improbable. He was his own attorney. He was adjudicated insane and ordered imprisoned for his natural life.

Richards believes Fiorino belongs in a mental institution. The maximum-security sanitarium on Canseco Bay, perhaps. But Fiorino's trial has become political leverage. Candidates vying for office in the next round of elections have made a series of demands, a list of promises to deal harshly with violent crime. Fiorino has been sent to Hongkongtown's SuperMax to appease the voters.

Now he is dead.

Warden Richards draws a deep breath. He can feel a migraine building behind his left eye. He is afraid. He again presses the *record* button on the touch interface.

"Testimony of Corrections Officer Lemmet, Ernest K., regarding the murder, this date stamp, of inmate Fiorino, Helio P., serial number 0451189, by alleged perpetrator Peyton, Ian W., serial number 0341674. Officer Lemmet was witness to an altercation in the prison yard, TDS, between the two inmates. Officer Lemmet. Go ahead."

Lemmet seems determined to do well. He is not particularly smart. So says his personnel file. He clears his throat.

"Fiorino was sitting in the yard," says Lemmet. "He'd been there all morning. He didn't talk to anyone. Nobody approached him. I think most of the inmates were scared. Fiorino's got a rep. Uh, you know, reputation. That's not uncommon with the high-profile cases—"

"What happened next?" Richards says, prompting.

"Peyton's yard time came up on the schedule. He walked out of the south entrance like he always does. They make a wide hole for the Monster. The inmates, I mean. They call him—"

Richards presses *pause* and glares. Lemmet nods vigorously.

Richards releases the button.

"Peyton crossed the yard," says Lemmet. "He didn't speak to anyone. He didn't pause. He just walked straight to Fiorino."

"Were you close enough to hear if they spoke?" asks Richards.

"He stood in front of Fiorino. Fiorino looks up at him and says, 'I'm not in the mood.' Like he was being hazed, you know? Peyton didn't wait. He just reached down and grabbed Fiorino by the neck. Then he dragged Fiorino across the yard."

"He dragged him by the neck?"

"Yeah," says Lemmet. "He walked right under the drones. We've got surveillance from six different angles. He crossed the yard with Fiorino and then stopped. And then, you know."

"I don't know," says Richards. "State it plainly."

"He just started . . . *turning* Fiorino's head. Like he . . . like he was *unscrewing* it. He just kept going until . . ."

"Until what?"

"Until it came unscrewed."

In his mind, Richards is composing a letter of disciplinary action for Lemmet's file. He is not expecting an answer when he asks, "Is there anything else?" He is surprised when Lemmet answers.

"Yes sir," says the guard. "It looked like . . . I mean, it was in all the recordings. I checked a couple of them. But I saw it when he was crossing the yard. He was doing it even before he murdered Fiorino."

"Doing what?" Richards asks.

"Crying, sir," says Lemmet. "Peyton was crying like a baby."

There Is No Safe

Peyton endured her brooding until they left their borrowed flat for lunch. Finally, at a sidewalk cafe on Dragon Street, he tapped a thick forefinger on their table to get her attention.

"What, Daddy?" she asked.

"Annika, you've been pouting all morning. What is it?"

She looked up at him, then away, distracted by a flight of turbofan drones drifting overhead. Peyton followed her gaze. He shielded his eyes with his hand.

"I don't see any parcels," said Annika.

Peyton looked to her. "What?"

"Delivery fliers," she said. "I like them. I like to think about all those packages flying around the city. Sometimes I picture all the robots in the city as people, and I think they all talk to each other. They watch us and they trade information. The smartest of all the robots knows everything."

"Annika," said Peyton. "You're changing the subject."

She stared into her bowl of *kaeng phet pet yang* for several moments. "I really want a tab," she said.

Peyton's eyes widened. "That's all?" he said. "I thought something was wrong."

Annika shook her head. "But I don't *need* one," she said. "It's selfish to want things you don't need. In school we learned a story about a lion who wanted to be the king of the jungle. When he found out there was another lion who was just as strong, he fought him and he lost. He didn't need to be king. He was still a lion. But he was selfish and so he died."

Peyton thought about that for a while. Finally, he said, "It wasn't selfish to want your watch. It makes you happy. And the tools you use for your watch. They helped us to help Gabriel."

She smiled. "I miss Gabriel," she said.

"Things that make you happy," said Peyton, "make *me* happy."

"Are you sure?" she asked.

"What do you mean?"

"You never seem happy," she said. "You always seem worried."

Peyton frowned. "I'm sorry, Annika. You always make me happy. There are other things I worry about."

"Like the police."

He paused again. "Yes," he said. "Like the police. But Annika, it's *my* job to worry. That's what fathers do. It's all right to tell me you want things." He reached into the pocket of the exercise pants she had bought for him, then handed her a small stack of plastic chits. "We have plenty of money."

"There's a kiosk at the other end of Wernerplasse," she said. "Next to the Funodrome."

He had learned that tone. "Would you like to stop at the Funodrome before or after?"

She laughed. "Before."

"Eat your lunch and we'll go."

Traffic was heavy as they walked down Wernerplasse. An army of hydrogen cycles, runabouts, pedicabs, and solar unis vied for position in and around the larger ground cars and cargo trams. The streets were full of people, too, some of them wearing the oversize wicker headgear that was, Annika informed him, very fashionable right now. He wondered how long it would be before she asked him for a hat the size of a fruit basket.

More rolling couriers passed them than seemed normal for mid-morning. That could mean another flash mob. The last one they'd seen had been a live commercial for Vitamin Jelly. The costumes and dancing had delighted Annika. If he could give her that experience again, he would be pleased. Yet another wheeled robot shot past Peyton, and he tried to spot a corporation sponsorship on its chassis.

Annika had eyes only for the Funodrome. To Peyton it looked like a corral and, on some level, he supposed it was. Shoppers were encouraged to leave their children to play in the contoured pit, which was lined with kinetic foam, while they went about their business in the area. Long-term robot supervision was available for a fee. *No Overnights*, proclaimed a prominent sign.

For Annika, Funodrome and places like it afforded a rare opportunity to play and interact with other children. With Peyton's permission she made for the entrance, left her shoes in one of the racks provided, and entered the pit. Soon she was a blur amidst the other children racing about inside, climbing over foam obstacles and atop pliable jumping platforms. A network of cushioned tunnels ran beneath the pit, too, with viewing windows spaced throughout their length.

"Tag!" Annika shouted. After touching her target—a boy her height—she ran for the entrance to one of the tunnels. "Safe!" she declared. "The tunnel is safe!" Eventually she left her hiding spot, was tagged, and pursued her quarry in return. The "safe" spot seemed to change depending on where in the pit Annika stood. Peyton thought that seemed convenient.

Parents who wished to remain while their children played could use a bench that ran the perimeter of the pit. Peyton opted to lurk in the shadow of the adjacent building, at the mouth of an alleyway parallel to the pit. Here he could see Annika but was largely screened from view himself. He was also next to the kiosk where he assumed she would buy her tab. Several of the forearm tablets, in fact, were sized for someone as small as Annika. Many were larger. He did not imagine a data sleeve was made that could accommodate his own wrist, much less his forearm.

A turbofan drone flew past at head height. Peyton had to duck to avoid it. Drone collisions were frequent enough that they seldom made news in Hongkongtown.

He watched Annika play for more than two hours. Eventually, she started to slow down, but not before engaging in one last, frenetic bout of "tag" with another little girl. Annika's playmate was roughly her size and age, with striking platinum hair. She wore a school uniform. They chased each other in circles so quickly that Peyton thought his daughter might fall and hurt herself. Finally, though, Annika dove for the perimeter bench, causing a mother in a wool jollysuit to move out of the way.

"Safe!" said Annika. "The bench is safe. I'm safe."

The girl with the platinum hair stopped running. She walked, very deliberately, to where Annika was perched on the bench. Without hurrying, she reached out and placed one hand gently on Annika's shoulder.

"There is no safe," she said.

Peyton was impressed. Cold as ice, that one. She would make someone a lovely contract wife one day. Annika opened her mouth to protest and looked to Peyton. He shook his head and beckoned.

"Come on," he said when she reached him, still tugging on one shoe. "You can buy your computer."

"I lost at tag," she said.

"You got *served* at tag," said Peyton. Annika laughed. "I'll wait here," he said. "Go ahead and get whatever you like."

"Okay, Daddy," she said. She disappeared into the queue outside the tech kiosk.

Peyton was not sure how long she would need to make a decision. He was not concerned. He stood a little farther back in the alley, resting against the wall, scratching his back through the fabric of his shirt.

Another drone drifted into the alley. It stopped next to Peyton, hovering at chest level. Annoyed, he reached up to grab it. He would snap the blade from its fan and leave it in the alley for the scavengers.

The drone began to spray him with gas.

The caustic smell burned his throat. He swatted the drone with one large palm, shattering it against the paved alleyway, rupturing the canister of numbing agent it bore. Holding his breath, he ran to the middle of the alley with his face in the crook of his arm. His eyes watered badly.

Six more drones descended on him. At the opposite end of the alleyway, robots on wheels began to close the distance. The robots were law enforcement models, armed with automatic weapons. As they came toward him, the flying drones laid down a fog bank of neural paralyzer.

He could not fight them. If he paused for even a moment, the nerve agent would put him down. Only his accelerated metabolism, his elevated adrenaline, was keeping him going.

His eyes ached. Annika was somewhere past the robots. Somewhere past the gas. Somewhere, alone. She needed him. She needed him and he could not get to her.

Peyton ran.

The Treasure Is Mine

"This suggests," said the man on the kiosk screens, "that to foster amity among our differently unique fellow citizens is to pave the way for a future in which we are united within and without . . ."

Peyton glanced up at the bank of screens. The bazaar was full of them. They were placed at intervals among the open stalls and in the pedestrian walkways. Some bore scrolls of travel data, weather adjustments, and business links. Many displayed the same feed of a well-dressed man at a podium. Peyton was indifferent to politicians. He assumed this was one.

He scanned the throngs around him. The crowd moved slowly, a creature of concentric circles. Every kiosk had a layer of customers around it. Casual observers moved around these, and pedestrians made circuits around that middle tier. The bazaar was a lung that breathed at its own pace. Only Peyton's size allowed him to skirt the lines. Where he moved, people parted.

It had been an hour. Had he lost her? He looked left, then right. A robot courier passed him. It was old, rusted. The law enforcement units had given up overnight. He had seen only two flying drones since then.

There! He saw the flash of blonde hair and he dove through the crowd, spilling more than a few bazaar-goers. A few muttered their outrage. Their indignation turned to silence when they put eyes on him. None of these things were important.

The girl ducked between two mirrored buildings bordering the bazaar. He had to turn sideways to make the opening. The alley scraped his back and chest. She was just ahead of him. He reached for her. The space between the buildings began to narrow.

No. It was too tight. The walls pressed him from either side. He couldn't move forward. She was going to escape! As if she heard his thoughts, she stopped, turned, looked at him. He reached out. His fingers brushed her blonde hair.

It wasn't Annika.

"Mister?" said the little girl. "Are you all right?"

"I'm sorry," said Peyton. "I saw you in the crowd . . . I'm looking for my daughter. Her name is Annika. She's twelve."

"I'm twelve," said the girl. Her hair was the same shade and length as Annika's. "I'm Aubry, not Annika."

Peyton lowered his arm. "I'm sorry if I scared you. I thought you were her."

She started to say something and then looked at him oddly. "Mister . . . are you stuck?"

Peyton felt his face grow hot. That was new. "I think I am," he said.

"Sometimes when it seems like you can't go any farther," said Aubry, "that's when you have to try your hardest. Because you just might be really close to what you're trying to reach."

"Wait," said Peyton.

"I have to go now, mister," said Aubry. She turned, hurried to the end of the alley, turned the corner, and was gone.

Sometimes when it seems like you can't go any farther, that's when you have to try your hardest. Peyton frowned. Forcing air from his lungs, he relaxed his shoulders and pushed off with his feet. The buildings in front and behind scraped his flesh through his clothes.

Suddenly he was free.

The alley mouth widened. He moved quickly. There was a pair of trash androids scooping up debris near the next cross-section. He tripped over one and, annoyed, shoved the other against the wall, out of his way. The robot continued hooking trash with its metal arms, beeping quietly. It was probably twenty years old and looked the part.

When Peyton cleared the intersection he emerged on Third at Ouroboros. He found himself staring at a Screen Service shop. The front of the shop was a wall of displays receiving different data streams. Some of them were of the politician he had seen before, a replay loop of the same speech.

He looked up the street. He looked over his shoulder. A hydrogen-cycle gang rolled past him, moving fast, the riders settled low in their saddles.

The center screen in the shop display went blank. A gold pocket watch danced across it, then vanished. Peyton's mouth opened. Had he seen it?

The watch appeared again. It drifted from left to right. When it reappeared again, it was on the screen farthest to the right. It blinked, a computer-generated image that sparkled as it turned.

Peyton turned right and began to walk.

He was crossing Ouroboros when he saw the watch on a traffic-control panel. It directed him left. He followed the watch on news visors and weather stands, on kiosks and passing pedicabs, on robot sandwich boards and drone banners. Finally, he turned into yet another alley, this one dark and cluttered with empty shipping containers.

There were two men here. One was squat, with thick, oiled, curly hair. He looked like a toad to Peyton. He was sallow and broad, wearing gray synthetics that were textured to look like pavement. The squat man was hiding behind a metal cargo flat in the middle of the alley. Peyton was tall enough to see him there.

The other man was closer to Peyton. He was taller and too thin to be well; his skin was laced with broken blood vessels and pocked with craters. If he was not a Sleep addict he was taking something similar.

"It's mine," said the thin man. "The treasure is mine." He held a knife in his hand. He extended his arm, waving the blade at Peyton.

Opportunists. They had followed the watch as he had. This was Hongkongtown. The behavior of such street vermin was not surprising. Peyton reached out and folded his hand over the knife, feeling the blade cut his palm. He shook his fist.

The tall man's wrist snapped loudly and he screamed.

Peyton swung the drug addict by the arm, dislocating the limb. He mashed the poor devil against a shipping container until the man stopped moving. The squat man was already running and Peyton let him go. The toad was not important.

Blood spattered the pavement. Peyton looked at his hand. The wound was closing.

He found her at the end of the alley, against the wall, fingers tapping on the touch screen of her computer sleeve. He stood over her. The animated watch danced across the forearm tab's face.

He reached down and brushed a lock of blonde hair from her face.

"Hi Daddy," said Annika.

Apartment 81B

Annika yawned. “He’s never going to come home,” she said.

“They always do,” said Peyton.

Annika tugged the chain of her gold pocket watch, which was fastened to one of the buttons of her sweater. The watch she kept in the pocket of her tapered leggings. She snapped open the timepiece, read it, stared at it for a moment, and put it away. Then she went back to tapping at the screen of her forearm tab, causing inscrutable glowing blocks to roll around and touch or stick to other, equally inscrutable glowing blocks.

“What is that?” Peyton asked. He sat with his back to the wall of the corridor. Facing them was the sealed door of Apartment 81B.

“A game,” she told him. She moved closer to him, sitting next to him on the floor, using his massive arm as a pillow. She continued to tap the screen. Some of the glowing blocks moved to connect with others.

“How is it played?”

“You have to recombine the amino acids to make stronger peptide chains,” she said. “The longest polypeptide wins. Some of the carboxyl groups have hard-coded weaknesses in them, though, so you have to learn to work around those.”

Peyton considered that. “Is it . . . fun?”

“Yes,” she said. She never took her eyes from the screen.

"What do you want for dinner?" he asked.

"We could get Mister Mustard."

"I didn't like Mister Mustard," said Peyton. "Everything tastes like curry."

"You don't like anything the first time," said Annika. "You always change your mind."

"Hmm," Peyton said.

A man in an overcoat walked toward them. Peyton tensed, wondering if this was the owner of Apartment 81B. It wasn't. The man continued past them and turned the corner, never once looking their way. They were deep in Gunpowder Heights here. People saw nothing they did not have to see.

"Daddy?" Annika asked. "What was your favorite game when you were a boy?"

Peyton looked at her, surprised. "I didn't have one," he said. "Hide-and-seek, maybe. I don't know."

"No, silly," she said. "Your favorite tab game."

"I didn't have a tab," he said. "I didn't have a computer, either."

"Your parents were too poor?" She was still making peptide chains.

"I didn't know my parents," said Peyton. "I grew up right here, in Hongkongtown. I lived in the city orphanage until I was fourteen. Then I got a job at the fish market. When I was big enough I started working for the Triads."

"Triads?"

"Bad people," said Peyton. "The Triads ran street crime in Hongkongtown back then. I guess maybe they still do, but not as much. I haven't seen as many gang tags as I used to. A lot has changed."

"Changed since what?"

"I was in prison for fifteen years," said Peyton. He found himself staring at his hands. "Since before you were born."

Annika switched off her tab and looked up at him. "Why did they put you in prison?" she asked.

"I was very bad."

"What did you do?"

Peyton rubbed one palm across his face. It took him a moment before he could make eye contact with her. "I was a very bad man, Annika," he said. "I hurt people. A lot of people. And back then I didn't care about the bad things I did."

"But you care now."

"Yes," said Peyton. "I care now."

"And it makes you sad."

"Yes."

Annika leaned against him. She put one hand on his forearm. "It makes you sad," she said, "because you worry that you're still a bad man. You're worried that you are the things you did."

Peyton looked up. The night sky was not visible beyond the pall of illuminated haze that hung over Hongkongtown. "Yes," he said again. "You're very smart, Annika."

"I know."

"When we were separated," he said, "back at the Funodrome. How did you know where to hide? How did you get away?"

"Daddy, we were at a *playground*," she said, as if that explained it all. When he continued to look questioningly at her, she said, "Playgrounds are full of children. I just went home with one of the big families. Their robot minders don't check for extra kids. They're programmed to know that their charges could have playmates. They just make sure they aren't missing their primaries."

"What then?"

"We had a sleepover," said Annika. "I came back in the

morning and used my tab to enter the area networks. Then I just programmed the watches. It's a simple algorithm that jumps around all the available screens in the local node. I knew you would be looking for me. I knew you would have to see it eventually."

"You had a sleepover," he said.

"They were nice," said Annika. "I had pancakes for breakfast."

"You can use that to enter any network you want?" he asked, jerking his chin at the tablet device.

"Most of them," said Annika. "It depends on their security. There are some hardwall systems I can't get past. Those are physical barriers. Hardware appliances."

"But how—"

"School," she said.

He would have asked her more, but another figure approached. The man glanced at them curiously, fumbled his key, and kept staring at them as he unlocked the door marked 81B. Peyton stood. Annika trailed him as he crossed the corridor.

"Who are you?" asked the man. "I checked in with my caser yesterday."

Peyton slapped the man in the side of the head. His skull struck the door and cracked. The owner of Apartment 81B was dead before he met his front step.

"I'll put him in the basement," said Peyton. "The brochure said these units have basements for storage." He bent and picked up the dead man by the corpse's feet. His hand was more than large enough to surround both ankles at once. "What's a 'caser'?"

"A case worker, Daddy," said Annika. "Because he's on the sex offender registry."

"Oh," said Peyton. "When I was young we called those 'sollies.' They were social workers back then."

"All languages evolve, Daddy," she said.

Once the dead man was safety stowed, Peyton and Annika opted to skip dinner. She brought him an extra blanket from the hall closet and tucked him in on the couch, which was large enough to hold most of him.

“Good night, Annika,” he told her.

“Good night, Daddy,” she said. Before she had left the room, however, she stopped.

“What is it, Annika?”

“Daddy,” she said, “I don’t think you should be sad. I think you should be proud. You’re doing a good job.”

He had no words for that. He did not offer any.

“I hope his bed is made,” Annika said, opening the bedroom door. “I hate it when their beds aren’t made.”

Does It Hurt?

The squat man with the oiled hair resembled a toad. He smelled of Hongkongtown garbage. When he entered the interrogation chamber, thick fingers nervously plucking at his own shirt, VanClef did not look up. The Intelligence operative instead peered deeper into the scrolling data from the reader-chair. Strapped tightly into the chair was a twelve-year-old girl. Cables ran from a sensor collar around her neck. Her hair was so fair it was almost white.

"Mister VanClef, sir. Begging your pardon, sir, but—"

"Do you honestly think, Temken," said VanClef, "that your use of such pleasantries in any way mitigates your failure?"

"Uh, no, sir."

"Good," said VanClef. "I would hate to build our relationship on a lie." He made an adjustment to the terminal connected to the girl's collar. An almost subliminal hum filled the room. Secured in the reader-chair, the blonde girl squirmed and frowned. She looked at VanClef, then at the ceiling, then to Temken. Temken looked away.

"I'm feeding you a series of weather data," said VanClef to the girl. "I want you to interpolate. Give me forecasts for six months from now and a year from now. Use only the numbers in the matrix supplied."

The little girl nodded. Temken took a step closer.

"Is it . . . ?" he started. "I mean . . . Should you be torturing them?"

VanClef turned to Temken, his hands still on the dials of his terminal. "Yes, of course," he said. "That's precisely what I'm doing. I'm endangering close to thirty trillion in development funding because I enjoy inflicting pain on children. Shall I bind her and leave her for the monorail when I'm finished?" He waved black-gloved fingers. "Honestly, Temken. Leave the thinking to people who possess the necessary equipment for it."

"Sorry, sir," said Temken.

"We're still calibrating the equipment," VanClef said. Whether he was speaking to Temken or to himself was not obvious. "It's maddening. Sometimes we're able to map their brainwaves. Sometimes we get nothing. Sometimes the machine tells us they're plotting to take over the world. Sometimes it says they like ice cream. Maddening."

"What does it say now?" Temken said.

"It's another hallucinatory episode," said VanClef, waving his hand. "The sort of meaningless imagery that makes no earthly sense. According to the machine, she's picturing a robot spider with cameras for eyes, sitting at the center of a spiderweb, using the strands like telegraph wires to communicate with other robots throughout its spider city. Clearly this has nothing to do with weather interpolation."

"Telegraph?"

"Shut up, Temken."

"Does it . . . hurt?" Temken asked. The blonde girl had her eyes closed now. Her lips moved, but she made no sound.

"I'm told it requires a great deal of concentration," said VanClef. "And that it is tiring. But no, she is not being 'tortured,' as you put it. Now either keep silent or make your report, damn you."

"Sir! Yes, sir," said Temken. "I've been shadowing the Peytons for two weeks now, sir. I've also been trailing the girl through the virts that she frequents. Games, chathouses, that kind of thing. We were able to establish location and pattern. The raid went off as planned. We successfully separated them. Our drones were able to drive the father off."

"And yet you brought me nothing," said VanClef. "No Annika. No Peyton. Nothing."

"She disappeared somehow," said Temken. "Completely off the grid. We're still not sure how she did it. When she resurfaced she found a way to hack the local nodes. She inserted an animated signal in local displays."

"Which you followed," said VanClef.

"Yes, sir," said Temken. "The signal also drew a third party, a street-level predator. Peyton killed him."

"The father."

"Yes," said Temken. "The father killed him."

"You were within meters of Annika Peyton," said VanClef, "and you simply . . . left."

"Her father would have killed *me*, too, sir," said Temken. "There was nothing I could do."

VanClef sighed. "Which means now we'll have to reacquire them. The ability of Ian Peyton to remain hidden in Hongkongtown defies all logic. The man must be 270 kilos. He stands half a meter taller than any human being. Hell, he's *wider* than some people are tall. How do they do it? How do they remain undetected for so long each time?"

"We're not sure," said Temken. "My electronics team are working on it. They think maybe one of Peyton's implants produces an electromagnetic field that interferes with surveillance."

"He's biological," said VanClef. "There's nothing in his specifications that would account for that."

"I don't know, sir," said Temken. "That's just a theory. I can have a new team on them as soon as we place them. We could stage another raid."

"No," said VanClef. The girl in the reader-chair was sweating profusely. VanClef took a black silk handkerchief from inside his suit jacket and gently dabbed at her forehead. "Focus on the virts. Perhaps you can draw her out voluntarily. Technologically propositioning a minor should be nothing new to you."

Temken stared at the floor. "Sir," he said, "I hardly think—"

"That," said VanClef, "is an understatement." He wiped the girl's forehead again, pressed the handkerchief to his lips, and tucked it away. "Did you speak to Maintenance?"

"They're working on the problem, sir," said Temken.

"Good. I need our internal network restored. I can't have this facility isolated from the rest of the grid."

"Yes, sir."

"What about Level G? Is that door still sealed?"

"The hydraulics are frozen," said Temken. "I'm told it's going to take at least two more days to drill through the hardened pistons manually. But Level G houses the auxiliary kitchen. The children should have enough food and water for much longer than that."

"Tell the work crews I want them putting in mandatory overtime until the problem is solved," said VanClef. "The Project cost the taxpayers a small fortune. It's ridiculous that I should have my progress hindered by mechanical issues."

"Yes, sir," said Temken. He turned to leave. As he did, he saw VanClef lean over and kiss the blonde girl's forehead.

"Temken," said VanClef. "One more thing."

"Yes, sir?"

"If you fail again, I'll kill you."

"Yes, sir."

A Bad Man

Peyton closed the door of the kiosk, shoulders hunched inside the religion vendor's plastic cylinder. Rainwater from his overcoat drummed on the tiled floor and left a puddle under his boots. He did not know what to do with his hands. He folded them in his lap.

A small dome light switched on. It was set in the divider that bordered his half of the cylinder. Beneath the light, a plastic door slid sideways. The mesh screen beneath that bore the symbol of the Univariance Church: a star on a cross within a sphere beneath a crescent.

"Child of all gods," said the man behind the mesh, "know that you are in a safe place, among friends who are here to help you."

Peyton had no answer. The man behind the mesh wore the LED collar of a priest. The priest cleared his throat.

"I don't know how this works," said Peyton.

"You paid for the confessional," said the priest. "You may unburden yourself to me." The priest was middle-aged. His head was shaved. His features were very soft. One of his eyes drooped. His face was dark with beard stubble.

"I need to talk to someone," said Peyton.

"I am listening," said the priest. "You may input more funds if time expires before you're finished."

Peyton rubbed his hands together. "I worked for the Triads," he said. "It was twenty years ago, here in Hongkongtown."

"Many have fallen into the trap of easy earnings from organized criminal enterprise," said the priest. "I want you to say the Mantra of Forgiveness twenty times and make a donation to the Church of—"

"I'm not finished," said Peyton.

"My apologies, my son," said the priest. "Please continue." The LED of his collar turned from white to blue.

"There was something wrong with me," said Peyton. "An imbalance in my brain. I was born with it."

"There is no wrong in being what the gods made you," said the priest.

"I killed for the first time when I was nine years old," said Peyton. "A boy at school. He wouldn't stop hitting me. I stabbed him in the eye with a stylus."

The priest's LED changed from blue to green.

"I killed again when I was fourteen," said Peyton. "A Hongkongtown prostitute who tried to rob me. By the time I was nineteen I was performing executions for the Triads. And at twenty-six I killed a man named Wo Jao."

"These are great evils," said the priest, "but a donation of suitable size may—"

"Jao was running Sleep for the Triads," said Peyton. "He was a distributor whose job it was to supply street dealers. A mid-level member of a very powerful organized crime family. But Jao was greedy. He was skimming profits, shorting the Triads their share of the money. So they told me to kill him."

The priest's collar turned red. "I'm afraid that means time is expired," he said. "But if you insert more chits—"

"I was small back then," said Peyton. "Normal. Not like now. I took a gun to Jao's house. Shot his dog. Shot his guards."

"Uh," said the priest.

"Jao was hiding in his bedroom. It was hardened. Safe from attack. I stuffed the ventilators with strips of fabric from his furniture. I set them on fire. I smoked him out."

"I really think—"

"When he came out, I put my gun under his chin. I told him the Triads had ordered his death. I told him it wasn't personal. It wasn't. I didn't care about him. I didn't care if he lived or died."

The priest's red collar started blinking. "My son, you'll need to insert more chits to continue," he said.

"He begged me. He told me he had a daughter. 'I'll never see her again if you kill me,' he said to me. 'She'll grow up alone. You'll take me away from her forever.'" He stopped and pressed his fingers together. His knuckles turned white. "I remember it exactly. 'You'll take me away from her forever.' That's what I did. I put my gun under his chin and I put his brains on the wall."

"My son," the priest began.

"And I didn't care," said Peyton. "I felt nothing. Killing *never* made me feel. But then came the Project."

"My son, the gods love you, but I must call security," said the priest.

"Something about my endocrine system," said Peyton. "It had to be rebalanced. Before they could implant the hormone sacs. 'Building on a level foundation,' they called it."

The priest was furiously pressing a button on his side of the wall. Peyton reached out and poked one huge finger through the mesh screen. He pulled the screen free and dropped it on the floor.

"My son, you can't do that," said the priest. "The Church will have to charge your account for any damages."

Peyton rubbed the back of one huge hand across his eyes. His hand came away wet. He looked at the priest. "Your panic button won't work," he said. "I pulled the cable before I got in."

"Young man, if you refuse to work with the Church, the Church cannot help you." The priest frowned at him through the opening in the barrier.

"I just had to tell someone," said Peyton. "There's no one I can talk to. I can't tell Annika. She can't know that I murdered a father. That I took him from his daughter forever. She told me I should be proud. That I'm doing a good job. But I'm not. I'm not doing enough. I don't know what enough would be."

"It is time for you to go," said the priest.

"My little girl," said Peyton. "For twelve years I thought she was dead. What is her life now? What will it be? She lives on the streets of Hongkongtown. In flophouses. In the homes of sex offenders. She sleeps in the beds of people who are so horrible they deserve what I do to them. But I'm no better."

The priest had turned pale. "Please go," he said quietly.

"They call you 'father,' said Peyton. "But a father is a protector. A father does absolutely anything he has to do. To protect his child. To give her what she wants and needs. To make her safe."

"Please," said the priest.

"You're on the offender registry," said Peyton. "You like little boys. That's why I came here. I needed to talk. But I can't talk to anyone."

"It's not my fault," said the priest. He was crying now. "I'm sick. The doctors said so."

"Maybe I really am no better," Peyton said quietly. "Maybe I deserve to die. But I can't. Not while I have a job to do."

Peyton reached through the opening. The priest tried to run, tried to open the door on his side, but he was not fast enough. Peyton's grip crushed his throat and snapped his spine.

"I'm a bad man," said Peyton to the dead priest. "But I'm also Annika's father."

Friends

"You're pouting again."

Annika looked up from the touch screen of her forearm computer. She was sitting upside down on the end of the sofa, her legs braced against one of the armrests, her head on a pillow on the floor. She spared him an exasperated glance and then went back to the machine.

Peyton looked back to the wall screen. He had been watching a documentary on the Steamway Riots. To say he did not feel a certain kinship with creatures considered less than human, creatures not fit to live within "normal" society, would be a lie. He jerked his chin at the screen, and the wall went blank before switching to a simulation of the weather outside. The sim was always better than the reality. The sky was a deeper blue. The clouds were a fluffier, brighter white.

The flophouse in which they sat was a prepaid unit, nicer than many in which they usually stayed. The kitchen was stocked and the carpets were self-cleaning. They had enjoyed several peaceful days here. Peyton had spent most of those days sleeping on the couch. His accelerated metabolism ran in long cycles. He had entered one of his brief ebb phases.

Peyton leaned back on the sofa and closed his eyes. He felt her get up; heard her walk to the kitchen; heard her enter a set of instructions at the printer. When she returned she had a plate of soy cubes and a sphere of applesauce. She was also holding a mug of coffee. Coffee helped blunt his fatigue.

"Thank you, Annika," he said. He sat up, took the food, and balanced the plate on his leg while sipping coffee. She had sugared and lightened it zealously.

"There aren't any Ogs here," she said.

"Augments?" Peyton asked. He popped a couple of soy cubes in his mouth and chewed. "No. Hongkongtown has always been too far out of the way. Augments like to be in the thick of things. Only the largest population centers, like Central City, have an Augment District. When I was a boy, Hongkongtown also had vigilance committees. They killed Augments and drove them out of the city."

"Could there be riots here?"

"Like in Steamway, you mean? That was a specific protest about specific things. But riots can happen any time. If enough people stand up and fight for something, there will be a riot."

"So a riot is when a group of people fight for something they want," said Annika. "Against people who want to stop them. Like the people in charge."

"Yes," said Peyton. "Pretty much." He gulped coffee.

"Did you learn about the Augments in school?"

"No," said Peyton. "I didn't go to school. I had to take 'tolerance' classes in prison. They used the Augments as an example because there weren't any inside. Less chance of starting problems among the prison gangs."

"How do you make a gang?" Annika asked him. She climbed up on the arm of the sofa and stole a piece of soy from his plate.

"You need a bunch of friends, I guess," said Peyton. "Those friends agree to work together toward a goal. If somebody tries to hurt one of your friends, all the others hurt him back."

"So that it isn't any fun for the bully," said Annika.

"Yes." He finished his coffee and offered her the last piece of soy. She shook her head. "Annika, what's bothering you today?" he said. "Is there something you want?"

"No," said Annika. "It's just that none of the members of my gang are in the virts, so they can't play games with me."

"Your *gang*?" Peyton asked.

"Like you said." She began counting on her fingers. "My friends. We talk in the virts. Play games. Sometimes we explore in 3D. But none of them can get onto the grid right now. So I'm by myself."

"You can't make new friends?"

"There are always people who want to make friends in the virts," said Annika. "Some of them are even my age."

"But it's not the same," Peyton said. "I think I understand. Look, Annika, I should get out and move around. Let's go do something. Something fun."

"It's late," said Annika.

"This is Hongkongtown," said Peyton. "Nothing closes."

Peyton was too large to ride any of the rides. He did not mind. He stayed in the shadows, walking along the perimeter fence, keeping a close eye on Annika as she ran from machine to machine. So far she had ridden the Tiltrotor four times. It seemed to be her favorite. He had given her enough chits to ride it a hundred more if she wished.

The all-night amusement park sat in the center of the Lion Arc, a stretch of commerce and entertainment franchises accessible to multiple Hongkongtown neighborhoods. It was extremely busy, which made for plentiful crowds in which to disappear. It also boasted anything a customer could want. There was no manner of diversion that could not be had here, no exotic foodstuff or contraindicated consumer product that could not be purchased. When travelers from the rest of the world thought of Hongkongtown, this was what they pictured—not its slums, not its peninsular prison, not its street life. To travel agents and the ignorant, the Lion Arc was Hongkongtown in all its fetid wonder.

He watched as his daughter stopped at the spun-sugar vendor and procured another cone of blue fibers. She was going to make herself sick, at the rate she was going. But she looked happier than he had seen her in a while.

Some of them are even my age. The comment concerned him. There were predators enough in Hongkongtown. There was no reason to think these could not occupy virtual space as easily as reality. He was not conversant in computers. He had made his way in the world with knives, with guns, and—after the Project—with his enormous fists. He was not good with technology.

Annika had made a couple of friends tonight. They were a boy and a girl, roughly her size, wearing clothes that did not seem to quite fit them. Cast-offs. He recognized the symptoms easily enough. They were street children. Annika invited the pair to join her on the Tiltrotor and paid for their admission.

"Your daughter is very generous," said a voice. Peyton tensed, ready for a fight. But the slim figure in the hooded rain slicker hardly looked like a threat. The newcomer seemed emaciated. Peyton could not see his face past the hood, but the slicker was draped on his frame like canvas hung out to dry.

"How did you know?" Peyton asked. He could smash this interloper with a finger, should he choose.

"The way you watch her," said the man. "Always looking. Always close. There is no place for you in there, beyond this fence. But you watch because you want her to be happy. It is the same for me."

Peyton understood, then. The newcomer shifted beneath its hood slightly, and Peyton caught a glimpse of its face: A metal mask. Cameras for eyes. A neck made of hydraulic servomotors. An Augment.

"I thought there were none of your kind here," said Peyton.

"There aren't," said the Og. "This is why I hide."

"Those children," said Peyton. "Yours?"

"Yes," said the Og. "Certifiably human. But having me for a parent . . . It is not easy for them. I imagine it is no easier for you."

"I'm not an Augment."

"You are not human, either," said the Og. Its neck servos whined as it looked up at Peyton. "I mean no offense."

"I know," said Peyton. He looked back across the fence to watch the children. Now the siblings were offering to buy Annika more sugar. Fortunately for everyone, she declined.

"Many things hide in the shadows of Hongkongtown," said the Og. "It does not hurt to have friends. Friends who understand." The Og reached into its slicker and produced a circuit card. Peyton accepted it.

"I don't have one," said Peyton.

"*You* will have to do me the honor of calling on *me*, then," said the Og, "the next time your daughter would like playmates."

"I might do that," said Peyton.

The Og somehow signaled to its children, or they were on a set timetable. The siblings made their good-byes to Annika, who hugged them. She returned to the Tiltrotor. The boy and girl exited the park, nodded to Peyton politely, and took their parent's outstretched pincers. The Og made a bow with its neck servos and turned to go.

"Such a difficult mystery," said the Og over its shoulder. "Be mindful of the added challenges, my large friend."

"Challenges?" Peyton asked after it.

"Little girls," said the Og, receding into the dark. "The smarter they are, the more interesting they will make your life."

Montauk

Peyton woke on the floor next to the sofa. He had been sitting on the carpet, using the couch as a backrest, watching screen and drinking coffee. He must have fallen asleep. Annika had draped a blanket over him.

He sat up. His mug was gone. He looked over his shoulder and saw it sitting on the counter in the kitchenette. Annika again. He rubbed one huge hand across his face and through his hair.

His head felt thick. It always did when he woke. His metabolism moved very fast when he was awake, but asleep, it was almost dormant. It reminded him of the old days, before the Project, when he spent his nights drinking and his mornings hungover.

The wall screen had reverted to a twenty-four-hour display of the time. He realized that it was much later than it should be. He had slept almost through the day. Where was Annika?

The door to the bedroom was not shut completely. He eased this open. Annika was asleep in her clothes on top of the bedspread. She had at least removed her forearm tab. It was on the floor. He picked it up, thinking to place it on the night table for her. He stopped.

She slept heavily—so heavily, based on her breathing, that she must be exhausted. He stared at the tab in his hand. In the last days she had done nothing but stare at this computer, using it to play her games and occupy the virtual spaces where she interacted with her friends. He had no idea what she really did with those friends; he had no concept of the conversations she might be having.

He was not smart. He should have worried about this before. This was a problem he could not solve on his own.

From the pocket of his shirt he took the contact circuit the Og had given him. This he inserted in the socket next to the wall screen. There was only a moment's delay.

"It's you," said the Og. The lighting on its end of the connection had been adjusted to put its face in shadow. The silhouette was vague. Peyton recognized the voice.

"I need your help," he said. "You know machines. Computers."

"You might say that," said the Og. It had cameras for eyes and a metal face. Its hands were motor claws.

"I need to know what my daughter has been doing with her computer," said Peyton. "Is this possible?"

"Yes."

"Do you need the computer to do it?"

"No," said the Og. "There should be a number on it. A serial etching. Read it to me."

Peyton did so. The Og nodded and recited an address. "The ozone warning is elevated of late. Do you require a rebreather?"

"I don't know what that is," said Peyton.

"Of course you don't," said the Og. "My flat is two blocks down and one block over. I'll have what you want when you get here."

Peyton nodded. He pulled the circuit. Checking once more on Annika, he put her computer on the night table before closing the door, gently, behind him.

"I'm twelve," said the little girl who opened the door. "My name is Aimee." Her hair was a lustrous dark blonde, almost auburn, that reached to the middle of her back. In her outsized, cast-off clothing she looked like a waif, but there was a measured intelligence behind those eyes. Aimee looked Peyton up and down as he stood in the doorway. He felt uncomfortably transparent.

The Og appeared behind the girl. Without its slicker, its form was more apparent: It was an alloy skeleton, all gears and pistons and cubes of metal, walking on arched and spring-loaded feet. A full-body mod, with a human brain somewhere behind the camera-lens eyes and hammered facial mask. Somewhere in the skeleton, clad in metal, would be the Og's human spine, perhaps some of its other organs. The creature's cameras whirred and extended as it changed its point of focus.

"Greetings, Peyton," it said. "Aimee you've met. She is my adopted daughter. Samuel is out procuring groceries for himself and his sister."

Peyton stepped inside, easing himself through the narrow doorway with some difficulty. The flat the Og and its family occupied was an irregular unit among a cluster of similar dwellings. Peyton knew the type. They were prepaid and unregistered—the kind of place someone not actively wanted by the police could live quietly for an extended stay. Aimee closed the door and skipped out of the living room. The room was cluttered with clothes, toys, and packing cartons. There was no furniture, but there were two wall screens.

"Groceries for himself and his sister," Peyton repeated.

"I don't eat," said the Og. "Not in the conventional sense. My organic systems require very little in the way of nutrients." It gestured with a metal pincer toward the center of the living area. "Please make yourself comfortable." It made a slight bow. "My name is Montauk."

"How did you know mine?" asked Peyton. He sat cross-legged on the floor.

"An educated guess," said Montauk. "There is very little in the grid unknown to me." It waved a pincer at the screen, which illuminated with a scroll of text. "This is every virt and extended chat your daughter's tab has processed in the last week. You will be relieved to know that it is largely innocent."

"How did you know that's what I wanted?" Peyton asked.

"It is what any father would want," said Montauk. "But please note that I said 'largely.' Annika has one contact whom I believe may be a predator. He uses an identity nominally attached to the name 'Billy,' but that is not his name. I've tried to trace the identity to its source, but it is too well masked. This is rare enough to be noteworthy. A predator accustomed to successfully engaging victims through the grid might know how to do this."

"So you can't give me a name or an address."

"No," said Montauk. "But based on the frequency of Annika's conversations with 'Billy,' I think he may try to arrange a meeting with her soon. He is very adept. Somehow he has spurred Annika to contact him more often than he contacts her. This plants in his victim's mind the notion that it is *her* idea to seek him out, and thus ensures compliance."

"Annika is smart. She won't fall for that."

"Annika is twelve years old," said Montauk. "Peyton, she could be a genius on the order of Einstein or Hollyfeld, but she lacks your knowledge of the criminal world. She is not 'street smart,' as they say. Although I suspect she is much more so now than when you first found each other."

There was a knock on the door. It came in code—three, a pause, two more, another pause, and then a single knock. Aimee appeared from the bedroom hallway and unlocked the door. Samuel was almost dwarfed by the bag of groceries he carried. He placed this on the table in the kitchenette.

"We'll make spaghetti," said Aimee. "Spaghetti is good when you need a lot of food all at once."

"I think that's an invitation," said Montauk. "Would you like to stay for dinner?"

"I should get back," said Peyton. "Annika doesn't know where I've gone. If she wakes up she might be frightened."

"Send her a message, silly," said Aimee. "She has a messaging account, doesn't she?"

Montauk looked to Peyton. Its cameras dialed out. "I could do just that," it said. "I can also explain the circumstances, should she doubt the provenance of the message."

"All right," said Peyton.

"We'll be ready soon," said Aimee from the kitchenette.

Peyton watched the children cook for a time. Montauk went back to the wall screen, shunting through feeds so quickly Peyton could not track them. "If Hongkongtown had the grid capacity for subliminal bursts," said the Og, "I could do this in a fraction of the time it now takes. But this is not exactly Central City."

"What are you doing?" asked Peyton.

"I check the 'nets every day, node to node," said Montauk. "Looking for any sign, any clue, that my whereabouts have become known." It paused. "You'll be pleased to know that the recent hydrogen platform explosion in Southasia was *not* the work of terrorists. Or so the terrorists would prefer the authorities believed."

"Who is searching for you? The police?"

"Not as such," said Montauk. It never took its cameras from the screen. "It is a very long story. One I will tell you eventually, should you wish to hear it. Listening to my long, boring stories will be your repayment for my assistance."

Peyton considered that. "Why *are* you helping me?" he said.

"The fact that I am a persecuted member of a marginalized demographic is insufficient?" asked Montauk. "Solidarity among the other-than-normal?" The Og made a kind of ratcheting sound deep within its metal chest. Peyton realized this was laughter. "Very well, Peyton. You are not wrong."

"What, then?" Peyton said.

"I am not so rich in friends," said Montauk, "that I can afford to pass up the opportunity to make one. Can you?"

"No," said Peyton. He again watched the children preparing dinner, which seemed to involve a lot of whispered conferring. "How did you find them?"

"Samuel is actually my son," said Montauk. "His birth predates the day I took the name Montauk. Before I shed my human shell. Before my *becoming*."

"Is that what an Augment calls it when he is converted?"

"Some do," said Montauk. "Some don't." The Og waved a pincer. "I came to Hongkongtown with Samuel to escape certain . . . consequences."

"Will he change his name and become an Og? Peyton asked.

"We've discussed it," said Montauk. "I refused to make the decision for him. One is either born with the 'sickness' they accuse us of carrying, or one is not. The conversion itself is nearly instantaneous, barring a few coding issues and the time required to synchronize wetware with hardware and its governing programming.

When a boy as young as Samuel decides he wishes to follow his parent's path, however, it can be difficult. Northam law does not permit minors to make this choice. Certain government agencies will intervene."

"Consequences," Peyton repeated.

"Just so," said Montauk. "We have been here for five years. Half of that time we spent alone. Then we encountered Aimee. She was living on the streets, poor thing, eating out of garbage bins."

"She's so much like Annika," said Peyton. "What happened to her family?"

"She says she doesn't know," said Montauk. "There are many orphans in Hongkongtown. Some are the victims of trafficking rings. Others are . . . leftovers. There are so many murders here. The real numbers are suppressed by the reputable media agencies. Some of these killings claim entire families. From the moment I met Aimee, I knew she was alone. I knew I wanted to help her. And in the time she has lived with us as my own child, I have come to love her as I love Samuel."

"Aimee's parents were killed?"

"I've had no success tracing her DNA," said Montauk. "Her vital signs, skin responses, pupil dilation . . . these do not change when I ask her about her family. She is either the world's most accomplished liar, or she truly does not know. My theory is that whatever happened to her traumatized her so badly that she blocked out the memories. There are certain therapies that could help her recover them. I see no reason why I should put her through that."

"Dinner's ready," called Samuel from the kitchen.

"Someone could be searching for her," said Peyton.

"They might be. And if they are, keeping her with me and Samuel endangers our freedom. Makes our lives more difficult.

One might say she is a liability."

Peyton felt his chest tighten. "But you wouldn't," he said.

"No," said Montauk. "I know that one day very soon, she will leave us. She has her own path to follow. Her own work to do. But while she remains in our company, no matter how much danger comes with having her with us, no matter what we must do to ensure her safety, we will gladly do so. Aimee could never be a liability."

"Why not?" asked Peyton.

"Because she is my daughter," said the Og.

Something about Clocks

"I'm going out, Daddy," said Annika.

"Where?" said Peyton. "It's late."

"Hongkongtown," Annika said, as if this explained everything. "We need more proteins for the printer. I'll get some. You should try to sleep."

Peyton looked at her carefully. "All right," he said. "Be careful. Screen me if there's any trouble."

"You're becoming very modern, Daddy," she said, smiling. Twice now, she had relayed messages to him from her forearm tab—which she always wore—to the wall screen in their flat. She now took for granted this method of communicating with him. She hugged his leg, waved, and was out the door before he could say anything else.

He counted to one hundred.

When he was finished, he went to the bedroom. On the top shelf in the closet was the pasteboard box in which he kept Marachuck's cut-down shotgun. He had added to this a plastic sack of shells. Briefly he considered taking the weapon with him.

No, he thought. *It isn't that bad. She's too smart.*

He put the gun back in its hiding spot.

Go or stay? He was running out of time. He did not argue with himself much longer. It took him only minutes to catch up with her, using the traffic between them to screen himself as he paced her from the opposite side of the street. His height worked for him and against him. It enabled him to watch her while she could not see him, but threatened to expose him whenever the traffic cleared.

When it became obvious that she was heading to the amusement park, Peyton circled the block, jogging past pedestrians and pedicab pilots who were quick to give him a wide berth. He came up behind the park. The Tiltrotor, Annika's favorite ride, was at the rear of the fenced space, placing its maintenance channels against the wall. This meant a deep, wide pit, of sorts, backed the ride and separated it from the fence.

He saw neither drones nor mounted cameras. The slats of the fence bent easily. They were much worse for wear after he bent them back, trying to conceal his breach. The Tiltrotor was very loud, groaning and wheezing as its hydraulics spun alloy carriages at high speeds.

Peyton spotted the man almost immediately. He was squat and round and waiting near the ride's entrance, standing against a light post. Peyton thought he looked familiar.

He saw Annika approaching before the man did. Placing his hands against the lip of the maintenance pit, Peyton prepared to hoist himself up.

Temken shifted his weight. His left foot was asleep. He forgot this when he saw the little blonde girl. Annika Peyton was approaching, just as they'd agreed. He braced himself against the light pole.

She would be looking for a boy her age, not a grown man. They had arranged to meet at this ride. When she saw no boy, she would circle around the ride, wondering if he was nearby. Once she did, once she got close enough, he could grab her. His fingers found the bottle of anesthetic spray in his pocket. Any moment now.

She did not look at him when she walked past, but she was too far away. He did not dare tip his hand too early, for she was bound to be faster than he was. If she bolted, he would never catch her.

He had not dared deploy a backup team. He thought the presence of so many police had tipped the Peytons before. He was therefore alone. It should not take more than one operative to scoop up a single twelve-year-old girl.

He moved farther from the light pole, into the center of the walkway. She would reach the dead end behind the Tiltrotor and then come back. When she did, no matter which side she took, she would be within reach. He waited.

She did not appear.

Five minutes passed. Ten. At fifteen, his nerves were shot. Had she found some other exit? Was there a path behind the ride, something small enough for a child? If he had missed her, she might not fall for his lure again.

There! In the recessed area behind the ride, he saw her blonde hair, even in the darkness. They were alone here. She was cornered. There was no more need for caution. He ran for her—

A hand, twice the size of his head, stopped him.

Lightning bolts fired in his vision. He tasted blood. The blow from Peyton's open palm had driven the breath from his body.

He had run into a wall once. This was worse.

He gasped, rolled, tried to gain his feet. Someone drove a hot iron through his back. He collapsed to the pavement on his stomach. From the side of his eye he saw Ian Peyton pinning him to the ground with a single finger. Peyton's finger flexed. Something, a rib, cracked in Temken's chest.

"Please," gasped Temken. "Please! I won't tell anyone I saw you."

"Annika," said Peyton. His voice was almost a whisper. The girl appeared from the shadows next to him. "Go home. Go right home, no stopping. I'll be there soon."

"Okay," she said. "Are you all right, Daddy? You seem upset."

"I'm fine," said Peyton. "But you and I will have to talk about this."

"Because of that man?" said Annika. "He's bad, isn't he? He's a bad person and you're going to fix him."

"I'm going to make him go to sleep," said Peyton. "Because he's bad, yes."

"Okay, Daddy," said Annika. "I'm going home now."

Temken tried to speak. Blood poured from his mouth. He could feel broken ribs grating together. The stabbing pain in his side was unbearable. He could not breathe.

The girl left. She was skipping. Singing a song. Something about clocks.

The government operative managed to drag the contact circuit from his pocket. It fell to the ground. Temken's fingers were numb. Peyton took the chip.

"She's mine," said the big man. "She's not for you. How many like her have you taken?"

Temken tried to speak. Air hissed from between his lips. "Help," he managed.

"There are so many of you," said Peyton. "I'll never be able to get you all. Never be able to make the world safe for her." He placed the palm of his hand against Temken's skull. "That's why I'll never stop." He began to push.

Oh God, thought Temken. *He's crushing my skull.*

"I shouldn't enjoy this," said Peyton. "It's wrong to enjoy it." He pushed harder.

He's crushing my skull! Stop! STOP!

"But I'm going to," said Peyton.

It hurts so much and he's going to crack it open please God it hurts please I'm sorry—

Billy

"Eating spun sugar," said Montauk. His cameras were at full extension. He made some kind of adjustment. The cameras turned and whirred. "They look perfectly content."

"You're sure you can watch them from here?" asked Peyton.

"Certain," said the Og. "Samuel has an electric baton. I've taught him to use it. Aimee carries a phone. We will know should anything go awry."

"Electric baton," said Peyton. "Wouldn't that be . . . ?"

"Deadly to me?" Montauk supplied. "Yes. In short order. Samuel is fourteen. Almost a young man, if small for his age. It has been sadly necessary to give him great responsibility. What did you tell Annika about the incident?"

"I explained to her that the person she came to the amusement park to meet was a bad man who wanted to trick her," said Peyton. "That he lied to her when they spoke through the computer. That there are more like him out there and she must be careful. I also told her it isn't safe to agree to meet new friends without me."

"That sounds reasonable," said the Og.

Peyton and the Og sat at a table next to a robot soy-dog vendor. They were across the street and diagonal to the amusement park. It had been three days since the death of the man pretending to be "Billy." His death had not appeared in the news. Montauk had explained that this was unusual. It had taken all three days for the Og to finish deciphering the complex encryption carried by Billy's contact circuit.

"Your message said we're in trouble," said Peyton.

Montauk's voice was completely synthetic. It had a lilting, almost mocking quality to it. Neither male nor female, it was carefully neutral, its vowels clipped and its consonants crisp. Only when the Og laughed was the illusion broken. The ratcheting noise it made when amused was wholly alien.

"Trouble," said Montauk, "is the vaguest of adjectives for your peculiar predicament. I would like your permission to destroy the chip."

"Why?"

"Because if you had simply put that contact circuit in the wall," said the Og, "you would have heard police sirens three hundred seconds later. It is DNA encrypted to the owner. It connects to only one other party. Neither 'Billy' nor the man whose attention this chip summons is someone you wish to know. If I were a creature of fewer precautions, the authorities might already have found and deported me."

"I don't understand," said Peyton.

The Og took from within its slicker a pair of plastic printouts. They were photographs. The first was of "Billy," the toad-faced man. The second was a lean, hollow-eyed figure dressed in black.

"This 'Billy' was a man named Temken," Montauk reported. "He works, or worked, for Government Intelligence. His civil service record goes back twenty years and is utterly unremarkable. He is what we would call 'legs.' He does grunt work for the Powers That Are. In this case, that is the Intelligence service."

"And him?" Peyton tapped the photo of the man in black.

"For our purposes, that is the Intelligence service," said Montauk. "That is Marion VanClef. The details of his service record are sealed. His current rank is listed only as "Agent," which means he's very highly placed. I believe Temken worked for this man."

"So Annika wasn't targeted by a predator," said Peyton. "She was being stalked by a government operative."

"It would seem so. There is an interesting complication."

"What?"

Montauk tapped the photo of Temken with one metal pincer. "Temken is a convicted sex offender. As a man of nineteen he propositioned two young girls and was intercepted. It's possible his government service was a plea deal. It would explain why he's never excelled." The Og checked the children again, scanning with its cameras. It turned back to Peyton. "This VanClef is a very powerful man. If Temken sought Annika, he may have been doing so for his own purposes. Or he may have been doing so for VanClef."

"Why would Government Intelligence want my daughter?"

"As a means of getting to you?" asked the Og. "From what you've told me, you are not vulnerable to much else."

"My escape is a matter for law enforcement," said Peyton. "I know nothing that could be of use to Intelligence. I sat on Death Row for more than a decade, and never once did anyone question me. The Warden and I reached an agreement based on my cooperation. It was easier for him, easier for his bureaucracy, to give me small considerations if I waited out the automated appeals and made no trouble. If not for the legal maze he was forced to navigate, I'm sure the Warden would have simply evacuated the air from my cell. It would have been easier."

"You are missing the obvious," said Montauk.

"What do you mean?"

"I mean," said the Og, "if the government has no interest in *you*, there is only one person they could possibly be hunting."

"Annika," said Peyton.

"Annika," said Montauk.

145 Months Ago

He is alone in the heavy-gravity room of the prison. The room is controversial. Many civilians have protested its existence.

There is no property in prison. Any personal effects are confiscated on entry. A man's clothes are borrowed, worn and laundered and shared with all others of the same size, recycled and reissued each week. He is allowed to accumulate nothing in his cell. His books are borrowed. His diversions are few. His vices are not tolerated.

In such an environment, some turn to violence. The weak become property; the soft become sport. There are more reasons than boredom to use the gravity room. To build one's body. To increase one's strength.

The prison sits on a peninsula at the edge of Hongkongtown, buffeted by the ink-black waves of a dead ocean. It is named the Promontory, though none call it that. It is simply *the prison.* Thirty percent of all Hongkongtown's citizens will end their days inside it. That is the price for the city-state's freedom. It is a place of chaos, a refuge for the worst the mainland can funnel to its shores. Its freedom is the freedom of the penal colony. In Hongkongtown, one may make whatever life one can.

Some lives are short.

If he is honest with himself, he knows that lifting the electronic gravity bar, even on its highest override setting, does nothing to make him stronger. The growth hormones, the enzymes, the adrenaline coursing through his body—these chemicals and more flow through him, pumped to his cells by transplanted organs grafted to his endocrine system. The Project has made him what he is, has caused him to gain height and weight, has given him power like no human has ever possessed. For him, exercise is superfluous. It burns energy but does little else.

His cells heal quickly. He has been set on fire and shrugged it off; he has been stabbed and walked away; he has been shot with prison-built firearms and laughed. When he came to the prison, he was a victim. Then came the Project.

Prisoners are not stupid. Individually, they may commit foolish crimes—crimes that ruin their lives and the lives of others. Collectively, they possess a keen intelligence. It is an intelligence that looks ever inward, policing the organism that is the prison, searching out and destroying any threat to the body. Cancers are cut out. Sickness is attacked. If the body must suffer the fevers of a bloody riot, then a riot it will have.

They came for Peyton as he grew. They understood what he was becoming. Their efforts were too little and too late. Every attempt failed. Eventually, even the Warden stopped asking after his well-being.

They call Peyton the Monster. They are not wrong.

The Warden is a coward; the Warden understands bureaucracy. Bureaucracy rewards the absence of disorder, not the assertion of reason. Bureaucracy keeps Peyton alive. The Warden begs him to kill as few inmates as possible; to show mercy; to make no trouble. He purges Peyton's records accordingly. Peyton does his best to cooperate. The craven Warden does other small favors for him in return. It is an adequate arrangement.

Peyton lifts the bar again. He wants the effort to strain him;

he wants the effort to hurt him. It does neither.

Tears stream down his cheeks.

He hates himself for crying. He hates himself for feeling regret, for knowing anguish. He has never felt such things before. He has never known emotional pain.

It is the Project. They have changed his body chemistry. They have restored something, given him something he was born without. He does not want it back. He does not have a choice.

The Warden has come to him today. The Warden is a messenger. The Warden resents the role he has been asked to play. Powers above him, powers that have decreed the Project will take place within the Warden's domain, have pressed him into service. The Warden does not understand the message he has been asked to relay.

Peyton understands. Peyton has been waiting for this day. The Project has offered him much. In exchange he has given his cooperation. He has let them test him. He has let them evaluate him. He has let them take his blood and scan his organs.

He has given them a sample of his DNA.

That sample has been used to make a child. Peyton does not know why the Project wished this done. At the beginning, he did not care. But that was before they changed his body.

That was before they gave him back *remorse*.

Tears continue to pool on the bench. He cannot stop them. He can do nothing to escape the pain. The awful, clinging guilt, the regret, the wish never to have been . . . These pass into him, through him, and over him. It is an ache. It is a torment. It is drowning him.

His child and his child's mother are dead.

The Warden can be forgiven the indifference with which he has delivered this coded news. He does not know. He cannot know. The Project has not shared the information with him.

Word has come to Peyton all the same. The child created using his DNA, the surrogate mother chosen to bear this child . . . they have died on the operating table. He has never met the woman. He grieves for her. He has never seen the child.

He mourns.

When he was told a child would be created, a child that would become the custody of government scientists, he felt nothing. What was this child to him? He was Ian Peyton. He cared for nothing. For no one.

Now, knowing this son, this daughter, this baby is dead, he wants only to die.

He pushes the bar up and down. He prays for fatigue to come. It does not.

He has asked the Project to kill him. They have refused. He has asked the Warden to snuff him out. The Warden has said no. Peyton is to live out his days here in the Promontory. He will sit in a cell alone. He will spend each day knowing that his child is dead.

He can't do it. He won't do it.

He has formed a plan.

He will watch. He will bide his time. He will choose a victim who deserves to die. Here, in prison, he will commit one last murder.

They will put him on death row. The appeals process is automatic. It will take years.

When he has committed his murder he will ask the Warden for a final favor. Ian Peyton has been no monk; he has known his share of women. Somewhere in the world he may have a living child. He wants to know. He *needs* to know. He has never cared before. He cares now.

He will barter his cooperation. He will ask that a search for his

DNA be conducted. The price will be years of quiet occupancy—years on death row in which he will do everything he can to take no more lives. Bureaucracy will reward the Warden for these years of peaceful residence. Bureaucracy is the Warden's only god.

Years stretch before him. They are years he must endure. At their end is the death he so desperately wants.

He will wait.

Violet Speakeasy

"Annika, I'm worried about something."

"You're *always* worrying, Daddy," said Annika, looking up from her plate. "We've talked about this." With her fork, she attacked the second of two enormous waffles.

"I'm serious," said Peyton. "Because you're with me, you're not going to school. I didn't want you to go back. I didn't want you to leave. But I think I was selfish. You're so smart. I've been thinking about this, and I feel like it's wrong for you not to get an education."

The waffle house on Dragon Street was dimly lighted, boasting plenty of alcoves and recesses. The booth they had selected was configured on one side for customers using mobility scooters. Peyton sat cross-legged on this side, while Annika sat in a chair across from him. While he watched, Annika took the hose from its clip on the table and doused her plate with syrup.

Peyton scanned the room but saw nothing to concern him. The waffle house had been recommended by Montauk. "It caters to a diverse selection of differently realized beings," the Og had said of it. "They'll give you no trouble. Should the authorities visit, they'll have no memory of your stay." Peyton suspected that the serving robots moving quietly among the tables were, in fact, Ogs. It had never occurred to him that an Augment might pretend to be, or disguise itself as, a robot. Watching them closely now—an irregular step here, an overlong pause there—he thought he saw telltale signs of individual behavior in the serving staff.

"I'm learning a lot while I'm with you, Daddy," Annika told him. "Things I couldn't learn in school. I'm learning how the world works. I learn just by watching you."

"That's what worries me."

"You're doing it again," she said. "You're all frowny and wrinkled. Stop it. At school they taught me math and circuits and networks and geography. But they didn't teach me about lying. They didn't explain mean people, or bad people. They didn't show me what to do, or how to find someone who can do what I can't. *You* taught me all that."

He wasn't sure what to say to that. He waited while she finished her meal, then left a small stack of plastic chits on the table and walked her out.

"Please come again," said the robot by the door. Peyton looked at it carefully. It inclined its head to him. One of its glowing optic sensors flickered.

"I will," said Peyton.

On the street, they struck out in the direction of home. It was not a terribly long walk, but it was not short. Several times Peyton had wondered if they might secure a vehicle. Stealing one was easy. Buying one would not be difficult. But he had seen no ground cars big enough to fit him. Short of obtaining a hydrogen lorry or dragging Annika around in a pedicab, he did not see an alternative to walking.

"That robot winked at you," said Annika. They walked through the street throngs easily. Peyton walked ahead, separating the crowd, creating a wake in which Annika could have run circles. He looked down at her and winked.

"Yes," he said.

"Robots don't wink," said Annika.

"That's because it was an Og," said Peyton. "I think most of them were. Maybe all. It's hard to tell when they don't want you to know."

"There are robots everywhere," said Annika. "I wonder how many of them are really Ogs?"

"Montauk might know," said Peyton.

"I like him."

"I'm not sure he's a 'him,'" said Peyton. "But I'm not sure he's not, either." He turned right, leaving the stream of pedestrians to cut through an alley. Their paid flop was on the other side. "Do you like playing with Samuel and Aimee?"

"Of course," said Annika. She was walking beside him now, skipping. "Aimee and I are teaching Samuel trigonometry."

"Why would you do that?" Peyton asked.

"You can't understand triangles until you understand trigonometry, Daddy."

"I'll take your word for it," said Peyton. Perhaps Montauk could explain. He would have to ask.

Movement farther up the alley made him stop. Annika, without prompting, fell in behind him, shielding herself with his thigh. The two men who approached had been hiding in the shadows of a stack of disposer tubes—compressed cylinders of dehydrated, deodorized garbage, the effluvia of the in-sink units found in most dwellings. The men approached almost in lockstep, walking next to each other. They were dressed shabbily, like street beggars or Sleep addicts. One wore a threadbare overcoat. The other was bald and dressed in layers of beige rags.

"Evening, big guy," said the bald man. He passed by, nodding, almost bowing. The other man nodded as well. They seemed in a hurry to put distance between themselves and Peyton.

Annika turned to follow their progress. The two men stopped some distance away. They were now engaged in a furious, whispered argument. Peyton could make out their faces in the light from the street beyond, but he could not hear their words.

"Come on, Annika," he said. "Let's go."

"They're talking about us," said Annika.

"What?" He looked to her. Her mouth was forming words silently. "Are you . . . are you reading their lips?"

"Yes," said Annika. "Aimee taught me."

"Why would—"

"Daddy," said Annika. "The bald one wants to know why the other one didn't use his knife. They're arguing about mugging us. The bald one says the other one is a coward. He says you might be big but your guts come out as easy as anybody."

It was the casual way she recited it that caught him, burned him, stoked the fire of his temper. His rage erupted. He pointed to the wall of the alley and she pressed herself against it, eyes wide, missing nothing. He took a step forward.

The two men saw him coming. They started to run. There was no way they could match Peyton's long strides. He caught them easily, digging his fingers into their clavicles from behind. They fell to their knees, moaning. The blade of a knife caught light from the alley mouth.

Peyton flexed his right hand. The bald man screamed and dropped his knife. Peyton snapped the bald man's collarbone and then pressed a thumb into the back of the man's neck.

"Please!" said the bald man.

"Please what?" Peyton asked. "Please don't stab a man while he walks home with his daughter? Please don't murder strangers? Please don't make the streets of this filthy city the kind of place where the gutters clog with blood?" He snapped the man's neck with his thumb. The bald man made a noise like a deflating balloon. When Peyton let go, the corpse fell on its face.

The other man had stayed very still. He risked a glance over his shoulder at Peyton. "I never seen you," he said. "I don't know you. I don't know *him*." This last came with a jerk of the chin to the dead man.

"Thinking," said Peyton.

"I like a drink," said the man in the overcoat. "Maybe a few pills. I steal. I never killed nobody. Please, mister, I never did."

"Liar," said Peyton. He grabbed the man by the back of the neck and shook him. Bones snapped. When he was satisfied, Peyton dropped the body. He went to rejoin Annika, who took the edge of his hand and skipped beside him as they left the alley.

"I could go to school through the virts," she offered.

"People do that?" said Peyton. "It's real school?"

"Yes," she said. "All I have to do is register. The name can be anything. Anything made up."

"A fake name?" Peyton asked. They were close to home now. Annika skipped more vigorously. "Something common."

"Bo-ring," she said in sing-song. "Violet," she said. "It should be Violet."

"You'll need a last name," said Peyton.

"Violet Speakeasy," said Annika.

Peyton actually laughed. "That's . . . distinctive. You're sure? They'll expect you to answer to that, won't they?"

"I like it," said Annika. "In the virts you can be anyone."

"If you're sure," said Peyton.

"I am," said Annika. "Besides"—she looked up at him as he paused to unlock the front door of their flop—"if I go to school in the virts I won't meet anyone you'll have to put to sleep."

People Are Funny

"Best waffles in town," said Neiring. He dug in with his fork. "You'll regret missing them."

"I ate at Row's," said Getty. He took a rebreather from his nostrils and tucked it away. Most residents of Hongkongtown had long ago adapted to the ozone bursts. A few, particularly those with respiratory ailments or who were elderly, required nose filters for the worst periods.

"I thought the same thing," said Neiring. "But they really are delicious."

"First things first, Inspector."

Neiring looked around. A robot server bearing a tray of drinks trundled past. He reached into his coat and produced a plastic envelope full of chits. This he passed across the table to Getty.

The prison guard took the envelope, slit it with a fingernail, thumbed the chits. He nodded.

"As agreed," said Neiring.

"I could lose my job for giving you this," said Getty. From his own rain slicker he produced a data chip. Neiring took it. "There isn't much. I warned you there wouldn't be. But I got what we had."

"What does it say?" Neiring asked. He took another large bite.

"Annika Peyton's records don't exist," said Getty. "At least, they *didn't*. A week before her father's execution, a recursive data error starts propagating through some of the nodes on the grid. It had barely resolved across all of the 'nets when Richards, that fool, saw the display at the gallows and announced it to the world. Even then, the records aren't complete. There are no medical certifications. No other family ties. No entry for a birth mother. No address history. That little girl just winked into existence at twelve."

Neiring sipped from his coffee mug. "So what *is* there?" he said.

"There's a listing for her school," said Getty. "With an address near the Redlight, which doesn't make any sense. The neighboring zones are all industrial. There are no schools there."

"Could it be a decoy?" asked Neiring. "The data, I mean. Planted by—"

"By VanClef, you mean?" said Getty. "If it is, you don't know me. I was never here."

Neiring held up a hand. "Seriously," he said. "How badly are you putting yourself at risk to get me this information?"

"Not too badly," said Getty. "I'm near my pension. There aren't too many at the Promontory who are senior to me. The data error isn't directly traceable. I'll be fine as long you don't throw my name around."

"I won't," said Neiring. The guard started to get up. Neiring held up a hand. "Getty," he said.

"Yeah?"

"Thank you."

"Inspector," said Getty, "I could have drawn death-house duty the day Ian Peyton escaped. Instead, I called in sick. That's the only reason I'm alive today. If you ask me, hunting Peyton and his daughter is a mistake. And not because Intelligence warned you off."

"That's what everybody keeps telling me," said Neiring.

Getty tipped an imaginary hat, turned, and left the waffle house. Neiring cut another slice from his waffle.

"He's not wrong, you know," said the man in the booth behind him.

Neiring finished his dinner. Behind him, Moxley got up from the adjoining booth. He tucked the revolver he carried back into its holster under his coat, then sat down across from Neiring.

"You were sitting there with your gun out?"

"You're damned right I was," said Mox, sticking a vapor tube in his mouth. The tip flared blue as he inhaled. "You've got to learn to think less of people, Neiring."

"Meaning?"

"Meaning that if VanClef had gotten to him, it wouldn't be beneath an Intelligence operative to send somebody to hose you down. I had my gun on him from the moment he walked in."

"Which is why you suggested we meet in the most remote diner in the city," said Neiring, "with only robots on hand as witnesses."

"I suggested this place because the food is good," said Mox. "I like to eat." He flagged down a passing robot from within a growing cloud of byproduct mist. "Gimme a plate of eggs and bacon. Over hard. *Real* eggs, too, not that synthetic crap."

The robot beeped and rolled away.

"I guess we're lucky," said Neiring.

"Why?"

"VanClef didn't send an assassin. Getty came to get paid. We're lucky that he's as corrupt as everybody else in this town. Everyone's got their hand out."

"Hongkongtown," said Mox. "While you were playing strangers in the night with Getty, I spent the day chasing down something odd." He took a stack of plastic prints from inside his coat and spread them on the table. "See something odd?

"Annika Peyton," said Neiring. Each of the photos was of a blonde-haired girl, small enough to be twelve years old.

"No, see," said Mox, "that's just what I thought, too. These are surveillance pulls from the city patrol drones."

"Those records are supposed to be destroyed," said Neiring. "Privateer law."

"They are," said Mox. "They purge the files every two days. These sightings are all over Hongkongtown. From Dragon to the Promontory and back again. And all within the last forty-eight hours."

"But that's crazy," said Neiring. "Annika couldn't possibly be in this many places at the same time over just two days."

"No," said Mox. "She couldn't. And she wasn't. You macro those shots, every one of them comes up negative for Annika Peyton's facial recog. Not enough points of similarity."

The serving robot, or one like it, wobbled over with Moxley's food. The detective took his plate and began digging into the eggs. He grinned widely.

"How can you eat around that vape tube?" said Neiring.

"The same way I can drink while I do," said Moxley. He took a silver hip flask from his coat and knocked back a long swallow. Neiring shook his head when Moxley offered him the flask.

"So what are you saying, Mox?" Neiring asked. "That a small army of little blonde girls is running around Hongkongtown, fouling the surveillance algorithms?"

"No," said Moxley. "These are . . ." He trailed off. The serving robot still sat patiently next to the table. "Get lost," he told it, rapping on its housing with his knuckles. "We're set for now." The robot rolled slowly away. To Neiring, Moxley said, "Old circuits. I bet there's a robot graveyard out back."

"The little girls," Neiring prompted.

"Right," said Mox. "See, we've both been wondering how Peyton and his kid are walking around Hongkongtown without tripping any automated surveillance markers. Should be simple enough, right? Well, I talked to a guy down in the tech center. He says the surveillance drones and all the public cameras have cut-out programming to prevent false positives. Cuts down on the nuisance reporting, right? Well, I figure Peyton or his kid, probably the girl, knows enough about computers to introduce ghosts. Simulated little blonde girls, carried throughout the local nodes by a virus."

"That sounds far-fetched," said Neiring.

"It did to me too," said Moxley. "Until I checked facial recognition against the DNA database. *None* of these kids exist, Mox. Not one of them. Sure, a few kids slip through the database every year. But every last one?" He expended his vapor tube and dropped it on his now empty plate. "That's how they're doing it. I'm certain. You'd need somebody on the ground tracking them, eyes-on, to acquire them."

"So where does that leave us?" Neiring asked.

"Need you ask?" said Mox. "We take that chip and we go look at this school that isn't supposed to exist. Detective work one-oh-one, buddy."

"And if that's a dead end?"

"Don't get ahead of me," said Mox. "I'm on a roll."

"All right," said Neiring. "Let's go."

The pair headed out of the waffle house. Just outside the exit, some wag had draped a hooded rain slicker over the tall, skinny robot minding the door. It looked almost human that way. The thought was amusing.

"What are you chuckling about?" Neiring asked. "Doors."

The passenger and driver-side doors of his ground car, parked at the curb outside the waffle house, opened themselves.

"Nothing," said Moxley. "People are funny, that's all."

As the car pulled away, neither man saw the cloaked figure turn its metal head to watch them go.

Not Recovered

"He's rebooting now," said the medical tech. His name tag declared him "Foster" and bore a serial number.

VanClef looked up from where he sat reading reports on a pocket tab. He tucked away the device and went to stand next to Foster. His boots rang on the white tiles of the government medical center, located in a heavily guarded and classified annex of Hongkongtown's largest private hospital.

On a hydraulic table wide enough to accommodate a ground car, ORN84821796 lay quietly. The armored carapace of the battle machine was streaked with oxidation. VanClef ran one gloved finger across this. His fingertip left a runnel in the orange lattice.

The "patient," if that word applied here, was surrounded by the armatures of robot medical equipment. Various tubes and couplings were connected to access ports on his metal frame. There were open pods on his shoulders and forearms. Refueling hoses snaked to his legs.

"What is his prognosis?" VanClef asked.

"Good," said Foster. "You realize that once they're decommissioned, they're not supposed to be recoverable."

"I'm aware," said VanClef. "He's viable nonetheless?"

"He will be," said the tech. "I'm running a glucose and stimulant suspension through his organic systems now. It should shake off the cobwebs and get him fully conscious again. The mental conditioning appears stable, and his brainwaves show no sign of degradation. Once we designate you as his unit commander, he'll follow your orders with . . . reasonable reliability. I can't guarantee that his cognition hasn't suffered. His brain has been in the equivalent of a coma for several years. There's always some fall-off of higher function."

"How will that affect him?"

"His reaction times will be slow," said Foster. "Reflexes will be similarly retarded. He won't possess much in the way of independent problem-solving skills. It shouldn't affect his hierarchical protocols."

"Good," said VanClef. "Slow is not a problem. Insubordinate . . . *that* would be a problem."

"I still haven't received the necessary authorization paperwork," said Foster.

"It's coming through channels," said VanClef. "You'll have it."

"I hope so, sir," said Foster. "Without it I'm obligated to report the misappropriation of military resources. We're not licensed to field this equipment."

"It's being taken care of," said VanClef. "The weapons pods will function?"

"Once you've supplied the necessary munitions," said Foster. "They can't be had commercially. This model is obsolete." He handed VanClef a plastic print. "These are the specifications."

"Yes," said VanClef. "I anticipated as much." He gestured to the door of the surgical chamber. "And our guest in the next room?"

Foster sighed. He gestured for the Intelligence agent to follow. The door slid quietly aside as they approached.

The smell of chemical antiseptic stabbed VanClef's nostrils.

Undergirding this was something much worse, something rotten and cloying. He coughed. From his pocket he took the black silk handkerchief he always carried. This he placed over his mouth.

"The damage is considerable, as you can see," Foster reported. The man in the hospital bed was swathed in pressure bandages and wore an oxygen helmet. Machines breathed for him; machines processed and treated his blood and bodily wastes. Several machines whose purpose VanClef could not divine were connected to the squat figure's limbs, chest, and pelvis.

"Will he live?"

"The better question, Agent VanClef," said Foster, "is whether you want him to."

"It's that bad?"

"Yes, sir," said Foster. "You should consider euthanizing him, in my professional opinion."

"As long as Temken is alive," said VanClef, "his salary accrues in my operating budget."

Foster shrugged. "That's your call to make, of course. Mister Temken's skull has been cracked and his brain evulsed. We're fairly certain he is awake in there, to the extent that he retains higher brain function, but there is almost certainly some damage. I'm circulating a full spectrum of painkillers through him, as much as we can without risking renal failure. As it is we've had to install heart and lung machines. The trauma he endured provoked several organ failures. There's also the long-term risk of infection."

"Is that why he smells so badly?"

"We're fighting a necrotizing bacteria in his extremities," said Foster. "That's something he picked up here in the hospital, to be honest. He should be dead already. I'm astonished he survived the medevac here. I don't think I've ever seen a living man as badly damaged as this."

VanClef pressed his handkerchief more tightly to his face and leaned over Temken's helmet. "Where are his eyes?"

"Not recovered," said Foster.

"The pressure of having his skull split did that?"

"I assume as much."

"All right," said VanClef. "How much pain is he in?"

"As much as there is," said Foster.

"Pity," said Foster. "Let me know if his condition changes. In the meantime I want you to conduct an analysis of Ian Peyton's physical specifications. Find me a vulnerability. His metabolism makes it extremely difficult to tranquilize him, for example. If you can concoct something we could use to do that, I can close this case."

"You want to take him alive?"

"It would be preferable," said VanClef. "But it is not a requirement. And let me remind you that Peyton's specifications are classified." He took a print from his coat and handed it to Foster. Foster held it up to the light.

The outline of a hypertrophic man dominated the print. Several call-outs indicated organ locations and contained columns of statistics.

"I may not find anything," said Foster.

"Every system has a weakness," said VanClef. "So does Peyton." He shot a last glance at Temken and then swept from the room.

The medical tech shook his head. Looking more closely at the medical records VanClef had given him, he realized that the patient's name was not listed as Ian Peyton. It said, instead, "Stillwater, William."

Foster frowned. He would just ignore the discrepancy.

The schemes of Intelligence agents were none of his concern.

The Monster

The pavement fell away beneath his feet. His lungs burned. A stabbing pain gripped his side, gnawing at him, trying to pull him down. He could not stop. He could not give in. He dared not slow.

Everyone says it can follow you anywhere.

Jonas Mayer flew through alley after crossway, past glass facades and lighted portals, through intersections clogged with overnight traffic. Four times he was nearly hit by ground cars and pedicabs. A rider on a hydrogen cycle clipped him with the handlebars. He tripped, stumbled, scraped his face on the paving. He practically tore out his own fingernails clawing his way back to his feet.

Everyone says that it never gets tired.

He was crossing the RotenStrasse when he thought he saw its eyes glaring at him from a doorway. On Marshal, he was convinced he caught a glimpse of it, trailing him amidst the crowd. Near the Bowl, he ducked into a photo kiosk that was out of order. The robot salesman mumbled nonsense to him while the flash fired again and again. He scanned the passing crowd, looking for some sign of it.

There. Had he seen it? Was that the monster? He couldn't be sure. Everything was too dark. The photo flashes had ruined his night vision. Did that shadow move? Colored blobs danced in his sight.

He wanted to scream. He looked left. He looked right. Where was he? Somewhere in the middle of Dragon Street. Where could he go? Where was safe?

Everyone says it won't go in small spaces.

He saw it. Row's, it was called. A public diner. There would be other people there. It was well lighted. The monster wouldn't dare take him there. It couldn't. The doors were narrow sliders. The diner burned with artificial brightness. He would be safe.

He would stay until it was light. Then he could use the morning pedestrian traffic, the foot commuters, as cover to get home.

Stupid. So stupid to get caught anywhere down here after dark. Word was out. From Dragon to the amusement park, and maybe farther out than that, you weren't safe.

Everyone says it needs darkness to hide.

He almost collapsed when the sliding doors closed behind him. He smelled coffee and the deep fryer and bowls of spicy soup. There were plenty of other people here. Groups, couples. No way the monster could take him in front of all these witnesses. Everyone said that. Everyone said that it stayed in the shadows whenever it could, hiding until it chose a victim.

He slid into a booth and peered out the window. The lights inside made it hard to see through the darkness. He cupped his hand over his eyes and tried to watch the street.

Row's was famous for its human staff. The waitress jostled his elbow, impatient for his order. Jonas turned and said, "Coffee—"

The monster had found him!

He screamed. The figure next to the table didn't move. He realized the towering being wasn't a monster at all. It was just a gaunt figure in a rain slicker.

"Are you all right, sir?" it asked.

He rubbed his face with his palm. Some kind of robot. He'd

never seen one that looked so human. The robot sat down without asking. It stared at him from beneath its hood.

Everyone says that it crushes your skull.

He looked around, wondering if anyone had noticed him shout. No one had or, maybe more likely, no one cared. This was Hongkongtown. You couldn't throw a brick and not hit a Sleep addict screaming from withdrawal.

"I'm . . . sorry," said Jonas. He stared at the robot. "I thought you were someone else."

"That's understandable," said the robot. It sat very still across from him. "If you don't mind the observation, sir, you seem more than a little troubled."

"I'm . . . I'm under a lot of stress. I'm Jonas, by the way. Jon to my friends."

Everyone says that it follows the List.

"Perhaps you would let me purchase you a meal, Jon," said the robot. "I've spent many years on the streets of Hongkongtown. I know weariness when I see it."

"Thank you," he said. "I'm sorry. I don't know how to return the favor."

The robot made a strange ratcheting noise deep within its metal chest. "I do not eat," it said. "Rest easy, friend." It gestured with a pincer-like hand. Drops of rainwater fell on the table.

"Do you come to Row's often?" Jonas asked. He had no idea how to small-talk a robot.

"No," it said. "I came in here to get out of the storm. You're lucky. It was much worse out there an hour ago."

The waitress arrived. She took his order without interest. The coffee, when it came, was strong and hot and burned. He drank it black. "Yeah," he said at last. "Lucky."

"Tell me, Jon," the robot said. "What exactly is it, out there, that you're afraid of? You keep watching the windows."

Everyone says it may wait in your home.

"I . . ." Jonas said. "You wouldn't believe me. The stories people tell. About the monster."

"The monster," said the robot. "The one that kills sex offenders in Hongkongtown."

Something cold, something the coffee could not touch, settled in the pit of his stomach. He put his mug down. "How do you know that?" Jonas asked.

"I've heard about it too," said the robot. "I told you, Jon. I've spent a lot of time on these streets. I hear things."

"I *heard* it," Jonas said. "I heard the monster today. A block from my flat. I heard it talking about someone it was going to kill. Me. It came for *me*. So I ran."

"And now you're afraid you'll be killed," said the robot.

"Everyone says that happens."

"Everyone?" asked the robot. "Who is everyone?"

"My friends," said Jonas. "The people I know."

Everyone says that you'll never be missed.

"I can help you, Jon," said the robot. "I've heard the stories. I know a place that's safe from the monster. It's not far."

"How . . . ?"

"I like to think my purpose," said the robot, "is to help weary travelers find their rest at last."

It made no sense. It was a *robot*. How was it even *having* this conversation with him? What could it possibly know that could help him? And why would it bother? The logical part of his brain told him to run, told him to get out of Row's, told him to leave this strange machine far behind him.

But he had nowhere else to go. He could go home. But he'd tried to do that once today already.

He could travel to another part of the city. But there was no one he could stay with, no one he could count on. Not if he got too far from home. He didn't have the money for a hotel stay of any length.

Everyone says it's already too late for you.

Tossing a chit on the table for his coffee, he stood. "I want to be safe," he said, close to tears. "I just want to be safe."

"I can help you, Jon," the robot said again. It placed a metal claw on his shoulder and guided him to the exit. Once on the street, it pointed. "Go that way for two blocks," it said. "Turn left when you get to the cross street with the mail kiosk. There's a tram stop there. Wait there for the four o'clock tram. You should find that this gets you where you need to go. You'll be safe."

He wanted to believe. He had no other choice. He muttered a thank-you to the strange machine in the hooded slicker and ran into the night.

Everyone says that it puts out your eyes.

He barely saw the people and vehicles passing him. The tram stop bore a pair of benches, their backs conjoined. He sat facing the street.

He had made it. He was here. He glanced at his watch. It would be four soon. He was going to make it.

He felt the couple that sat down on the opposite side of the bench. The metal seat vibrated beneath him. Tourists got fatter every year. He almost laughed at his own joke.

"These are good grades, Annika," said a rumbling voice.

"Thank you, Daddy," she said. "I like the virtual school. It's better than my old school."

There was a pause. The cold ball was forming again in Jonas' stomach. He tried not to move.

"You're sure?" asked her father. "You learned so much before

I found you. The way you describe it, I think your old school must have been pretty special."

"I guess," said Annika. "I didn't like it so much when they hit us with the stick."

Jonas swore he heard the deep-voiced man spit in surprise. "Hit you with . . . They did *what?*"

"You know," said the girl. "Whenever we got something wrong. To help us learn better. Never where anyone could see. That's what sleeves are for."

Their tram would come. Their tram would come and they would leave. It was going to be okay.

Everyone says there is no hiding place for you.

"Annika," said Peyton, "Your old school. Do you think you could find it on a map for me? Do you know where it is?"

"Of course, Daddy," said Annika. "That's one of the first things they taught us. They weren't even mean about it all the time."

There was smoldering wrath in the man's voice when he spoke again. "Good," he said. "I think I want to go there."

"I don't want to go back," the girl said quickly.

"No," said the man. "You won't have to. I just want to visit. Once."

"We'll need to finish with Mr. Mayer first," she said. "He probably thought he was pretty smart, running into the crowd like that. He probably thought we would lose him."

It couldn't be happening. They could not be talking about him. It was a bad dream. He was supposed to be safe. He was supposed to get on the four o'clock tram.

"He was fast," said the man. "I hate that he got away. He's a bad man, Annika. He may hurt more children. His repeat offender index is very high."

“I know,” said Annika. “I don’t want him to hurt anyone else. I don’t understand why these bad men aren’t kept in prison. They aren’t like you. They couldn’t just leave if they were in prison.”

It wasn’t fair. He didn’t deserve to die this way. It wasn’t right.

“I don’t understand that either, Annika.” The big man shifted on the bench. “Mayer has to come home someday. Maybe we go back and just wait.”

“Oh, you don’t have to,” she said. “He’s sitting behind us.”

Jonas turned in his seat. His eyes met hers. She smiled at him.

The monster had found him.

The monster had brought its father.

He turned to run. The big man’s hand grabbed his neck.

Everyone picked by the little girl dies.

Uh-Oh

"Lock," said Neiring to his car. Behind him, Moxley hitched at his trousers and then checked the weapon before arranging it under his overcoat. Much as he hated to admit the private detective was right, Neiring took out his own service automatic and press-checked it. He put it back in its thermoplastic holster, making sure his own coat would not foul his draw.

The neighborhood was one of the worst in Hongkongtown, three blocks from the Redlight. Here, the night sky was dominated by the silhouettes of dormant mini-factories, which rose in spires all around them. Hongkongtown's industry was highly modular and always scalable. Factories that were turning out goods today might be cold and shuttered tomorrow, only to be reactivated for increased capacity a month later.

The structures around them were sealed. Neiring didn't like the look of the street. It was cluttered with debris. There were shipping containers, stripped ground cars, the burned-out skeleton of a hydrogen cycle. Garbage rose in mounds and blew in scraps and chunks with the howling wind. They were close to the sea wall here. That proximity drove gusts between the factories and whipped them to painful velocities.

"This is the one," said Mox. He pointed to the nearest of the darkened spires. "This is the address. There's no way there's a school here. According to the public registry, this is a robot plant for making tool-holders."

"Let's take a closer look," said Neiring. "Maybe we can pry up one of the shutters and get a look inside."

"Works for me," said Mox. He took a step forward and froze. The sound of a bottle skittering across pavement echoed across the street.

"Who's there?" Neiring called out. He drew his weapon, staring into the darkness.

"Uh-oh," said Moxley.

Someone they could not see began banging a metal object against the paving. The sound was deliberate and rhythmic: *Thump, thump, thump*. A pause. *Thump, thump, thump.*

"Who's out there?" Neiring demanded.

"Get back in the car," said Moxley. He was near the driver's side. He curled his fingers around the handle.

"Mox?" said Neiring.

"I said get back in the damned car!" shouted Moxley.

"Doors!" shouted Neiring. "Ignition!" He threw himself in the passenger side as Mox climbed in, grunting as he squeezed himself between the wheel and Neiring's usual seat. The detective slammed the throttle forward and the directional back, spinning the vehicle around, trying to point the nose back the way they had come.

A chunk of paving the size of a trashcan lid bounced off the windshield, leaving a stress fracture. Mox poured on the power, but now there were figures blocking the road. Where they had come from, where they had been hiding, Neiring could not imagine. This wasn't a few people; this was practically a flash mob. They were dressed in rags. The headlights of Neiring's car caused them to flinch and snarl.

Mox hit the brakes and wrenched the directional back. The

car began to reverse, picking up speed. Behind them waited the dead end that was the cul-de-sac of factories. Before them, the crowd of disheveled men and women began to walk, then to jog, then to run.

"We are so holing screwed," said Mox.

"What is it?" Neiring asked. "What are they?"

"Sleepers," said Mox. He shifted directions once more, bouncing up and over the lip of the drive path, clipping one of the menacing Sleepers as Mox accelerated past. A steady stream of rocks, bottles, and other hard refuse was now bouncing from Neiring's car, denting and cracking its polymer shell.

"You almost killed that one," said Neiring.

"I'll try harder next time," said Mox. "Sleepers aren't people any more, Ray. You don't see it. You don't come down here enough."

"Look out!" shouted Neiring.

Too late, Moxley saw the metal cable. The Sleepers had pulled it taut between a pair of shipping containers, using the alloy boxes to brace the cable. The detective had time to slam the brakes while reaching out to shove Neiring's head below the level of the dashboard.

The cable scythed through the windshield a hand's width above their heads. Fragments of transparent plastic showered the two men. The car slammed to a halt, the cable caught on the A-frame of its roof struts.

"Out," said Mox. "Out, get out, get your gun ready! Now, Ray!" He all but pushed Neiring from the other side. Neiring drew his automatic again. He had never seen Moxley this agitated. It took Neiring a moment to realize why.

Mox was terrified.

The Sleepers encircled them. The ring of shuffling addicts

began to close right away. They held a variety of weapons, from pipes to knives to chunks of pavement.

They never made a sound.

Moxley threw himself over the hood of the car and landed heavily next to Neiring, stumbling and swearing. Neiring dragged the detective to his feet. Moxley, revolver in hand, then put his back to Neiring's. "Don't shoot until I say," he said. "When they come they're gonna come for blood. You shoot for the head or the pelvic girdle. You got it? The eye box or the waist triangle, Neiring. Nothing else is going to stop them. Pray we've got enough."

"Enough?"

"Enough bullets for all of them."

Neiring's nose twitched. He could *smell* them now. Sleep smelled of lilacs. It was cloying and thick, completely out of place.

The Sleepers themselves had pallid skin and eyes so bloodshot they looked like rabbits. Prolonged use of Sleep didn't just break capillaries in the eyes; it cut off the supply of blood to the epidermis, slowly killing the addicts from the outside in. Like lepers, they would flake and crumble, dropping fingers and toes before entire limbs went missing. Neiring had never seen a Sleeper as far gone as these.

The Sleepers charged. Neiring flicked the selector on his pistol to three-round burst and began pumping rounds into the crowd. Moxley's revolver barked again and again. The detective's hand-cannon was deafening at his back, but Neiring was grateful. Mox was deadly accurate. His revolver's heavy caliber split skulls two at a time. With most of his shots, Mox managed to drill a Sleeper and take down the one standing behind him.

Neiring's pistol started to beep. He dropped the magazine and replaced it with a practiced motion, a motion he had learned and used only on a government target range. Dead addicts were piling up at their feet now, but the ones behind the wall of corpses simply climbed over their comrades. Neiring kept firing. He felt his weapon begin to grow hot as he emptied the magazine, reloaded again, and emptied the gun once more.

Then the Sleepers were all dead.

Ears ringing, Neiring turned to see Moxley breaking his revolver, dumping its spent cartridges, and sliding in a fresh moon clip. The top-break weapon fired explosive, rocket-propelled rounds. It was considered wildly impractical by most professionals. Moxley disagreed.

Neiring scanned the circle of dead. Some of the Sleepers were missing fingers. Many had rags tied to their feet. Some were barefoot, displaying missing toes.

"They were so *quiet,*" said Neiring. He was holding his empty pistol as if he might fire it. Its charging block was locked back. He was out of reloads. "Why were they so quiet?"

Moxley's hands were shaking. He managed to get a vapor tube in his mouth and thumb it alive. The blue light cast odd shadows on his moon-pie face. "Their vocal cords dry out first," he said. Even his voice was trembling. "You meet a Sleeper who can't scream anymore, he's not coming back, even if you put him in rehab. He's taken the night train. The skin turns to ash not long after." He pointed his gun at the circle of corpses. "This isn't normal. When we pulled out they should have been satisfied. They should have just watched us go."

"I don't follow," said Neiring.

"Sleepers are territorial," said Moxley. "You invade their space, they'll come at you. Get gone and they'll let you go. They don't like you; you don't like them. It's mutual. But they're more skittish than combative. There's only one reason they'd try to kill us while we were fleeing, and that's because they thought we wanted to steal from them. Like a rabid animal guarding the only watering hole."

"I don't understand," said Neiring. "What does this mean?"

Moxley spat. He took a long drag from his tube.

"It means," he said, "that somebody's been *feeding* them."

Discretion

"Is this all of them?" VanClef asked, peering through the one-way pane. From the other side it was a mirror. From this side, it was an observation port, set high above the open space of a converted warehouse in the Redlight.

"As many as we could round up, sir," said Bridger. "Two dozen, less the one who died in the truck on the way over. An allergic reaction to the stimulants."

VanClef nodded. He had come to expect concise reports. Bridger was a competent agent. Certainly he boasted a better service record than Temken's. He was healthy, toned, even tan, with perfect hair and perfect teeth—in every way Temken's opposite. Why, then, did he seem so dull?

VanClef surprised himself. He had not expected Temken's loss to affect him.

No matter. Having an assistant allowed him to delegate certain tasks, freeing him to devote his attention elsewhere. Agent Bridger was therefore a necessary tedium.

"You administered the dosage I instructed?" VanClef asked.

"I did," said Bridger. "We've also left a pallet of unwrapped rations in the center of the warehouse. I assume this has something to do with their post-addiction proclivities? The stimulants will obviously make them stronger, amplifying their already considerable danger and making them more challenging foes. The food is therefore the motivator?"

"Correct," said VanClef. "When they reach a certain stage of addiction, Sleepers cease to be what we think of as *people*. It is as if the drug has burned away anything you or I might consider . . . human. In certain parts of Hongkongtown they run in packs like wild animals. The locals quickly learn to avoid the areas these gangs of Sleepers claim as their dens. Until they begin to lose appendages from the drug, the amplified speed and strength it gives them, the complete numbness to pain it confers, conspire to make them extremely dangerous."

Bridger was a transfer from the mainland. Sleepers were a new phenomenon to him. "You were using a pack of Sleepers to guard the factory," he said.

"Yes," said VanClef. "The most dangerous thing you can do is feed a Sleeper in the final, feral stages of the drug. He becomes habituated, much like a . . . a *bear*, or some other wild animal. Even the smallest child in Hongkongtown knows not to give a beggar food. It is never worth the risk."

"Which is why we use the tunnels to enter and leave the facility," said Bridger.

"Exactly," said VanClef. "Early in Hongkongtown's history, when the opiate trade built the city and the Triads grew to prominence, it was common practice to use vicious dogs to guard one's stashed fortunes and stockpiled drugs. You simply locked the animal or animals in the area to be secured."

"That's logical," said Bridger. "No one would think of a pack of Sleepers as a security system, but they would discourage unauthorized personnel."

"Unfortunately," said VanClef, "I did not anticipate the interference of determined meddlers such as Raymond Neiring and Harold Moxley. Have you pulled their files?"

"I have," said Bridger. "There's nothing Intelligence knows about them that I don't."

"Good." VanClef allowed himself a moment's satisfaction. Perhaps, in his disappointment over losing Temken, he had been unkind to consider Agent Bridger boring. "See to it that appropriate arrangements are made."

"Yes, sir." Bridger put two fingers to the transceiver in his ear. "They're ready for you downstairs, sir."

"Good," said VanClef. "Tell them to send in the Sleepers first."

Bridger did so. He tapped his transceiver again and said, "Sir. I'm curious about something."

"And that is?

"Why round up the survivors?" said Bridger. "I understand wanting to eliminate any possible links, however tenuous, to Intelligence. Once security was breached, it makes sense to mop it up. But why not simply cleanse the Sleepers Moxley and Neiring didn't kill? Why use them for this test?"

"Waste not, Agent Bridger," said VanClef. "Waste not."

On the warehouse floor below, a door opened in the East wall. The pack of Sleepers came running out of it. They gestured wildly, pulling at their rags and at the flesh of their fellows, none of them managing so much as a moan. VanClef was impressed. These Sleepers moved with real purpose. They made immediately for the food, falling on it and tearing into it.

"Unleash the test subjects," said VanClef.

Bridger made the order. On the West wall, another set of doors opened. It took a moment for any movement to register.

Three men came lumbering out.

VanClef watched through the observation port. Every one of them was hypertrophic. The largest of them was as big as Ian

Peyton, while the other two were not much smaller. They held themselves low to the ground, centered, ready to strike. VanClef marveled at the easy familiarity they shared. This was not the first time these three had stalked and killed as a group. VanClef had been testing them for weeks. Their progress was remarkable.

"Who are they, sir?" asked Bridger.

"The alpha we call Big Bill," said VanClef. "The other two are Perry and Mulligan. All three were in cold storage until a month ago. That's when I realized they might be useful."

The Sleepers had noticed the oncoming trio. The addicts fanned out to protect their new territory, placing themselves between the three huge men and the rations. It was not the food the newcomers wanted, however. They had their orders. This was not their first time in VanClef's makeshift arena.

"But where did they come from?" asked Bridger.

"They're stepping stones," said VanClef. "Each one got us closer to the specific set of procedures that would produce Peyton."

The giant men tore into the Sleepers. VanClef watched in amazement. A heavily armed tactical team, even a military unit, would have been hard pressed to fight off the addicts. The Sleepers were vicious, they were mindless, and they felt neither pain nor fear. The amphetamines coursing through their bodies made them stronger and faster still. None of that mattered. The Sleepers were torn limb from limb.

Bridger turned away, looking nauseous. He went to the wall screen and began calling up files on the three subjects. This pleased VanClef. The man might be horrified at what he had just seen, but he was determined to be useful. Bridger was definitely an improvement on Temken.

"Big Bill's medical statistics are identical to Peyton's," said Bridger. "If anything, his projections are *better*."

"Yes," said VanClef. "But he had certain psychological deficiencies that caused us to drop him from the program." He turned away from the window. The carnage below was almost over. "These three are almost ready," he said. "I have a few more drills I'd like to run them through. In the meantime, I want you to organize a tactical team and put them on standby."

"We're still having trouble acquiring the Peytons. Surveillance thinks maybe someone's slipped a malicious algorithm into the system that's fouling the screening process. We're getting one percent of the hits we *should* be getting."

"But we *are* getting hits," said VanClef. "Hongkongtown is large, but its territory is finite. Sooner or later we will find them, just as we did before. And when we do I want to be ready to move on them with all possible firepower."

Bridger examined the wall screen, where Big Bill's image was captioned with his birth name: Stillwater, William.

"What about Big Bill and his friends?" asked Bridger. "If I and my team take the Peytons the next time they surface, you'll have trained your preliminary subjects for nothing."

"Not for nothing," said VanClef. "They are a fallback. One that I feel it is only prudent to have, but an option I would rather not use. I had the surviving Sleepers eliminated for the same reason."

"Sir?"

"Discretion, Bridger," said VanClef. "Discretion. We have enough problems to resolve at the school. I would rather not bring any more attention to Project Violet than is absolutely necessary."

The Factory

Peyton shook his head. "This can't be it," he said. "These are closed factories. There are no schools here, Annika."

"It's there, Daddy," she said. "That one." Annika pointed to the factory in the center of the cul-de-sac.

"I don't understand," said Peyton.

"It's in there," Annika insisted. "But there's going to be a problem."

"What?" Peyton asked.

"I don't see any of the Sleepers," she said. "We should have seen them by now. That means somebody came and made them go away."

"There were Sleepers here?" asked Peyton. His hand fell to the butt of the sawed-off shotgun in his belt.

"People don't understand the Sleepers," said Annika. "Not as well as they should. When they claim a territory, that group becomes a pack. The pack has weak members. The weakest ones stay hidden so they can dream."

"How do you—?" Peyton started.

Something scraped across the pavement behind them. Peyton turned. He watched as a man with milk-white skin crawled from beneath a stripped, burned-out automobile frame.

"When they get desperate," said Annika, "the weak ones get very strong. Very fast. Most people don't know about this stage.

Only people who live on the streets of Hongkongtown have seen them, and many of them are killed by the Sleepers."

A sewer cover shifted in its receptacle. It grated against the paving as something beneath it pushed it aside.

"Annika," said Peyton. "Get ready to run."

"No, Daddy," she said. "If I run they'll find me. Faster than you can stop them."

Peyton drew the shotgun from his belt. "When I was blind," he said. "When I was blind, and the police came. Do you remember how we worked together?"

"Yes, Daddy."

"We have to do that now. Hurry."

The sound of glass breaking reached their ears. A metal barrel was thrown from one side of the street to the other. The sound of unseen fists hammering shipping containers filled the cul-de-sac.

Peyton knelt. He felt Annika's fingers curl into the fabric of his shirt beneath his enormous overcoat. She climbed him like a tree, hooking her arms around his neck, positioning herself next to his left ear the way she had done when she acted as his eyes.

"Annika," he said. "Am I stronger than them?"

"One of them," she said. "Five of them. Ten of them. More than that . . . I'm not sure, Daddy. Montauk says their teeth have—"

"Montauk?" he asked. The Sleepers came out of the darkness, first one at a time, then in twos and threes. "Don't let go," he whispered to her. "Stay behind me no matter what."

The addicts formed a knot in the street before them. Peyton backed up a pace. The shotgun held only two shells. He had more in his pocket, but reloading would be slow.

"They won't feel it if you hurt them," whispered Annika in his ear. "Some of them are missing arms and legs already. A few have started to eat themselves."

She was right. The Sleepers were pale as albinos. A few were missing at least one eye; others had yawning sockets where both had been. The ones missing legs crawled and hobbled as best they could. Those with only stumps for arms still had teeth. The marks of their own bites were visible in their ashen flesh.

"They must be so lonely," Annika said. "When the others got taken away, these were left to rot in their hiding spots."

"Shotgun shells in my pocket," said Peyton. "Get ready to reload for me."

"Yes, Daddy."

The Sleepers charged. Peyton held himself low, waiting for them to get close enough. When the first of the creatures came within arm's reach, he grabbed it by the neck, lifted, threw it aside. The next one he shot in the face. The Sleeper behind that one took a blast to the throat.

"Take the gun!" Peyton shouted. He handed the gun up to Annika.

They were on top of him now. Peyton balled his fists and began smashing them. He shattered jaws. He broke ribs. He burst desiccated organs. The Sleepers kept coming.

Peyton snapped legs. He ripped arms free from their sockets. He crushed skulls, pulped brains. He broke knees, ankles, pelvises. The Sleepers kept coming.

Annika handed down the shotgun. He blasted an addict in the face, spun, shot another one in the heart. He handed up the weapon and shoved his fist completely through a Sleepers' chest, feeling air on his bloody fingers. The Sleepers kept coming.

He began cutting arcs in the air with his fists. He felt their crumbling skin against his knuckles as he smashed them, toppled them, battered them. Annika gave him the shotgun once more. He shoved the barrels into the mouth of the nearest addict and pulled both triggers, blowing the creature's head apart, cleaving the face of the Sleeper behind it.

The Sleepers kept coming.

"There are so many," he heard Annika say.

She reloaded for him. He fired the weapon twice, broke it, handed it up. He punched a Sleeper in the neck, rammed his rigid fingers through the eyes of another, clapped his hands and crushed the skull of a third. The shotgun appeared in the air by his ear. He reached up, grabbed it, fired both barrels with one hand. The Sleepers kept coming, and now they were driving him back, pushing him into the V formed by a pair of abandoned shipping containers that stood corner to corner. Peyton risked a glance back as he handed Annika the gun. The steel walls of the containers were stained red with blood and orange with corrosion. The Sleepers had used this corner before. He was being herded into a trap, funneled into a dead end. They would swarm him and—

Annika screamed.

She dropped the shotgun. Peyton saw it fall. It was trampled by the Sleepers still pushing him back.

"Daddy!" she shouted. "Daddy, I'm sorry!"

The barrels. He cursed himself, cursed his stupidity. The barrels had grown hot. He had barely noticed through his thick skin. She had burned herself.

He started to reach up, to put his hand on his daughter, to assure her that it was all right, that they would be okay without the weapon. He felt it, then: one of the addicts had sunk its teeth into the flesh of his arm. A jolt like electricity traveled up his arm, seizing his shoulder, making his arm go dead. He roared in surprise and smashed the addict with his other hand, breaking open the Sleeper's face and sending its teeth flying.

He continued to back up. He started kicking, low to crack

their knees, lower to break their ankles. The ones whose limbs he snapped started to drag themselves along with their rotting stumps. He fought with his good arm, throwing vicious hooks and uppercuts, breaking and smashing.

Pain. He looked down. One of the Sleepers had bitten him in the thigh. He grabbed the top of its skull and ripped its head off, throwing the head, kicking the body aside. He was too late. The electric shock spread through his leg. He felt the limb go rubbery.

"Daddy!" Annika screamed.

Peyton fell to one knee. Annika's back was now pressing against the steel V of the containers. They had nowhere to go.

He began swinging his good arm in wide arcs, using his fist like a morning star, smashing the crowd of rotting Sleepers as he swayed from left to right. This tactic worked for a little while. He managed to keep them at bay until they started coming at him from above and below, jumping over the level of his fist while others crawled along the ground beneath it. He met the leapers, striking them down, but he felt ashen fingers brushing his good leg. They were getting through. They were going to swamp him. He could not stop them all.

Annika made a sound in his ear. It was not a word. It was fear.

The image of Annika at the mercy of these creatures, torn apart, eaten alive, blossomed in his mind.

No. Not like that.

He reached up with his good arm. He wrapped his fingers gently around her, feeling the pulse in her neck, feeling her hair against his palm.

"Daddy?"

"Close your eyes, Annika," he said.

"I love you, Daddy."

A pneumatic hiss filled the air. Peyton's eyes widened. The

Sleepers crawling toward him were torn apart, blown to bits only inches away. Each shot raised a cloud of dried flesh. The shooting intensified. A pair of figures wearing hooded cloaks began to close from the opposite side of the mob. They held belt-fed bolt guns, powered by cylinders of compressed air. The guns trailed long sleeves of conical bullets.

"Get down!" said Montauk. The Og's voice was electronically amplified.

Peyton curled his arm and clutched Annika to his chest. He dropped to knee and elbow on the pavement, shielding her with his body, making himself as flat as he could. The bolt guns opened up on full automatic, filling the air above his back with searing projectiles.

The shooting stopped.

Peyton waited. He held Annika to his body, afraid to move, unable to stand, knowing only that while she was protected by his body, she could not be harmed.

"Daddy," she said quietly.

"What, Annika?"

"You're squishing me."

"It's all right," said Montauk. The Og moved to stand over them, holding the bolt gun with its barrel pointed to the sky. The other hooded figure stood a pace behind him. Peyton could not see its face clearly, but it was obviously another Og, more machine than man.

"It's you," said Peyton.

"That's my line," it said. "Don't try to stand, Peyton. Your knee will give out. Give me a moment, please."

The Og took a pair of contact pods from its cloak and held them out to Peyton. Peyton stared at the half-spheres, each the size of an eyeball.

"What?" Peyton asked.

"Lick them, please," it said. "The flat side."

Peyton did so, feeling foolish. Montauk placed one of the spheres against Peyton's thigh and the other on his arm. "The bleeding doesn't look too bad," said the Og. "I don't think we'll need to do anything there. Your own endocrine system should take care of any mundane infection these things had to offer."

A feeling like standing on pins and needles began to spread through Peyton's numbed arm and leg. "What did you do to me?" he asked.

"It is what I *undid*, actually," said Montauk. "When a Sleeper reaches this final stage, his blood and his saliva are laced with the drug. More accurately, it is a drug by-product—Sleep distilled, robbed of its narcotic and hallucinogenic effects, replaced by a Sleep-derived neurotoxin that paralyzes muscle tissue. The effects would have worn off quickly enough on their own, but the stimulants I've given you will counteract the fatigue this causes. You should be able to stand now."

Peyton rose. He wobbled a little, but his arm and leg were already starting to feel normal. He flexed his arm and ran a finger across the bite mark. It was scabbing over.

Annika scrambled to her feet and leaned against one of his legs. Around them, the dead Sleepers—the ones Peyton had not pulled apart—had been shot to ribbons.

Peyton looked at Montauk. "How?" he said.

"I must admit," said Montauk, "that your daughter and I have been in close communication for some time. But you did not give us much warning of this adventure. We barely made it here in time."

"You've been talking through the computer," said Peyton. He looked to the sleeve tab on Annika's arm.

"Yes," said Montauk. "Once I had her unit's serial number it was easy for us to stay in touch. She told me just before you departed that you were both coming here. I warned her about the Sleepers and arranged to be here with support when you arrived. There was every likelihood you would need help to make it past these leftovers. They're more dangerous than the main pack."

"But why?" Peyton asked. "What is your involvement here? And why didn't you or Annika tell me?"

"It is complicated," said Montauk. "But I assure you, Peyton, that none of my secrets are held to harm you. Mine is a difficult world. As for why I am helping you and will continue to do so, this is an act of friendship."

The other Og had found Peyton's fallen shotgun. It offered the weapon without a word. Peyton took it.

"This is more than friendship," said Peyton to Montauk. "Tell me it's not."

Montauk paused. It took a step closer and placed one pincer on Peyton's arm. Peyton looked down at the metal digits and back into the Og's camera eyes. "You can trust me," said Montauk. "Not only because we're friends. But because helping you is an investment in my future."

"I don't understand," said Peyton.

"Now's not the time or place to explain further," said Montauk. "But you will have your answers." It gestured to its fellow Og. "This is Loran. Another friend. Its voxbox is new and not yet initialized, so it cannot speak. But it is thinking complimentary things, I assure you."

The other Og nodded. A servo in its neck whined.

"Loran has been keeping this location under surveillance for me," said Montauk. "Two days ago it witnessed a pair of men blunder into the area. They were attacked by the main pack of

Sleepers and shot many of them. The remainder of the main pack were rounded up by government troops last night, leaving only these stragglers." It spread its metal arms. "But that is not what is important."

"What is?" Peyton asked.

"The two men who nearly lost their lives investigating this location," said Montauk. "They are an Inspector Neiring and a Detective Moxley. These men are looking into your case, Peyton. They are hunting you. And that means they have found Annika's school."

"What school?" Peyton demanded. "What school is this? This is a factory!"

"Please, friend Peyton," said Montauk, bowing its head. "Allow me to show you. Or perhaps more accurately, allow Annika to show you."

"He's right, Daddy," said Annika.

"All right," said Peyton. "All right. But I still don't understand." He broke the shotgun, reloaded it, snapped it shut, and tucked it in his belt. Kneeling next to Annika, he said, "Are your hands all right?"

"Yes, Daddy," she said. "My fingers are a little red, but not too bad."

With Loran bringing up the rear, watchful with its bolt gun, Annika led her father and the two Ogs to the side of the factory building. "We always used the tunnels," she said. "But they taught us how to get back in from the surface if there was ever an emergency."

"They simply failed to mention the habituated pack of ravening drug addicts they had encouraged to take up residence in the neighborhood," said Montauk.

Peyton looked at the Og. Montauk looked back, its metal

mask unreadable.

Annika pressed a series of bricks in the molded facade of the factory. Something clicked inside the wall. The facade parted, revealing a pneumatic door. This opened silently.

Checking her pocket watch, Annika smiled and closed the lid.

"What is it, Annika?" said Peyton.

"We're right on time," she said. She started to take a step forward, but Peyton stopped her with his hand.

"No," he said.

Montauk motioned to Loran. Loran took up a sentry position by the door. Montauk said to Peyton, "I will guard your daughter with my life."

Peyton put his massive hands together and cracked his knuckles.

Close your eyes, Annika.

"Daddy?" asked Annika. "You're all red. Are you okay?"

Montauk moved her gently out of Peyton's way. "Your father has some things he needs to fix, my dear."

"Or some people," said Annika.

"Just so," said Montauk.

"Wait here until I'm finished," Peyton rumbled.

"How will we know?" asked the Og.

"The screaming will stop," said Peyton.

Hur, hur

The doors have been ripped off the hinges.

There are three sets of doors, set within a security corridor leading to the surface. Each door is thicker than the last. Each door incorporates a series of heavy bolts, within channels on the opposite side, to seal the portal.

These bolts litter the floor, twisted, misshapen. A few bear oval imprints where giant fingers have pressed them, indented them, crushed them.

The foyer from the surface corridor is a kill box.

A turret firing collapsed-uranium slugs at the rate of 800 rounds per minute has been mounted at the end of the box. Pits concealed in the floor are lined with razor-sharp alloy spikes. The touch of a single button inside a far away control room can open the pits, fire the gun, turn everything within the box to ground meat in fractions of a second.

The gun has not been fired. The floor pits have not been revealed. These are electronic mechanisms, controlled remotely by a series of circuits, relays, and digital controls. All have been disabled.

The facility is far underground, fully twenty meters below the dormant factory that conceals it. It is separated into wings. The wings can be hermetically, hydraulically sealed from each other. This is because the facility was originally designed by the government to develop chemical and biological weapons. It lay vacant for twenty years before its conversion into a psychological testing facility and, yes, nominally a school.

The doors leading from the kill box have also been wrenched aside. They are warped, bent, dented. They bear the indentations of enormous knuckles. There are two ways, once beyond the mounted gun, to descend to the active levels of the facility. The stairways have been flooded by a curious plumbing problem, caused by a cascade-failure of the facility's climate control network. The lift appears to be functional. A strange computer malfunction has caused the lift not to operate, when called, for the last three days.

It worked today.

On the lower level, the lift doors are open. Two dead men, dressed as security personnel, lie here. Their guns have been taken. Their bones have been broken. Their skulls have been crushed flat. Their eyes are out.

This hallway leads to an intersection. To the left, a wing of the facility has been sealed off from the inside. The secured doors leading to this wing show the signs of extensive work to breach them. A work crew has struggled for days to separate the alloy panels. The doors remain intact. The work crew does not.

It should not be possible to punch a hole through a human being, to dig with blunt force past a man's ribs, to hollow his chest with a blow and grab his spine through the cavity created. It should not be possible to split a man's brain by chopping at his skull with the edge of one's hand. It should not be possible to punch a man so hard his jaw is ripped from his head. It should not be possible to attempt the same punch and succeed in knocking the entire head clear of the neck. All of these things were, nonetheless, entirely, horribly possible.

The walls of the chamber are crimson. They are so thick with blood that in the years to come, when the facility again lies empty and vacant, the very poured stone of the walls will be permanently stained. The men who died here will remain part of this tunnel until time turns the tunnel itself to dust.

The wrath, the fury, the monster that has invaded these halls is not patient. He is not kind. He is not forgiving. But he is thorough. Before he breaches the sealed chamber, he reverses course, finds the wing of the facility that has not yet been blocked off. Here, terrified men and women, operatives of the government, cower behind desks and under tables.

Not all of these operatives are wholly "bad" people. All have done bad things, yes. All have been party to the mistreatment of children—children held within this "school," children taught according to governmental whim, children interrogated and tested and imprisoned, treated as property because that is what they have become. Many of these operatives have known guilt. Many have suffered regrets. None have sought to correct their misdeeds. It is this failure that has condemned them.

There are wall-mounted robot guns. There are security barriers. There are electricity fields. None of the automated systems are operable. None of the manually activated systems have activated. It is as if the very machines have turned against the occupants of this government laboratory.

Here, a woman in a lab coat no longer wears her head. There, a man similarly dressed has had his arms and legs ripped free. The expression on the dead man's face is one of surprise, one of incredulity, one of pain. The dead man has seen terrible things. Terrible things have been done to him. No one in the laboratory has escaped.

The floors are awash in blood and human organs. A severed

hand lies on a table; it still holds a pen. An eyeball stares from the center of a desk. A man with a crushed skull flails amid a puddle of his own blood, trying to move his feet. He makes a noise that sounds like, "*Hur, hur.*" The last words he *chose* to speak were, "Why? Why?"

The question "Why?" has been asked by more than one victim of this bloody rampage. It has not been acknowledged; it has not been dignified. A vessel of wrath has visited punishment on the facility's occupants. That vessel is indifferent to negotiation, to explanation, to pleas for mercy or suggestions of dialogue.

That vessel leaves heavy boot prints in an ocean of blood when it finally approaches, once more, the sealed doors leading to the sealed wing, the wing it has not yet visited. It flexes its arms. It balls its mighty fists, each the size of a basketball. It rears back its right hand, ready to begin battering down the barrier, knowing that in only minutes it can do what the work crew could not do in weeks. These doors cannot stop it. It will rip them apart. The wrathful giant draws in a deep breath—

A buzzer sounds. A green light winks alive on the wall.

The doors open on smooth hydraulics, never touched by the monster who walks through them.

A Hammer

Peyton marveled at the small crowd of little girls. They were all blondes, their hair colors ranging from platinum to Annika's gold locks to something like auburn. They were all exactly the same height; they had eyes that ranged from the blue of ice to a paler gray and even light green. Their skin was fair and flawless; their features were fine, even noble. They told him, one at a time: "I'm twelve years old."

"My name is Peyton," he said. "Do you all go to school here?"

The little girls turned to one another, exchanging wide-eyed glances. Something passed between them without words. They looked back to Peyton and nodded, almost solemnly.

"I'm here to help you," said Peyton. "Don't be afraid."

"We let you in," said one of the girls. Her voice was very quiet.

"Would you . . . would you like to leave?" Peyton asked. He could hear movement at his back. Montauk, Loran, and his daughter were entering the school.

Again the girls looked to each other. Finally, they nodded, their heads moving in unison.

Montauk approached. "Interesting," it said. Its cameras clicked and whirred as it examined the crowd of twelve-year-olds. The girls took a collective step backward, perhaps unsure what to make of the two cyborgs.

When Annika appeared behind Peyton and the Ogs, the transformation was abrupt. The little girls lost their hesitation. They rushed forward to greet her, called her by name, embraced her. Peyton was touched by the homecoming. Next to him, Montauk made an odd noise somewhere in its chassis. Peyton looked at the Og.

"I'm sorry," said the Og. "They're just so genuine. It would bring a tear to my eye, if I had eyes."

The girls began whispering to each other. Peyton found it unnerving, although he was not sure why. When they had come to what he assumed was consensus, nodding among themselves and turning eagerly to face him, it was Annika who came forward to act as their representative.

"Daddy," she said, "the girls opened the doors twice today. Once was for you, and once was for Dr. Foster. He ran here when you broke down the outside doors. The girls thought you might want to ask him some questions alone, so they told him he could come in and be safe."

The mob of little blonde girls moved as one toward a hatchway at the back of the room. It had a wheel lock on it, like something Peyton would expect to find in an undersea vessel. The whole time, the girls spoke to each other in animated tones. Their voices were so similar that Peyton found it impossible to tell who was who except for Annika.

"I gave Annabelle an appendectomy."

"Are your fingers burned? We have gel in the first aid kit."

"You just read the instructions and did what they said. That's not the same as giving an appendectomy. Anyone can read instructions."

"We got a field report from Aria two weeks ago."

"Mr. VanClef was so mad!"

"I like Aria," said Annika.

"Annabelle, you're just mad because there's a scar."

"We sealed off the networks and purged them."

"Am not."

"Aubry has the accounts set up now."

Peyton turned to Montauk as the girls set about opening the hatch. His look must have conveyed his confusion. "They've done much of the work necessary to liberate the school already," said the Og. "I gather they've been giving VanClef's minions considerable grief here. Several escapes predate the computer error that put Annika on a public transport, destined for the gallery at your execution."

"Your daughter," said Peyton. "Your daughter is one of the girls who got away."

"Yes," said Montauk. "You can imagine my surprise. It is one of the connections between us, Peyton. Both our daughters fled this place . . . and then worked to free their siblings. Those who remained here very cleverly—and recently—sealed themselves off from the staff. I think the pace of their lessons must have reached what the girls considered a critical point."

"Critical how?"

"Once I began speaking with Annika," said Montauk, "Aimee revealed some details to me. It seems the girls were selected for their brilliance. Obviously, VanClef has a type." He swept a pincer across the blonde crowd. "And it explains why Annika would have been among those chosen. With a father in prison and no mother in evidence, it was a simple matter to conceal her existence from you. At that point she became the property of the government, to experiment on as they would."

"Is that why you didn't tell me?" Peyton asked.

"Had it been only my Aimee's secret," said the Og, "I may

have. But Annika had her own reasons for waiting. I wanted to show her that respect. She has an incredible mind, Peyton. Don't let her appearance fool you. She is so much more than a little girl. That is the mistake VanClef made. He and the government underestimated the girls' ability to learn."

"Learn what?"

"As smart as they are, the girls came here as infants," said Montauk. "They had no frame of reference for deception. For violence."

I'm learning a lot while I'm with you, Daddy. Things I couldn't learn in school. I'm learning how the world works. I learn just by watching you.

"What deception?" asked Peyton. "What violence?"

"The girls you see here," said Montauk, "less the ones who escaped and disappeared into Hongkongtown, are only a fraction of the group Annika remembers. Over time the girls began to put it together: Fail certain tests, score below certain aptitudes, and you disappear, never to be seen again. Over time they developed what I believe is a fairly complex algorithm. What they concluded was that most of the work they needed to free them from the school they could do themselves, here and through their . . . agents, if you wish to call the escapees that. But they are, after all, only girls. They needed help. They needed someone to trip the defenses, to eliminate the physical resistance they could not overcome. They needed a hammer to drive the final nails."

"Me."

"You *are* quite the hammer," said Montauk.

"So they were expecting us," said Peyton. "That's what she meant about being on time."

"So it would seem. One presumes she mentioned certain practices here knowing that this would spur your response. And

I am quite certain she did so on a timetable of her choosing, with specific intent."

The girls were now standing in front of the hatchway, watching Peyton, Montauk, and Loran. Peyton beckoned to Annika. She came forward.

"What is it, Daddy?"

"What do we do now, Annika?" said Peyton. "We can't just turn these girls out into the street."

"I can make arrangements for them," said Montauk.

"Oh, you won't have to," said Annika. "They all know what they need to do. The ones that want to find their parents can. They'll be okay."

Montauk looked at Peyton. Peyton looked at the Og. They both looked at Annika. "Are you sure?" asked Peyton.

"Yes, Daddy," said Annika. She leaned in, shielding her mouth with her hand. In a loud stage whisper she said, "They're all very smart."

The girls started laughing. The sound prompted someone on the other side of the hatchway to start banging against the metal door. Two of the little girls moved the now-unlocked hatch aside, revealing a man in a white lab coat. His hands had been tied behind his back, and his legs were bound with electrical wire.

"That's Dr. Foster," said Annika.

"Montauk," said Peyton, "can you and Loran see the girls out of this neighborhood?"

"Of course," said the Og. "Annika can come visit with my children, for that matter. You can pick her up at my place when your . . . business . . . here is concluded."

"Oh, that would be fun, Daddy," said Annika. "May I do that?"

"Yes," said Peyton. "I won't be too long."

"My children and I shall prepare dinner again, then," said Montauk. "Come along, Loran. Girls? If you will join me?"

"See you soon, Daddy," said Annika.

"Good-bye, Mr. Peyton," said the other girls in unison. Peyton watched them leave. When he was satisfied that they were out of the facility, he turned his attention back to Foster.

Foster looked at him. His eyes were bloodshot. He stared in terror.

"Did you work here?" Peyton asked.

"I'm only a consultant," Foster said quietly. "One of the workmen injured himself with a power-bore. I was here to treat him."

"Did you help test my daughter? Take away the ones that failed the tests?"

"No," said Foster. "That wasn't me. I had nothing to do with that. That was VanClef."

"Where *is* VanClef?" said Peyton. "I want to talk to him. I want to talk to the man who put my daughter in this place."

"I don't know," said Foster. "I really don't. Please don't hurt me. I had nothing to do with your daughter, nothing at all."

"You knew the girls were here," said Peyton. "You knew this facility was secret. You knew they were prisoners."

"Please," said Foster. "I was just doing my job—"

Peyton reached out and grabbed the bound man. He lifted Foster easily by the neck and ankles, holding him against the ceiling of the underground lab.

"PLEASE!" Foster screamed. "I can help you! I can give you money."

"I almost snapped my own daughter's neck to save her from being eaten alive," said Peyton. "Can your money buy that back? Can your money erase that memory?"

"You can leave Hongkongtown!" Foster said quickly.

"Anything you want! You can go somewhere you and your girl will be safe!"

Peyton frowned at the medical tech. He brought up his knee as he let Foster's body fall.

"There is no safe," said Peyton, and broke the screaming man in half.

An Army

His joints hurt again. He could feel the fatigue deep in his bones, feel the Sleeper poison and the stimulants Montauk had given him, feel the punishment he had taken breaching the school and smashing its defenses. He paused to lean against the bloody wall of the laboratory. His hand left a broad print.

He wanted to rest. The lift door faced him. He pressed the button and the doors opened.

He cast one last look at the destruction he had wrought. His rage had cooled. The thought of what might have been, how Annika might have died, the abuse she had suffered at the hands of those working here, still ached inside him. But his fury was sated. He had made them pay.

He was not finished.

He would find this VanClef. He would find the man responsible for all of this. He would wrap his fingers around the man's throat and squeeze until the government agent had told him everything about Peyton's little girl.

And then there would be no more VanClef at all.

He slumped against the wall of the elevator as it traveled, slowly, to the surface. The girls had rigged the entire complex, interfered with its defenses, fouled its computers. There was very little Annika could not do with access to a computer. How much power could half a dozen Annikas wield?

Making his way through the defenses he had destroyed, Peyton reached the outer doors. Montauk, or those with the Og, had sealed the most external barrier. He moved this aside and stepped out.

"IAN PEYTON," said an amplified voice. "LIE DOWN ON THE GROUND AND PUT YOUR HANDS ON YOUR HEAD."

A howling wind pushed him back against the facade of the factory. The circle of light that fell on him was blinding. He looked up, searching for its source, trying to shield his eyes with his hand.

A hundred rifles clacked as their bolts were pulled back. Servomotors groaned as the turret of a multitracked battle tank trained its mounted gun on him. The men using the tank for cover wore light-scattering camouflage. Their outlines blurred against the asphalt and debris of the cul-de-sac.

Peyton looked up at the helicopter. A cold rain was falling now. It danced across his face as he squinted against the beam of the chopper's spotlight. He pressed his hands together. He flexed his fingers. He squeezed his fists.

"An army," said Peyton. "You need an army to stop me."

"THIS IS AGENT VINCENT BRIDGER OF GOVERNMENT INTELLIGENCE," announced the public address system in the helicopter. "IAN PEYTON, YOU ARE UNDER ARREST. COMPLY OR YOU WILL BE KILLED."

"You made a mistake," Peyton said to no one. "Annika isn't here. She's with someone who can protect her. She doesn't need me now."

Annika. What kind of father put his daughter in such danger? He had been selfish. It had been selfish to take her from the prison. It had been selfish to believe he could parent her.

"COMPLY OR WE WILL OPEN FIRE!"

He was big. He was strong. He healed quickly. But the battle with the Sleepers, the attack on the school, had taken much of his strength. As he stared into the guns of the soldiers before him, as he watched the black maw of the tank turret track him, he realized that he had come to the end. He could not beat them all.

Montauk, the Og, was a decent creature. It had adopted Aimee; it would adopt Annika. Peyton's daughter was a genius. Now she had her fellow students from the school for company. If losing him made her sad, it would only be for a little while. She had lived for twelve years without him. The few weeks they had been together would hardly matter to her.

One last fight. One last fight to give Annika and Montauk more time. With each passing minute, they got farther away from the school. As long as Bridger and his tank and his helicopter and his soldiers were here, murdering Peyton, they were not following Peyton's daughter.

"Come kill me," said Peyton, flexing his fists. He took a step forward, then another. He felt the cords of muscle in his arms tighten as he flexed his shoulders, rolling his forearms out and away from his body. Splaying his fingers, he spread his arms, as if he would gather up the government troops and crush them. "Come kill me, you cowards! I'm not a little girl!"

"OPEN FIRE," said Bridger.

Peyton took another step forward.

The gunfire that burned the air filled the cul-de-sac with thunder. The buildings vibrated under the onslaught, shaking loose fragments of themselves, creating a dust cloud that rolled over the battleground and turned Peyton and his enemies into shadows.

Bullets ripped his flesh. He felt them hammer him, felt them stagger him, felt them drive him to his knees. It was all right. He did not have to stop it; he could give in to the pain; he could lie down and rest.

But he was not ready to rest. Not yet.

He regained his feet, pushing up on one leg, forcing the other to support him. It was like climbing from a manhole into a sandstorm. Projectiles continued to gouge him, rip him, slice him. He took a trembling step. A man with a rifle ran to him, blazing away on full automatic. Peyton slapped the soldier's gun away and punched him so hard his face caved in.

He took another step.

He was nearly knocked off balance. He could no longer feel his legs. He could see his fingers flex, could see his fists close, but he could not feel them. His hearing was no longer working. The sound of gunfire was now a whining, the ringing of a bell that never stopped. His vision began to recede, blackening around the edges, turning a strange shade of orange.

He dropped to one knee, then to both. He fell forward onto his stomach. The ringing in his ears became the roaring of an ocean.

He did not hear the canister that fell from the helicopter, but he saw it. There was another. There was a third. He stared at the green cylinders, feeling his flesh tearing, feeling the blood pour from him.

The canisters struck the pavement and began to spew gas.

The gas was black and acrid. It was poison. It rolled over him, scorching his lungs, making his chest seize. He did not feel the pavement against his face. He did not hear the soldiers dying around him. He did not feel the downdraft of the helicopter as it hovered over him. Dark mist was everywhere.

There is no safe. But for Annika, there was. He should never have taken her with him. But now she was safe with the Ogs, with the other girls. He had made a mistake, but he had fixed it, and now he was going to pay for everything.

That was the funny thing about mistakes. Sometimes they got away from you.

Project Terminated

He's dead, thought Agent Bridger. *He's dead. Let him be dead.*

The chopper floated above the cul-de-sac, gliding in methodical crosshatches from north to south and back again. The pilot, half his face hidden behind a smoked visor, had not said a word. He simply did as he was ordered.

Those orders had included the release of the poison gas canisters filled with a synthetic neurotoxin. This toxin had been specially formulated by VanClef's medical team. It was based on Peyton's body chemistry. While never tested, several of VanClef's subordinates had, in the Project's files, expressed their hope that a poison of this type could kill even Ian Peyton. The man's implanted organs generated counteragents to injected and externally introduced toxins. A synthetic toxin was deemed the only option to overcome his natural defenses.

Equipping the chopper with the Project's full inventory of the gas had been Bridger's idea. He believed in being thorough. He had not asked permission to do so; he had not cleared the act with VanClef. In his opinion, VanClef spent too much time behind a desk or an operating table, preoccupied with his ghoulish experiments, to understand the exigencies a field operative faced.

The problems at the school were evidence of this fact. VanClef had long ago relinquished his grip on the place. How many computer and mechanical problems had to occur before someone realized it must be the test subjects doing it? VanClef had not wanted to see it, but this much was obvious to Bridger from his first moments attached to the Project. He had tried several times to convince VanClef to terminate the subjects, but the man would hear none of it.

Small wonder it was, then, when the alarm sounded within the converted warehouse, that VanClef was caught flatfooted. He was in the middle of another drill with his trio of pet monsters when the passive systems at the school signaled a breach. Given the considerable security in place, a breach could mean only one thing: Peyton himself had come calling. This had always been a possibility, and one for which they were supposed to be prepared. A breach immediately mobilized a detachment of the Hongkongtown Civil Defense Force, whose commanding officer had orders to defer to Intelligence for the duration of operations around the school site. VanClef had only to take a chopper from the warehouse to the cul-de-sac and oversee the affair.

The black mist still clung to everything. That was a function of the toxin's design. It stuck tenaciously to what it touched. The pilot was careful to keep the helicopter well above the effective range of the poison. The rotors of the chopper helped disperse the mist as they passed over, allowing Bridger to check the brief window that this opened. As the chopper moved on, the mist rolled back in to fill the gap.

He has to be here, thought Bridger.

No one could survive an onslaught like that. He had watched the soldiers' guns chip away at Peyton's body, had watched Peyton stagger and slow. But it was one thing to watch VanClef's monsters from a floor above and through a mirrored barrier. It was easy to look at surveillance recordings of Peyton fighting police. It was nothing to review the medical examiners' reports of the victims

Peyton had torn to pieces. It was quite another to see Peyton from scant meters distant, ripping the heads off armed men and wading through gunfire as if he did not feel it.

Bridger could admit to himself that Peyton terrified him. That was why he had released the poison.

They had to find his body. It *had* to be here somewhere.

The pilot jerked as if surprised. He put two fingers to his helmet and then looked to Bridger. "I have a transmission from Intelligence, Agent Bridger," he said.

Bridger nodded. He pressed the shunt button above his own seat. The radio switched on.

"Agent Bridger. We've received an automated report that you are on site to address a breach at the Hongkongtown laboratory. Report. Have you apprehended the intruder?"

"I'm afraid it's much worse than that, sir," said Bridger. "Agent VanClef has lost positive control of the facility. The test subjects have escaped or are terminated. Our heat sensors show nothing alive inside the lab."

"And Patient Four?" The reply from the radio was distorted electronically. This was not an error. Bridger had never seen his superiors in Government Intelligence, nor did he possess any information that would help identify these men and women. Concealment of successive layers of the Intelligence hierarchy was a way of life for those in the agency.

"I'm surveying the area now," said Bridger. He looked to the pilot. The pilot shook his head. "Ian Peyton . . . has been killed. To make certain, we used a neurotoxin specifically formulated for him. We have not yet identified any survivors."

There was a pause. "Say again, Agent Bridger."

"I repeat," said Bridger, "Patient Four neutralized using a wide-area neurotoxin specifically developed for this subject. We have yet to identify any survivors among the Hongkongtown Civil Defense unit. I made the call. Their collateral deaths were necessary to achieve mission objective."

There was another pause, longer this time. Finally, the voice said, "Understood,"

Bridger waited until his nerve gave out. "Uh, orders, sir?"

"Agent Bridger, we are activating containment protocol. Repeat, containment protocol. Project Violet is terminated."

"Acknowledged," said Bridger. "Sir," he added. "What about Agent VanClef, sir?"

"We repeat," said the voice. "Project Violet is terminated. Proceed accordingly. Out."

Bridger and the pilot exchanged glances once more.

Below the chopper, the black mist continued to roil. "We're running out of grid," said the pilot. "I don't think he's down there."

"That's impossible," said Bridger.

"Is it?" said VanClef, appearing on the small screen in the chopper's control panel. He was seated behind his desk in his office at the warehouse.

"Agent VanClef," said Bridger. "I didn't expect you—"

"You didn't expect me to have bugged the chopper?" VanClef asked. "You didn't expect me to have heard every word of your exchange with Intelligence?"

Bridger paled. "Sir," he began. "I—"

"No," said VanClef, holding up his hand. "Don't insult my intelligence with whatever you're going to say next. You're a deep disappointment, Agent Bridger."

"Sir, I'm only following protocol."

"I'm not talking about that," said VanClef. "I'm talking about your failure to kill Peyton. Had you simply let the military do its job, they could have brought him down through sheer firepower.

But you panicked. You released an unauthorized neural agent in a civilian sector, killing the very men who were supposed to be neutralizing Peyton for you."

"But sir," said Bridger. "You didn't see him. In my place you'd have done the same thing."

"Agent Bridger," said VanClef, "don't ever project your insecurities onto a man. Never assume he shares your weaknesses."

"The poison was *designed* to kill Peyton."

"And never tested," said VanClef. "Has it occurred to you that Ian Peyton can hold his breath for at least six minutes? Are you familiar enough with his charts to tell me his lung capacity, which is ten times that of what you or I would consider normal? You didn't just create a smoke screen to hide Peyton's movements. You also eliminated his enemies en masse so he could slip away under your nose."

"He's *here*," said Bridger. "I'd bet my life on it."

"You already did," said VanClef. "And you lost. We were just speaking of what you didn't expect, Vincent. I have one more for you. You didn't expect me to have my own chopper wired with enough explosives to turn it to ash."

"Sir—"

On the screen, VanClef pressed a switch on the panel of his desk.

Bridger never heard the explosion that killed him.

Out with the Garbage

His fingers dug into the pavement. His hands were cracked and bleeding. He could not feel them. His limbs were numb, his vision blurry. Blood leaked from a dozen half-clotted wounds across his torso. Even past the ringing in his ears, he could hear his own ribs grating together. His legs would not support him.

He had almost no memory of crawling away from the cul-de-sac. He had no idea how far he had come. His lungs burned with every breath. His skin felt like it was covered with stinging insects. No matter how much he blinked, no matter how he squinted, he could not bring his eyesight into focus.

He did not have long.

The alleyway in which he crawled was piled high in fetid garbage. He wormed his way through the refuse, not feeling the multipedes that crawled on him and stung him, not caring when he pulled himself through broken glass or sharp fragments of plastic. He should have died at the factory. He *had* died at the factory. He had breathed too much poison, taken too much damage, for it to be otherwise.

He needed to get to Montauk's flat. Annika would be there. He only wanted to see her. If he could just see her one last time, tell her he loved her, then nothing else that happened would matter. He could die. He could finally rest.

Throw the arm. Dig in. Pull. Throw the arm. Dig in. Pull.

Peyton's world was reduced to this. Each breath seared his lungs. Each meter he gained left a river of blood on the paving behind him.

Every twenty meters, by his count, he threw up blood. The vomiting became a rib-cracking dry heave by the fifth or sixth time; he had lost track. Whether this was his body trying to cleanse the poison or evidence of the injuries that were killing him, he didn't know.

Keep going, he told himself. *Keep going.*

There were bullets inside him. Projectiles had lodged in his body. Some might be self-propelled; they might even now be drilling their way slowly to his organs.

He just had to last long enough to see Annika.

He heard it, then: a rumbling, low and subtle, beneath the ringing in his ears. Rolling over, enduring the agony that shot through him as he collided with the wall of the alley, he tried to push himself to a sitting position. It took him a few moments to manage it. By then, he could see the source of the noise.

There were three of them. The big one was clearly the alpha. The other two were followers, scarred as the first one was, but hanging back as their leader sized up Peyton.

The feral dogs were mastiffs. Hongkongtown's wild dog problem ebbed and flowed. Cycles in which the animals were hunted were typically followed by periods of pack expansion. Complacency would yield as the dogs became a threat, prompting more public hunts.

The garbage. He should have avoided this alley. The dogs had probably claimed this place. They saw him as a threat, which meant they would—

The alpha leapt for his throat.

He could barely lift his arms. The animal hit him in the chest, bouncing his head off the alley wall, clawing and snarling. Its jaws sought his neck, ready to bite deep. Instead he shoved his fist down the animal's throat.

His own blood welled. He was grateful for the numbness in his limbs. He reached in as deeply as he could, and when his arm would not move farther, he willed his hand to open and close. He grabbed. He pulled.

The noise the animal made caused the other two to freeze where they stood. Their hair stood up and they whined in confusion. They had no frame of reference for Peyton. He was bigger than any human prey they had stalked, smelled like death, and was doing something to their leader they could not fathom.

Peyton wrenched his arm free. The mastiff alpha shuddered, convulsed. Blood poured from its mouth. Its eyes rolled back into its skull.

With the last of his strength, Peyton threw the dying dog. It took everything he possessed. He collapsed against the wall of the alley, slumping again. The other two growled, dancing back and forth, unsure. Their ears were pressed against their heads.

He wasn't going to reach his daughter. He was going to end here, killed by dogs. He could not lift his arms. He could not raise his head.

The dogs reacted to something he could not perceive. They turned and ran. The ringing in Peyton's ears had become a pulsing, skull-shattering tone. Was this what dying sounded like?

No. The noise was not in his head. The noise was coming from the blocky gray vehicle moving up the alley. Its square face opened, revealing the clockwork chasm of a trash maul. The noise was a warning tone. The vehicle was churning up the debris in the alley, consuming it.

A sweeper. He was going to be picked up by a trash sweeper.

His body would be crushed and carried to a trash recycling facility. He could not laugh; his lungs were empty.

Garbage, he thought. *I go out with the garbage.*

A pair of slim, humanoid robots detached themselves from the sides of the compactor. The helper androids had hooks for arms; it was their job to police up small garbage that the compactor missed, delivering the straggling bits to the chugging machine. The technology had not changed in decades. Garbage detail was neither complicated nor particularly demanding work. These androids had probably been sweeping the same grid of alleyways for thirty years. They looked old enough.

No one to hear my last words, he thought. *No one except a robot that won't know what they mean.*

That was all right. He started to close his eyes.

One of the robots paused. It turned to look in his direction. He wouldn't have believed it if he hadn't seen it. The robot actually cast a glance at its partner, which continued picking up garbage, before it hurried over to look at Peyton.

Peyton stared up at it. Its blank camera eyes were fogged with dust. As he watched, the robot reached up and thumbed lines of grit out of its lenses. It leaned in so close that Peyton could see his reflection in its cameras.

"Ian Peyton?" it asked. "You don't look well."

"Mon . . . *Montauk* . . ." Peyton whispered.

The android turned again to its companion. The sound it made next was no language Peyton had ever heard. It was static mixed with tones and beeps. The second garbage robot responded by turning and walking over. It beeped obediently.

The two figures—one a robot, the other something else—reached down, took his arms, and began dragging him toward the Sweeper. They carried him past the compactor toward the rear of the vehicle, where a large flatbed cargo area waited.

"What . . . ?" Peyton said. "Why . . . ?"

"Any friend of Montauk's," said the Og disguised as a robot.

Something to Sign

He is Ian Peyton. He fears nobody. He finishes every fight he starts. He is not a big man; he doesn't need to be. He's tougher and he's meaner and he's faster with a gun or a knife. That's why the Triads used him for dirty work. When you needed a tough guy, you called Ian Peyton. Everybody knew that.

They all looked at him like they expected him to wet himself. The guards outside the Promontory looked at each other and at him, snickering and making comments about how popular he'd be inside. Like that kind of cheap psych-out would work on anyone who wasn't weak. Peyton had never been weak. He wasn't going to start now.

They gave him the full treatment in processing: Strip search, delousing, UV and EM, organ screen. The whole time the screws and the support staff acted like they knew something he didn't. He took their attitude and gave it back to them. He knew he wouldn't be the big fish he had been on the outside. This *was* the Promontory, after all. To get sent inside you had to be bad news. Well, he was Ian Peyton. He *was* bad news.

They'd adjust to him and he'd learn to make some concessions to them. He would do his time and get out without running his mouth. Next time around, he'd run a little faster, try a little harder. He didn't intend to come back.

On his way to his cell, he dealt with the usual catcalls, the typical thrown bedding and body wastes. Hazing. You couldn't skip it. Everybody had to deal with it. His cellmate was a lifer debit-kiter who'd been caught draining bank accounts one time too many. He did Peyton the courtesy of getting stabbed three days into Peyton's term in the prison. It was nice to have a private cell. Peyton wondered when they would assign him somebody new.

The inmates left him alone for the first week. He figured he was doing a good job of putting out the vibe: Don't look like food and you won't get eaten. Prison wasn't much different from life. It was just a lot more boring.

On the eighth day, they came for him in the yard.

There were four of them. He never learned their names. They tried to sweet-talk him at first, tried to get him to meet them in his private cell after yard time, tried to tell him that if he cooperated, his time inside would be plenty sweet. He broke the closest jaw with his most vicious uppercut, ready to dive into the others and make them pay for their insult. You had to show these guys who was boss right way. You had to show them you weren't a victim, or it would never stop. The rules were simple. He liked simple.

Except that there weren't four. There were six. The two he didn't see snuck up on him while he was dealing with the other four. They grabbed him, pinned his arms. He tried to use his legs, but two of the others grabbed these. That left two grown men to beat him bloody, beat him until his spleen was ruptured, beat him until his ribs were cracked and his eyes were so badly swollen that he was practically blind. He spent three days in the infirmary, one of those in a robot tube getting his liver and spleen mended.

They were waiting for him when he got out. He had defied them. Now they were going to break him. They were going to show him his place. Then they were going to punk him out.

His second visit to the infirmary lasted twice as long. He had to have bones knitted that time. One of his eyes was out, hanging by its optic nerve. His orbital bone was cracked. They put the eye back, lasered the retina in place, and fused the bone closed.

The third time, he was in a coma for three days. When he woke, he had no idea what had been fixed. He only knew that every part of him hurt. His future stared back at him—an endless succession of beatings and violations, which could only end in his premature death at the hands of his tormenters.

Lying in his hospital bed, Peyton considered taking his own life.

That was when Warden Richards came to him. He remembered every word of the conversation.

"Looks like you've found yourself some trouble, son," said the Warden.

"It's your prison," Peyton had said through swollen lips. "You should do something."

"There's nothing I can do," said the Warden. "No prison can control its population one hundred percent of the time. It's all I can do to keep the prison service off my back, keep the place running smoothly, keep our rankings high enough that I don't lose my job. Do you realize how valuable it would be to me if you'd all just do your time and not make trouble? I'd do you some favors, son, if I thought you could give me anything in return."

"Name it," said Peyton.

"Well," said Richards, "as it happens, there is something you can do. I'm just a messenger. They don't tell me much about the program. But the government is running some trials and they've asked me if I can provide them with a suitable test subject. You could be that subject."

"Be a guinea pig? No thank you."

"You should reconsider," said the Warden. "If you agree, it

looks good on my record. And if my record looks good, I stay in charge around here."

"And in return you'll protect me?" asked Peyton.

"No," said the Warden. "That would set a bad precedent. "But there are other things I might be able to do for you. A little favor here, a little favor there. And the good news is that you won't *need* me to protect you. They tell me if you join this program, you'll soon be bigger and stronger than you can imagine. Once you join, Peyton, you'll be so powerful that nobody in here will ever mess with you again."

"What'll they do to me?"

"Something about implanting organs that will boost your growth, your strength. Like legal steroids."

"I don't want to be an Oggy."

"No, no," said the Warden. "Nothing like that. I'm not even sure that would be legal. This is entirely biological. The organs are grown in a laboratory."

Peyton thought about it. He thought about all the years he had ahead of him in this place. He thought about the damage his enemies had done. The next time they might kill him—or worse, permanently cripple him.

"Show me something to sign," Peyton said.

Jenni Syn

"Annika," called Peyton. "Why is there a man tied up on the toilet?"

Peyton fought the surreal thickness in his head. He had been dreaming about prison, about Warden Richards, about joining the Project. These were not pleasant memories, and he wanted to dispel them. Waking up on the couch in the paid flop he shared with Annika, he felt as if he was forgetting something. He could not place it. His mouth tasted like rust. He had a brutal headache.

"Mmmph," said the man tied up on the toilet. A large piece of friction tape had been used to gag him. He looked very frightened. Peyton closed the bathroom door.

He was abruptly aware of his hunger. He stumbled to the kitchen. He was barefoot and shirtless, wearing pants caked with dried blood and riddled with bullet holes. The printer was preset to dispense Baycon and soy cubes. He pressed the button twice and found a polymer sphere of water in the wall cooler. His throat was dry.

He would eat, he thought, draining one sphere and popping the top of another with his thumb, and then he would kill the man in the bathroom.

Annika's door was closed. He wondered when she had gone to bed. She stayed up very late sometimes. He felt uneasy about that, as if he should say something.

He put his plate on the kitchenette table, next to his sawed-off shotgun.

Peyton stared. The weapon brought him back. He remembered. He looked down at his chest, which was covered in bandage spray. How was he alive? How was he home? Was he dreaming?

He knelt next to the kitchen table and devoured his breakfast. The wall screen's time display told him it was late morning. The date told him he had lost three days.

The shotgun looked freshly cleaned. He picked it up, opened it. It was loaded. He had not seen the gun since the battle outside the school. He had assumed it lost.

There was a trash bin in the kitchen, one he had not seen before. Curious, he checked. It was full of bloody disposable towels. He shook the bin; it rattled. There was more than one deformed bullet in there. Once more he ran his hand across his chest.

Whatever had happened in the last three days, it was clear he had missed quite a bit. He snatched up the last of his soy cubes, swallowed them, and went to the towel dispenser in the kitchenette. He pulled a heavy wad of towels from the dispenser, soaked them in water from the kitchen sink, and wrapped the heavy, wet towels around the snout of the shotgun. He wanted to test the weapon, make sure it was still reliable. He could think of no better test than to kill the man in the bathroom.

"MMMPPHH!" said the man when Peyton opened the door again. Well, that figured. Peyton put the moist lump of towels against the man's face and thumbed back both hammers of the shotgun.

"Good morning, Daddy," said Annika behind him. She yawned. He turned to look at her over his shoulder. "Aimee, you know, Montauk's daughter? She asked me to say hi to you. She says she moved to Central City. That sounds so exciting. We were up late in the virts, talking."

"Annika, please go back in the bedroom for a minute," he said. "I don't want you to—"

"Oh, Daddy," said Annika. "You're silly. That's Dr. Musgrove. We've been waiting for you to wake up."

"You have?" Peyton asked. He took the shotgun away from Musgrove's head and eased the hammers down. The doctor's hair and face were wet. He glared.

"Yes, but we're running out of time," said Annika. "It's Sweeps week. That's when the paid flops get raided. Montauk told me it's also when its friends get roosted."

"Rousted," Peyton corrected automatically.

"Rousted," repeated Annika. "That's why we weren't there when Herm brought you to Montauk's apartment."

"Herm?"

"The robot garbage-man," said Annika. "One of Montauk's friends. He's the one that brought me your gun. I don't know how he got it." She smiled. "Montauk has so many friends."

"He does," said Peyton.

"Mmmpphh!" said Dr. Musgrove.

Peyton gestured with the shotgun wrapped in towels. Musgrove stopped making noise.

"Herm said he asked you where you lived," said Annika. "He said you told him."

"I must have," said Peyton. "I don't remember. I was very sick."

"I know," said Annika. "When Herm and the other robot brought you here, he told me you had toxic shock and that you needed a doctor to take the bullets out of you. He's the one that gave me Dr. Musgrove's computer serial number, so I could find him on the grid. Montauk knows everything about everybody."

"Where is Montauk now?" Peyton asked.

"Hiding," said Annika. "Herm said he would be back when it got colder."

"When the heat dies down?" Peyton ventured.

"Daddy," she said, rolling her eyes. "That's what I *said.*"

"So you asked this Musgrove for help," Peyton said.

"No," said Annika. "I couldn't risk that VanClef might find us somehow. That's why I didn't call the girls for help, either. I don't know what VanClef knows and what he doesn't. I'm not sure what communications he's monitoring. I bought surgical tools at the bodega on Dragon Street with the last of the chits I had."

"That was smart," said Peyton.

"I had to make sure nothing could lead back to us," she said, "and that meant Dr. Musgrove couldn't know that he was coming here to treat someone. He thought was going to meet a dancer named Jenni Syn. He doesn't like his wife very much."

Peyton took that in. He glanced to Musgrove, who was now carefully avoiding eye contact. "So you lured him here," he said. "By pretending to be someone else."

"I made an avatar for the virts," said Annika. "One of those ladies who take off their clothes for money. The ones Montauk told me not to grow up to be like."

Peyton coughed. "Uh," he said. "Yes." He made a note to have a chat with Montauk when the Og resurfaced. He considered the bound doctor. "Annika . . . how did you get him tied up and gagged?"

"I just pointed the shotgun at him," she said, "and he did most of the work. You already showed me how to load it. I watched screen to find tutorials on how to clean it and shoot it."

"Have you fired it?"

"No, Daddy," she said. "I was afraid to. It would probably

knock me down. But I practiced bracing it against the chair where I sat."

"Let's . . . let's get packed," said Peyton. "The sooner we get out of here, the sooner Dr. Musgrove can go home."

"You really feel okay, Daddy?"

"I do," said Peyton. "I can feel myself healing. I think Dr. Musgrove did a good job."

"Oh, good," said Annika. "I was going to make him go to sleep if he didn't."

Vagaries of Fate

The medical bay was quiet but for the whisper of the breathing machine. VanClef sat on a chair next to the bed, scrolling through notes on his pocket tab, occasionally looking up to check on the man in the life-support apparatus.

"Poor old friend," he said. "They tell me that you can hear me. What would you say, right now, if you could?" He reached out and put his hand on Temken's, mindful of the electronic sensors attached to the comatose man's fingers. "Not much of a future for you, is there? With your brain seeping out of your broken skull."

"Sir," said a voice behind him.

"How many?" VanClef asked. He continued to hold Temken's hand.

"Several, sir. Myself, Smith, Eames, Jefferson, Klyter, and Korth. Perhaps the two men in charge of the motor pool."

"What of other operatives in the hospital?"

"Eliminated, sir. The others have left in the second chopper, headed for the warehouse."

"Have we acquired a signature yet?"

"Not yet, sir. But that much depleted uranium will be easy to spot. The techs tell me Peyton's system will retain the radiation signature for several days, even if any lodged projectiles are removed. The satellite we retasked is scanning the city. We'll have coordinates soon."

"And Orrin?"

"On the chopper, sir. In power-save mode, secured in the cargo bay."

"Good work, Stevens," said VanClef. "Go down and bring the car around front. I'd like a few moments alone with my friend."

"Of course, sir." Stevens disappeared as quietly as he had arrived.

"My superiors have issued the clean-up order," VanClef said to Temken. "Loss of positive control, they say. I have Agent Bridger to thank for that. No doubt they think they'll cleanse me, too. But I'm a step ahead. I've purged the building of everyone who isn't loyal to me. You're the last loose thread, I'm afraid. Poor, poor Temken. You tried so hard. That's what I always appreciated about you, even though I spoke to you so harshly."

VanClef stood. He heard the doors of the medical bay open. In the reflection of the monitor above Temken's bed, he watched the government tactical team enter the room. They held rifles. These were pointed at the floor, but that could change quickly.

"Agent VanClef," said the leader of the tactical team.

VanClef's hand, behind the medical bed, slid slowly down to his belt. "You're here to bring me in," he said. "You're here to serve notice that my project is terminated."

"That's correct, sir."

"That's unfortunate," he said. "Because I'm left with—"

He spun, drew his automatic, and fired four times. Each shot was a head shot. The four men of the tactical team were dead on their feet and VanClef was easing his pistol back in its holster before the first corpse hit the floor.

His ears echoed with the sound of the single shot the tac-team leader had managed to fire. The shot had been wide. It had missed him by half a meter. The wall above the medical bed was splattered with blood and brain. The sensors and reporting devices connected to Temken's corpse began wailing their funerary tune.

VanClef sighed. Standing, he reached out and, quite deliberately, switched off the life-support equipment. He stepped away from the bed.

The shooting pain in his neck made him stop. Reaching up, he found the radio-oscillator dart jutting from his skin. The wound bled quite a bit when he yanked the dart free.

So. Not one shot, but two. He checked the corpses. One of them was indeed holding not a pistol, but a pneumatic dart gun. Well. No matter now. These four weren't going to track him anywhere, no matter what high-frequency waves his blood emitted. He pressed his silk handkerchief to the wound in his neck.

On his way out of the hospital, VanClef paused in the foyer. This portion of the building was separate from the hospital property. Officially, it was leased office space, used by a firm that specialized in the genetic engineering of floral and vegetable products. Unofficially, the office space here gave VanClef ready access to a variety of specialized medical testing and treatment equipment that could be had nowhere else. And because it was a private hospital, he had only to pass around enough chits to keep everyone quiet.

Project Violet had originally encompassed the school beneath the factory, his warehouse, and these offices. The extremely inconvenient cleanup order necessitated that he abandon all but the warehouse, which he had set up to be defensible. It was simply one of the vagaries of fate that those defenses would be deployed to protect him from his own government, rather than from one of his subjects run amok.

He was getting ahead of himself, however. It was necessary

to make sure no trace of his work, no evidence of Project Violet, existed here. A beautiful redhead sat at the reception desk. He approached her.

"Mr. VanClef," she said behind him. He stopped walking. "Are you all right? Did Lieutenant Lewis find you?"

VanClef turned. He walked slowly to the reception desk. The girl's gold holograph plate read "A. West."

"Ms. West," he said. "I'm fine. Please swivel your terminal for me."

"Of course, Mr. VanClef." She turned the screen to face him. With one hand, he tapped out a series of commands on the reactive display. Blinking warning lights began to strobe through the foyer.

"What's that?" she asked. "Are you doing that?"

"I'm shutting down the fire-suppression system in the rented offices," he said. "There's a redundant fire barrier between it and the hospital proper. I doubt any patients will be endangered."

"Mr. VanClef?"

"I am forced to assume that Agent Stevens didn't speak with you."

"Uh . . . no," she said. "He was here. He seemed distracted. Why do you ask? Should I be reporting that alarm?"

VanClef sighed. He drew his pistol and shot her in the face. The report echoed through the marble-floored lobby.

Holstering his weapon, VanClef produced a thermal charge from inside his coat. He thumbed it and tossed it onto the late Ms. West's desk. The explosive produced a high-pitched whine.

VanClef strode out of the building. He had just cleared the outer doors when he felt the heat of the flames at his back. Stevens was waiting in the car.

"Stevens," VanClef said. He closed his door. "The next time you're feeling sentimental?"

"Sir?"

"Don't," said VanClef.

A Tertiary Source

He drank deeply. The brown liquid was an old friend. It didn't burn when he swallowed. Not anymore. Not for a long time. When the glass was empty he poured another double measure from the plastic bag of bourbon, wondering if he should get more ice from the dispenser in the hall.

Moxley sat in his walk-up Hongkongtown office off Dragon Street. Here, he was most comfortable. Here, he was surrounded by the debris of his life. As often as he thought the phrase, this was a literal truth and not a metaphor. His every worldly possession was crammed into this single room.

His desk was positioned against a metal-frame bed. Next to his work terminal was a bench grinder. Opposite this was a bench bearing a variety of hand tools. Every wall boasted a mismatched shelf full of antique paper books and bound plastics—Moxley's eclectic reference library, most of which was irreplaceable. A footlocker at the end of the bed contained those items he deemed worthy of extra security. These included his guns, his knives, and his Hongkongtown credentials, the latter stowed in a fireproof insulator.

The blinds over the windows were drawn. The only gap in the sun shields was for Moxley's air-circ and cooling units. These were a necessity during Hongkongtown's summers. Any wall space not taken by the windows was devoted to framed photographs and certifications, some of which were quite inexplicable. Moxley's private detective license, certifications from hand-to-hand and weapons courses, his college degree, and several old photos of him with various politicians vied for space with lacquered mounted fish, woodcuts of Triad sigils, a painted shield bearing Indonesian blade patterns, and an impressive collage of pub and whiskey-bar coasters.

The remaining floor space was stacked high with suitcases, storage bins, a battered retail clothing rack that Moxley used for his coat and hat, his all-in-one printer-cooler-warmer, an industrial coffeemaker that didn't work (but which served to support a commercial coffeemaker that *did*), and a dresser that held the rest of his clothes.

Moxley's office chair creaked as he leaned back in it. On the desk before him, take-out cartons, wrappers, stacks of data chips, and several tab computers were stacked with obsessive care. These shook ominously when Moxley reached out to grab his drink from the desk. He nearly knocked over the threedy that sat by his keypad. It switched on.

It was the only photo he kept around. The hologram was of his son, Connor, and his wife, Judith. Well. Ex-wife. In the photo, Connor was smiling. Judith was not. Moxley raised his glass to the threedy, brushed the top of its housing with his finger, and drank his glass empty.

He felt his phone vibrate in his pocket, and his desktop terminal beeped. Neiring's face appeared on the desk screen.

"Ray," said Mox. "Late night for you, isn't it?"

"Don't you ever sleep?" Neiring asked.

"Why? You'd be happier if you woke me up?"

"No," said Neiring. "I'd be relieved you actually slept."

"No such," said Mox. "What do you need?"

"I've got a line on VanClef," said Neiring. "One of my contacts inside the corporation that runs the Promontory knows someone in Intelligence."

"A tertiary source," said Mox. He made a rude noise.

"Just hear me out," said Neiring. "Word inside of Intelligence is that VanClef just became persona non grata. Anyone close to him is scrambling to put some distance between themselves and his loyalists, to save their careers."

"So the Man in Black has the stank."

"The what?"

"The *stank*, Ray," said Mox. "Failure. One of these government types gets the stank on him, everybody else runs for the hills. Your source say why?"

"He's working on it," said Neiring. "And I've greased the tracks as liberally as I can."

"You've what now?"

"Let's just say you'll be buying lunch next time."

"Ray," said Mox. "I'm proud of you. Resorting to good, old-fashioned bribery. We'll make a detective of you yet."

"I have a *degree*," said Neiring.

"Don't we all," said Moxley. "That and half a chit will get you a handy in the Redlight."

Neiring rolled his eyes. "When my guy knows more, he'll call," he said. "In the meantime—"

"In the meantime," said Mox, "I'd say now is a great time to sleep and drink. Not in that order."

"Shouldn't we plan our next move?"

"*What* next move?" Mox asked. He fished for his vapor tubes in the pocket of his coat, which he was still wearing. The nights were chilly and he kept his heat set low. "VanClef already put you on notice. Not to mention threatened your life. You really want to poke around in the dark, hunting for clues to you-don't-really-know-what, until he notices you?"

"I don't know, Mox," said Neiring. "But I want to keep digging. We're *close*."

"Close to what?" Moxley said. "And when did this stop being about the Peytons and start being about VanClef?"

Neiring looked down. When he looked up at the video pickup again, he said, "Isn't it?"

"Yeah, well," said Moxley. "Something's fishy, that's for sure. But Ray, I get the distinct feeling we're not in the loop on this."

"You too?"

Moxley put a vapor tube in his mouth. He fumbled it and dropped it in his lap, which caused it to fall on the floor. "Hang on," he said, bending to retrieve it.

The window next to him exploded.

Moxley hit the floor as full-automatic gunfire punctured his window blinds and blew ragged holes in the plasticboard of the opposite wall. Pieces of polyglass sprinkled his back. Neiring's image was annihilated by a bullet. A long string of projectiles smashed the work terminal to shards and ripped up the surface of the desk.

"Great," he muttered from the floor. "This is just holing *great*." He crawled across the filthy carpet, toward the footlocker, while the gunman outside changed position and began raking the office from side to side. The gunfire was loud but not deafening. A nailer, he figured, judging from the alloy spikes embedded in his desk and walls.

He took a nail through the web of his left hand while opening the footlocker. Another nail nicked his ear, scaring him badly. Blood trickled down the side of his head. From inside the locker, he grabbed the one thing he wouldn't have to aim to fire, the one item he was absolutely not supposed to have here in Hongkongtown.

When he pulled open the plastic cylinder of the heat-seeking rocket tube, the projectile inside fired automatically. It filled the office with smoke and set the carpet on fire. Moxley coughed and stamped out the flames while the missile hove away, out the window and into the night—

Daylight flared as the missile hit the closest heat source that wasn't Moxley. The detective squinted, face in the scorched and bloody carpet. His hand ached. His ears rang.

The light died. Through the broken window, he could hear rain. Somewhere in the building, smoke- and fire-klaxons were hooting.

He stood. On his desk, the threedy sat untouched. A trio of nail rounds was embedded in the desk next to it.

Moxley bent and grabbed a laser rifle from the locker. His left hand hurt badly. Shouldering the laser, he went to the window, careful not to expose himself to a second shooter. On the ground two stories below, he saw what looked like the burning chassis of a hydrogen cycle. Scattered through the alley around the cycle were gobbets of cooked meat that he assumed were his would-be assassin.

"Amateur," Moxley said to the rain.

Willy Beaman

Peyton closed the door. "It worked," he said.

"I told you it would, Daddy," said Annika. She tapped her forearm tablet, shutting it down. "You just make them believe you're home alone and they'll show up anywhere. I don't think they stop to really consider what they're doing. It's like they're too desperate to get here."

"You didn't pretend to be anyone else?" Peyton asked, leaning against the door, hunching to avoid striking his head on the ceiling of the flop. "No Jenni Syn avatar?"

"No," said Annika. She took out her gold pocket watch, snapped it open, and stared at its face. "It works less well if I pretend to be grown up. There are so many that want children. I don't like thinking about that."

"No," said Peyton. "Neither do I. That's why this is important to do. Whenever we can do it, we should."

The man standing in the entryway began to shake. He looked back the way he'd come, at the door now closed behind him. Peyton caught the glance and shook his head.

"Who are you people?" asked the man.

"What's his name?" Peyton asked Annika.

"William Beaman," said Annika. "'Willy' to his friends. He works in the shipyards, running dock robots. He's pretty good with electronics. His grades were just average in school. He has bad credit."

"I just can't believe that worked," said Peyton.

"Uh," said Willy Beaman.

"Why, Daddy?" asked Annika. She was sitting askew the couch, her legs on the armrest, holding her watch in one hand.

"It just seems so . . . easy."

"Things aren't always hard," said Annika. "People make them harder than they need to be."

Peyton reached out and put one enormous hand on Beaman's shoulder. The scrawny man yelped. "Please let me go," he said. "I didn't see anything. I don't know anything. I won't tell anyone."

"You thought you were going to meet a twelve-year-old girl here," said Peyton.

"He *did* meet a twelve-year-old girl here, actually," said Annika.

Peyton shot her a look. Turning back to Beaman, he said, "How many?" With his free hand he encircled Beaman's right wrist.

"How many *what*?" asked Beaman.

Peyton frowned and, using two fingers, snapped Beaman's right pinky. The little man screamed.

Annika closed her watch, put it away, and walked to the kitchenette, where she began printing breakfast.

"You've never asked me about your mother," said Peyton. "I feel like I should tell you."

"Okay, Daddy."

"How many?" Peyton asked Beaman again.

"Please," Beaman said. Tears streamed down his cheeks. "I don't know what you're asking me."

"Wrong," said Peyton. He snapped the little man's ring finger.

Shrieking, Beaman fell to his knees. Peyton would not let go.

Beaman dangled there, held up by one arm, clutching at Peyton's granite fist.

"I never knew her," said Peyton to Annika. "I assume she was a volunteer to the Program, but I don't know that. They took the sample from me, and then . . . Then one day they had Warden Richards tell me she died. They told me you were dead, too. I've wondered before if that means your mother might be alive."

"Four!" Beaman shouted. "Four!"

"I don't think so," said Annika. "Montauk said the same thing. He told me that if I was alive, my mother might be. So I looked. I went on the grid and I searched. I found the death certificate. Not a fake one, either. She really did die when I was born."

"Four other children?" said Peyton to Beaman. "Four times you've done this?" To Annika, he said, "Does it make you sad? You've never mentioned it. I'm sorry if it does." To Beaman, he said, "I don't believe you. Try again." He broke Beaman's middle finger.

Annika had to raise her voice to be heard over Beaman's shrieks. "No, Daddy," she said.

"What?" Peyton asked. He put a hand over Beaman's mouth.

"I said," Annika told him, "no, it doesn't make me sad. That's why I didn't ask you."

Beaman was trying to speak. Peyton lifted his hand. "Twenty-four," Beaman cried. "Twenty-four. Oh God, oh God, it's twenty-four. I'm sorry. I'm sorry. Twenty-four."

"Before I found out you were alive," Peyton told Annika, "I wanted to die. I've been a bad man, Annika. I've done terrible things. I deserve to die for doing them. But then I learned you existed. It's my job to be your father."

"You feel obligated to be my daddy?"

"No," said Peyton. "I feel like my life is not my own. I'm

responsible for you, yes. But I also . . . I *want* to be your father. More than anything. Maybe by being a father I can repay a small part of what I've taken. But that isn't really why I want it. The moment I saw you, I knew I would die for you if I had to do it to keep you safe. But that meant something else. It meant . . . I had to *live* for you, too. Does that make sense?"

"I think so, Daddy," said Annika.

Beaman struggled. Peyton shook him lightly

"I need to do right," Peyton told Annika. "I need to do right by *you.*"

"Stop worrying, Daddy," she said, smiling at him. "You keep telling me how bad you were. But you were going to let them punish you. You were going to let them fix you. It's not your fault they couldn't do it. You're not in charge of everything."

"You're sure?" he asked.

"I've told you," she said. "It's selfish to want what you don't need. I don't need a mother. You're all I need."

Peyton's vision blurred. He wiped his eyes with the back of his hand. "Thank you, Annika." To Beaman, he said, "Twenty-four is a problem."

"What?" Beaman sputtered. "Why? Why?"

"Because you've only got twenty fingers and toes," said Peyton. He went to work nonetheless. When he got to twenty, he would just have to improvise.

"GOD PLEASE STOP PLEASE!" screamed Willy Beaman.

"What?" Peyton said, cupping his free hand to his ear.

"I said breakfast is ready," shouted Annika.

Shenzhen Boulevard

Neiring crossed Shenzhen Boulevard, dodging pedicabs and hydrogen bikes, to join his contact at a sidewalk hash-hut. The table was covered in grime, but outdoor tables always were. It was also wet. Everything was wet with morning rain, including his plastic chair. He did his best to ignore the seeping sensation in the seat of his pants.

"I'm not sure that's going to help," said Neiring. His phone buzzed. He tapped it with his thumb. If the caller was unimportant, the device would take a message. If the call was from one of his preferred contacts, like his supervisor, the phone would transmit his current location and explain that he was busy.

"It couldn't hurt," said Jase Calvin. He was sipping a hash latte and looked agitated. Calvin was a government administrator and looked the part. He was a thin, balding man in his late thirties, wearing a linen suit two decades out of fashion and half a size too small. Except for his hairline, he looked exactly the same to Neiring as he had at the University of Van Nuys.

"So what were you able to get?" Neiring asked. He waved away the slicker-covered serving android when it wandered past.

"Just so it's clear," said Calvin. "If it gets out that you got this from me, it's my job. So don't tell anyone. This report was . . . spontaneously generated by the environment."

"Right," said Neiring. "Can I see it?"

Calvin passed over the plastic folder full of prints. "This VanClef is a bad guy, Ray. Bad as they get."

Neiring started sifting through the files. "Have you read this?" he asked.

"Marion W. VanClef," said Calvin. "Fifty-eight years old. He's a xenobiologist with degrees in chemistry and physics. He was also a sergeant in the Border Wars. Saw combat in Arizona and New Mexico before Tucson went nuclear. Twenty years ago, Intelligence recruits him to head up a new division, nominally called Genetic Applications. It's a bioweapons division, Ray."

"That's all in the files?" Neiring asked. "None of it's classified?"

"There's been a data dump," said Calvin. "Half of this wasn't available two days ago. The government is disavowing VanClef. You know, painting him as a rogue agent? They've declassified his work and claimed he conducted it without official sanction."

"And that work is?"

"Project Violet," said Calvin. "Developing a reproducible biological weapon based solely on genetic manipulation. The idea was to create a small army of—"

"Peytons," said Neiring.

"That's really not what matters," said Calvin. "VanClef went off the reservation two days ago. Killed a bunch of government employees and tried to burn down the hospital they were using as a front. The government sent a kill-and-capture team to pick him up. They *tagged* him, Ray. He's walking around with a radio-transmitter singing in his veins. I've got the frequency right here."

"This is incredible," said Neiring. "Nobody would suspect . . ." He paused. "Calvin?" Calvin had put his head in his hands, as if he meant to sleep sitting at the table. His latte tipped over and spilled, splattering the back of his head. Neiring reached out for him. A furrow opened in the plastic table.

That time, Neiring heard the gunshot.

There were two killers, each armed with an automatic nail gun, walking in lockstep across Shenzhen with their weapons at waist level. They wore black body armor and their helmets had smoked visors. The armor was government issue. As Neiring threw himself down, pressed his face to the sticky pavement of the sidewalk cafe, he saw the shooters rake their weapons from side to side, heedless of the innocents killed.

They're here to kill me and anyone I might have talked to, he thought. *VanClef's making good on his threat.*

He managed, from his prone position, to get his service automatic out of its holster. The spray of sharp metal kept him pinned. The tabletop disintegrated in a shower of plastic splinters.

Working their way lower, he realized. *That's it. Nowhere to go.*

Neiring closed his eyes. There was so much more he had wanted to do with his life. He was afraid. He hoped it wouldn't hurt too badly.

The sound he heard next was not the meaty thud of nails in his body. It was instead the crash of something heavy into something heavier.

The rain of nails subsided. Neiring, gun in hand, stood, just in time to see Harold Moxley backing his car over the body of one of the gunmen.

The nose of Moxley's car was a bloody mess. Tires squealed and sprayed blood as the detective pushed his old vehicle over the dead man's body. Already, the second shooter—missed in what must have been a suicide charge by Moxley—started pumping nails into the rear of the car. The armored shooter's weapon held a large disc magazine.

Neiring braced his pistol in both hands. He sank into his stance, drew a breath, let half of it out. Holding the remainder, he let the trigger come back, let the gun fire itself when it was—

The triple burst *spanged* off the gunman's helmet, whipping his head back, knocking him down. Neiring ran for the fallen shooter, knowing that the hit was not lethal. He had to get to the man before the killer regained his feet.

Moxley's abused car was spewing black smoke fore and aft. The detective threw the door open and stepped out, trench coat whipping around his legs like a cape. As Neiring ran for him, Mox walked deliberately to the fallen gunner and kicked him in the head. The helmet went spinning across the pavement.

Moxley whipped his revolver from its shoulder holster, lined up the lower barrel, and fired once into the shooter's skull. Panting, Neiring reached his friend just as Moxley pumped a second explosive round into the fallen man.

"Stay down," said Moxley.

"You okay?" Neiring said. Moxley's hand bore a clumsily sprayed bandage. His coat was flecked with blood and torn by nails.

"Bad night," said Mox. He jerked his flabby chin at the dead men. "Bad morning, too."

"I know how to find VanClef," said Neiring. He held up the plastic folder Calvin had given him.

"Then let's make today worse," said Mox.

"You're sure you're all right?"

"Get in the car, Ray."

Count of Ten

"Put us at the curb," said VanClef from the passenger seat. "Keep power applied. We may need to reposition if they change course."

In the driver's seat of the truck, Stevens nodded. He put two fingers to the transceiver in his ear.

"Stevens," said the younger agent. "Go ahead." He waited for a few moments. "Get back here as soon as possible," he directed. Then he touched the transceiver to disengage it.

VanClef sighed. Without looking at Stevens, he said, "They've failed, haven't they?"

"All three, sir," said Stevens. "Smith last night. Klyter and Korth this morning. Moxley and Neiring remain at large."

"Perhaps we should assign Orrin to them. Assuming the capture and recovery goes as planned."

"It's a thought, sir. I'd rather we not get ahead of ourselves."

"Good man," said VanClef. "I may forgive you for the matter of Ms. West."

"Yes, sir."

They waited in silence for a few moments. Finally, VanClef pointed with one gloved finger. "There," he said. "Ten o'clock."

"Sir?"

"Sixty degrees *left*, damn you," said VanClef. "Unmistakably Ian Peyton."

Peyton stood head and shoulders above the rest of the crowd. He walked with one shoulder canted; that would be the side to which Annika was attached. She was not visible past the other pedestrians.

"Should I release the subjects, sir?" Stevens asked.

"Not yet," said VanClef. "Let's see where they go."

"They're headed for the amusement park," said Stevens. "They go there frequently."

VanClef nodded. "Move us down the street. Stay well back. But keep with them."

Stevens guided the truck down the street, hopping blocks slowly, moving around other vehicles with care. When they had paused once more to let Peyton and Annika enter the amusement park, Stevens turned to VanClef.

"Sir," he said. "I have an idea." VanClef stared at him. Stevens said, "If we send in the subjects, there will quite possibly be collateral damage."

"I would say that's certain," said VanClef.

"Let me go in on foot, sir," said Stevens. "Let me talk to them. It's the one strategy we haven't tried."

"Do I need to remind you of the damage Peyton did to the school?" asked VanClef. "With his bare hands?"

"Respectfully, sir," said Stevens, "he is with his daughter. I've studied his psychological profile extensively. He was willing to die, even *wanted* to die, until a mysterious computer error alerted the Warden to her presence in the gallery."

"Richards' big mouth," said VanClef, "has cost a great many people their lives."

"My point, sir," said Stevens, "is that I can play to his desire to protect her. Mentally he has almost no guile, sir. A purely average intelligence quotient at best. He's no match for me."

"Very well," said VanClef. "If it will prevent us from garnering any more attention, it's worth a try. Keep your transceiver open."

"Yes, sir."

Stevens left the heavy panel truck. He crossed the street and entered the amusement park. When he was a dozen meters from the front gates, he stopped. He saw Annika Peyton, alone, climbing aboard a ride called the Tiltrotor.

Of course. Peyton was too large to ride any of the rides with her. The crowds, the bright lighting inside the park . . . he would not be here. He would be outside, *just* outside, where he could keep her under watch. Stevens retraced his steps. He turned left, found nothing, and walked back toward the main gates. The right-hand path took him around the perimeter fence.

He never saw the shadows come alive. One moment he was walking, and the next he was being held aloft by the neck.

"Follow my daughter," said Peyton. "Follow me. That's not good for you."

"Wait," Stevens managed to say, gasping. "Please. I just want to talk to you."

Peyton threw him to the ground. Stevens felt something crack inside his chest. He coughed and instantly regretted this.

"Ten," said Peyton.

"I'm with Government Intelligence, Peyton," said Stevens. He tried to rise. Peyton planted one enormous boot on his chest and pressed him back into the pavement. Stevens' ribs ground together. He screamed and almost passed out.

"Nine," said Peyton.

"Listen to me," Stevens said, gasping. "You can't protect your daughter, Peyton. Not forever. You're one man against the endless resources of the Northam Federation. What happens to

Annika when they take you down? I can *help* you!"

Peyton removed his foot. Air, precious air, rushed into Stevens' lungs.

"Eight," said the giant. "Seven."

"VanClef is here," said Stevens. "He's ready to take you down. To take her into custody. He's got men who are still loyal to him. And he's got weapons you aren't prepared to face. This won't be easy for you, Peyton."

"Six," said Peyton. "Five. Four."

"If you give her to me, now," said Stevens, "she'll be safe. Turn yourself in. You can live out your life in the Promontory if that's what you want. We can pull a few strings, get your death sentence commuted. Annika could even visit you in prison."

"My daughter," said Peyton, "will *never* see the inside of that place. Three."

"Don't you understand?" Stevens said. "She's not *yours*, Peyton. Not in any way that counts. The two of you are nothing alike. You're an *ant* compared to her intellect. How long before she outgrows you, Peyton? How long before she leaves? She can't stay with you forever. She has a *destiny*, Peyton."

"Two," said Peyton. His voice was a whisper.

"What can you offer her?" asked Stevens. "You're a murderer, Peyton. A criminal. When she gets old enough to understand who and what you are, when she's smart enough to stare into your heart and see the monster that dwells there, will she still accept you?"

"One," said Peyton. "Stop talking."

"How smart is she *now*, Peyton?" Stevens went on. "How soon will it be before she reaches that level? Not long at all. Not at her current rate of development. What happens then? Do you think you'll still be her *father*?"

"I'll be her father until I'm dead," said Peyton. He raised his heel again.

"You'll become *nothing* in her eyes," said Stevens.

"You first," said Peyton.

He brought down his boot.

Hello, Annika

Daddy never came into the park. That was so strange. And he had changed his clothes. He always wore the same clothes, the ones she had purchased for him. She had cleaned them for him herself just yesterday. What was he doing? She took her pocket watch out and opened it. It wasn't nearly the time they had agreed to leave.

Putting her watch away, she climbed down from the Tiltrotor and hurried over. If Daddy was breaking all his own rules, bringing attention to himself and coming for her early, it must be some sort of emergency. She had better be ready to move quickly.

But it wasn't Daddy. It wasn't him at all.

The man was every bit as big as Daddy. His skin was the same pale color, his jaw as big and strong, his hands as huge. But he looked nothing like Daddy. He had red hair and a thick handlebar mustache. Who could it possibly be?

The big man saw her. When he did, he stopped walking and started running. He was coming straight for her.

Annika screamed.

Stevens shook his head. He used the fence to pull himself

to his feet. Congealed blood connected his nose and mouth. He wiped this away with the back of his hand.

Peyton had listened. Some part of him had, anyway. He could have crushed Stevens to pulp under his foot. Instead he had barely stomped the operative at all, opting instead to knock him unconscious.

He's thinking about what I said, Stevens thought. *He's wondering if I'm right.*

A little girl screamed.

That got Stevens' attention. With his palm he hooded his eyes, his left arm braced against his side. Every breath hurt. He was going to need his ribs knitted.

He saw them, then. Amidst the crowds inside the amusement park, he saw the alpha, Big Bill, lumbering toward one of the rides. The flash of blonde hair he also saw could not be a coincidence. Bill had acquired Annika and was bearing down on her.

He almost didn't see the blur that was Ian Peyton. He had never witnessed anyone or anything that large move so fast. The giant knocked down anyone in his way, cleaving a path through the crowd, leaving stunned, cursing, and fist-shaking patrons in his wake. He ran as if he didn't see them.

Big Bill sensed something and turned just as Peyton hit him.

The escaped giant collided with the alpha, wrapping his arms around Big Bill's waist, throwing his counterpart to the ground. Something that looked like a sawed-off shotgun spun away from the combatants and disappeared under a park bench. Stevens swore he could feel the vibration through the pavement as the two enormous men dug a furrow with their bodies. Big Bill roared in defiance. Peyton never made a sound—that was, until he spoke two words.

"Annika," he shouted. "RUN!"

Stevens started toward the two. He reached to his ear for his transceiver, but it was gone. VanClef would have been monitoring Stevens' conversation with Peyton. He had interpreted the abrupt end to their dialogue as failure. That must have prompted him to release Stillwater. The move struck him as reckless. This park was full of civilians, full of *children* and their parents. To release a psychopath like William Stillwater among civilians seemed needlessly messy.

The sound of bone crashing into bone reached his ears. Peyton was swinging mighty shovel-hooks into Big Bill's ribs. He had landed in the superior position, mounting Stillwater's waist, and he seemed determined to punch a tunnel through the man's chest. Bill bore the onslaught with cursing and howls of revenge to come. He was trying to protect his head with his own massive arms, but Peyton was sawing away at him, smashing the alpha's arms into his face, ramming elbows and forearm blows into Stillwater's abdomen.

It was remarkable, thought Stevens, how viscerally, how instinctively, the two realized they were enemies. They struggled with mortal ferocity, every strike a killing blow to anyone but Stillwater and Peyton.

Big Bill's laughter reached Stevens' ears.

It took Peyton a moment to realize what was happening, and that was enough for everything to go wrong for him. Perry and Mulligan appeared in the crowd, probably held back by VanClef for this very purpose. While Peyton was occupied with Stillwater, the other two subjects grabbed Peyton's arms and pulled him off their leader. They pinned Peyton against the corrugated wall surrounding the Tiltrotor. Stevens could *see* the pleasure radiating from Bill as he postured about, stepping this way and that in front of his now-captive enemy.

Big Bill began hammering away at Peyton's stomach. Peyton endured the blows in silence, his muscles tensing, sweat making his forehead and his bare arms shine under the overhead lights. The more Bill punched, the more Peyton flexed.

Sweat, thought Stevens.

The alpha realized it a heartbeat later, but Peyton was already moving. His right arm, slick with perspiration, pulled free of Mulligan's grasp. In the same motion, Peyton brought his arm around in a tight arc and drove his thumb into Perry's left eye.

Stevens watched, fascinated, as Perry's scream froze Mulligan in place. Bill was smarter; Bill was more aggressive. He didn't waste time surveying the injury to his subordinate. He simply threw himself at Peyton. But Peyton wasn't there.

Perry fell to his knees, clutching at his face, and Peyton used the man's eye socket as a stirrup to pull himself onto and over Perry's shoulders. He landed on the other side of the Tiltrotor's wall, inside the ride, which was still running. Passengers screamed. Bill looked momentarily confused, and in that moment, Peyton reappeared by the ride's entrance. He dwarfed the rusty bollard that bore the legend "You must be THIS tall to ride."

Peyton reached down, grabbed the post, and ripped it from the pavement. Bill stopped himself in mid-charge. Mulligan wasn't as smart. The subordinate closed on Peyton at full speed, perhaps thinking to shoot for Peyton's legs and bull him to the ground. Peyton swung the heavy metal bollard like a cricket bat. Mulligan's skull split like a boiled egg.

Perry was still screaming. Bill rounded on Peyton, arms out, circling.

Stevens crept closer.

"Gonna die," said Stillwater. "Gonna die screaming like Perry. Big Bill Stillwater gonna kill you."

Peyton did not answer. He turned, saw Stevens, fixed the man with a look Stevens could not identify. Casting a last, contemptuous glance at Stillwater, he turned away.

Then he ran.

He's realized it, thought Stevens. *He knows Bill and the others are a delaying tactic.*

Peyton tore through the amusement park, heading for the exit, with Big Bill Stillwater hot on his heels.

Annika hurried through the crowd. She thought about stealing a hydrogen bike; she thought about paying for a pedicab. But she was not sure where to go. The enemies Daddy faced were just like him. She did not know how to factor that, did not know precisely how to gauge that danger. She could not make a decision without—

She heard the big truck behind her. She turned in time to see it collide with the curb, bump up over it, then slide off. Its grille was bearing down on her.

The driver's door opened. A man in a black leather coat leaned out. He reached for her as the truck went past. He grabbed her by her sweater and pulled her into the cab.

"Daddy!" she cried out.

"Hello, Annika," said Marion VanClef.

Red Like a Beet

He was still carrying the metal post when they caught up to him. He felt his legs being taken from under him; felt his center of gravity shift; felt the sting of plastic and metal against his face and chest as he was pushed through the facade of a robot bodega. He and his enemy landed in a heap of shelves and broken merchandise, most of these cartons of dehydrated, preprinted food.

His hand found the post. He hefted it, standing. The robot proprietor beeped from behind its podium and Peyton turned to it. He hesitated for a moment. Perhaps this was—

Perry ripped the robot's head off. Sparks flew. The one-eyed man threw the head at Peyton, who dodged it. He charged Perry, swinging the club, smashing merchandise from nearby shelves.

"Go away," said Peyton. "I don't know you."

"You don't want to," said Perry. He pointed to the weeping mess that was his eye socket. "But I *owe* you now, Peyton. I'm not going to kill you. I'm going to take both your—"

Peyton hit him in the jaw with the metal post.

Teeth flew. Perry's bloody face was knocked sideways. Something cracked. The big man howled, holding his head, trying to straighten his neck. Peyton had never seen that happen before, but then, he had never before fought someone roughly his own size.

Big Bill loomed in the entrance to the shop.

"Think you broke him," he said. His voice was mockery and bass and nothing else.

"You're puppets," said Peyton. "Puppets of VanClef."

"I'm *nobody's* boy," rumbled Stillwater. He seemed content to watch Perry floundering on the tiles of the bodega's floor, pushing at his neck, trying to turn his head. It was as if Peyton's strike had locked Perry's neck off-center. "Never seen that before," Stillwater said.

"I was just thinking that," said Peyton. He let the metal post fall to the floor.

"Maybe he dies," said Stillwater. "Maybe he lives. Don't care. You're a job."

"I don't have to be," said Peyton. "You were in the Program."

"Just before you," said Stillwater. "They put me in the freezer. Thawed me out and gave me a job. You."

"You were in storage," said Peyton. "Why? You look just like me. Why not use you?"

"Tried," said Stillwater. "Sample rejected." The red-haired man tapped his skull with one large finger. "Something loose up here, they said." He smiled broadly beneath his handlebar mustache. "Could be true. Don't care."

"So you're nobody's boy," said Peyton, "but you let them give you a 'job.' Let them tell you what to do."

"Don't care about them," said Stillwater. "Don't care about *you*. Care about *me*. Big Bill Stillwater is the biggest. Big Bill Stillwater is the strongest. Prove it. Kill you, then go. Free now. Out of the freezer. Done taking orders."

"Does VanClef know you're not under his control?" said Peyton. "Maybe he'll send an army to kill you."

"He'll need to send two," said Stillwater. "Maybe more." Again the red-haired man grinned. "Kill Perry. Prove he's weak."

That got Perry's attention. He squirmed around on the floor, looking up at Stillwater as best he could. There was pleading in his eyes.

"He's not going to help you," said Peyton. "He doesn't have a kind heart."

"What?" Stillwater asked.

"Nothing," said Peyton. On the floor, Perry tried to say something. His words came out as a breathy moan. His face started to turn red.

"Dying," said Stillwater. "You holed him up bad."

"He could take a while to suffocate like that," said Peyton. "Maybe half an hour. Maybe more. You should put him out of his misery."

"Don't care about him," Stillwater repeated.

"Then I will," said Peyton. He reached for Perry. When his fingertips brushed the man's arms, Perry exploded, throwing furious punches, snarling and drooling with his head cocked to one side. His fists crashed against Peyton, incredibly strong, fueled by adrenaline and desperation. Peyton used his thick forearms to ward off most of the blows. Perry, still on the floor, tried to kick him off. The strikes against Peyton's shins were painful and, if he was not careful, Perry would break his leg or his ankle.

Stillwater chuckled from his spot in the doorway. "Doesn't want to go. Look at him. Red like a beet."

Perry was indeed turning a violent shade of red. Whatever damage had been done to him, he was not getting air, and the exertion was killing him as surely as if Peyton were choking him from behind.

Peyton fought past Perry's desperate guard and pinned the man. He was very aware of Big Bill standing there, and of the vulnerable position he would be in if Bill jumped in while Peyton was dealing with the wounded man. But Bill simply leaned against the wall. Annika had used a word the other day, a word to describe a television character she found arrogant and dismissive. Watching Big Bill, he thought of that word.

"Insolent," said Peyton.

"What?" said Bill.

"Nothing," Peyton said again. He managed to work his way around behind Perry, wrapping his arm under and against the man's damaged jaw. With his other arm, he braced the head. Perry moaned something Peyton could not understand. He was starting to move sluggishly now. There was no telling how long it would take him to die, lying on the floor of the bodega, but Peyton thought it would be a long time.

The loud *snap!* of Perry's neck signaled the end of his problems. Peyton threw the body off and stood.

Big Bill was gone.

Peyton stepped out of the bodega. He looked up and down the street. Where had his enemy gone? Had Bill given up? Gone to live whatever life he could, now that he was free of VanClef?

Standing on the street, Peyton swore.

No. That wasn't it at all.

Peyton looked up.

Big Bill was clinging to the roof of the bodega.

"Kill you now," he said.

He dropped.

Something I Can Grab

Peyton tasted blood. Stillwater's fist crashed into his jaw a second time, a third time, hammering him back, throwing him against the cracked facade of the bodega. Peyton sheltered his head, tucking his chin, feeling Big Bill's attacks crash against his forearms. Shards of the bodega's plaster dug into his kidneys.

He brought his elbows down on Stillwater's back. The sharp blows staggered the other giant, long enough for Peyton to ram his right fist into Stillwater's jaw. He threw shovel hook after shovel hook, left and right, left and right, chiseling away at Stillwater as if he would knock the man's jaw free of his skull. When he judged the timing right, he threw an uppercut that snapped Bill's head back. Then he threw a vicious front kick that pressed the air from Stillwater's lungs. The mustached giant staggered back, across the pedestrian walkway, into the street—

Big Bill turned in time to see the hovertruck that hit him. The collision crumpled the front of the vehicle and caused it to yaw into oncoming traffic, where it smashed a robot hydrogen cycle to pieces.

The screaming started.

Pedestrians fled when the hydrogen cycle detonated, creating a fireball that cast Bill's bloody face in orange relief. He staggered through the smoking, burning debris, headed for Peyton, who faced him through the chaos. Vehicles collided as they tried to avoid the flames. Several cyclists went down. Ground cars careened around the growing clot of fallen riders and their machines. An automated traffic klaxon began to sound. The stream of drones overhead was scattered by the whoops of a hovering traffic supervisor, a turbofan model equipped with cameras, loudspeakers, and strobe lights. The supervisor started shouting synthesized calls for orderly movement away from the crash area.

Stillwater jumped and caught it. The drone's fan screamed in protest. Bill swung the drone like a weapon, smashing aside a pedicab and knocking its driver to the pavement. The drone spun away as if thrown from a catapult. Stillwater was already charging Peyton again.

The two crashed against each other, chest to chest, grabbing for each other's arms, clinching up in a mammoth, standing brawl that saw them clawing and ripping at each other's flesh. Stillwater's hands found Peyton's face and he tried to gouge his opponent's eyes. Peyton broke his own hand up and through Stillwater's arms, slamming the heel of his palm against the other man's chin. Bill's head snapped back. Peyton drove the web of his hand into Stillwater's throat.

Staggered, Bill dragged Peyton to the ground with him, locking his hands around Peyton's wrists. Around them, people ran, shouted in alarm, even stood and watched in horror or fascination. Peyton rolled his wrists and grabbed Stillwater's, locking the two together at the arms. Both men exerted as much force as they could, their arms straining, the veins in their forearms and biceps swelling against their livid skin. Stillwater leaned in. His breath was hot and foul in Peyton's face.

"No room for you," said Stillwater. "I was *first*. Me. Big Bill Stillwater. *You* shouldn't be here. Now you won't be."

Peyton could feel his skin growing hot as he struggled against

Stillwater's grip. The two were so evenly matched that neither could break the wrist hold. "You don't owe them anything," he managed to say. "Your life is yours. Don't be their hammer."

"I was nothing before they changed me," said Bill. "Now I'm strong. But there's only one king of the mountain. There's only one top dog. That's *me*. You die so I can be me again."

"They'll hunt you," countered Peyton. "They'll kill you."

"They couldn't kill *you*," said Bill. "They made a mistake. Should have kept me asleep. I *liked* being asleep. But they woke me up, told me they made you. Couldn't live with that. As long as you live, I'm nobody. Only one top dog. Only ever one."

"They're using you," said Peyton. "Killing me won't get you what you want. It only helps *them*."

"Helps *me*," said Bill. "Killing you is for me. Takes the top dog to kill you. Takes *me*. Makes me king of the mountain. All I want."

Stillwater might have said more, but Peyton wrenched his arms apart. Tucking his own chin, Peyton drove his forehead up as Bill's face came down. The brutal head-butt drove Stillwater's nose back into his face, crushing it, spraying blood on them both. The maneuver caused Bill to lose his grip.

The sirens of private police cruisers were audible now. The crowd continued to swirl around the two men, while vehicles bypassed the widening ground zero of wrecked conveyances and fallen bystanders. The air smelled of copper and burning plastic.

"Police are coming," Peyton said. He stood, untangling himself from Stillwater, and turned to run.

"Don't care," said Bill. "I was nothing. Nothing until they made me Big Bill. They wake me up. They tell me they made *you*. Big as me. Strong as me. But you're not. When you die, Big Bill is left. Big Bill is the best. Nobody's better than me. I won't be nothing. Not again."

Stillwater lunged, grabbing Peyton's leg and pulling him to the pavement again. The two men rolled back and forth, finally rolling into the burning wreckage of the hydrogen cycle. Peyton felt his skin peeling back under the flames. Stillwater's howl of pain echoed his own. Still Peyton's fellow giant held on, tying him up, keeping him pinned to the ground. Heat from the burning cycle licked at his neck and shoulders.

A puddle of lubricant plasma began to spread around the bike. This too burned. Bill roared as the plasma reached him, igniting him, clinging to him like napalm. He began pounding on Peyton's chest with his clenched fists, trying to crush Peyton's ribs and collapse his lungs. Peyton shifted, catching Bill between the scissor of his legs. The two giant men strained against each other, locked in position.

The burning tire of the hydrogen bike was within Peyton's reach. He grabbed it, heedless of the pain, and ripped it free of the chassis, shoving the fiery tire into Stillwater's face. Bill began to cough and choke as he fought off the clinging, burning synthetic rubber. When the flames reached his eyes, he screamed.

Peyton had to get away. There was no telling how long he and Stillwater might stay locked in combat. They were too evenly matched. The flames turning his skin black were painful, so painful. He would heal quickly enough, but first he had to get clear, get free, roll the fire out, let his skin—

No, he thought.

Peyton fought his instincts. He reached into the burning wreckage of the hydrogen bike, breathless as the inferno took his arm, burning through his flesh, scorching him to the bone. The pain was . . . indescribable. He thought the word as he clawed deep into the burning corpse of the bike, deep into the oven that was baking his arm. He could not feel his fingers. He prayed he would still be able to will his hand to clench.

Hissing and spitting, the jellied tissues of his eyes weeping down his cheeks, Bill reached for Peyton's face. Peyton stretched, pushing his legs to full extension, holding Bill out and away from his torso. The wounded giant still would not give up. He dug his fingers into Peyton's thighs, trying to separate the muscles, pulling himself along Peyton's body. Blinded, he crawled upward, his fingers curled to pluck and rend.

He's going to claw out my eyes if he can reach them, thought Peyton.

Peyton would have screamed, but the boring of Big Bill's fingers was nothing compared to the tunnel of fire in which his arm was lodged.

Give me something I can grab, he thought. *Give me anything I can grip.*

There! His arm stopped; his shoulder joint registered the resistance. He forced himself to make a fist, to roll to one knee, to raise the burning hydrogen bike above his head. His vision began to blur, to gray, to turn deep purple. He was passing out. The pain was so intense it almost did not register.

Stillwater howled. Peyton could not hear his voice. The sirens, the screams of the bystanders, the downdrafts of the drones, the police and news helicopters now whirring overhead: he heard none of it. His head felt thick. He had only moments. He had to do it. He had to succeed. It was the only way to fight his way back to Annika.

It's selfish to want what you don't need.

"I WANT MY DAUGHTER!" Peyton screamed, swinging the burning bike like a club, crushing Big Bill's skull under the flaming frame of the vehicle.

Over and over he lifted the bike up and swung it down, smashing Bill's face, splitting his skull, smashing his brains to burning pulp and digging a furrow into the pavement beneath. Before he was done, the fire was almost extinguished. Finally, inevitably, he dropped the charred bike frame, extracting his smoldering, blackened arm and ashen hand. He stared at the limb and flexed fingers he could not feel.

It would get better. It would get better soon enough.

"Stop where you are!" came an amplified voice from overhead. "You are under arrest!"

Peyton was already running. Cradling his injured arm, he pumped his legs with all his remaining strength, crashing through the crowds and smashing aside trash containers in the alleys he forded. He barely felt the pavement beneath his feet. He ran faster than he had run in his life. He ran for his freedom. He ran for Annika.

"I want my daughter," he said again. But Annika was gone. He stumbled from alley to alley, his arm and hand aching, Annika was gone and he did not know what to do.

He stopped at a public medical kiosk. He had chits in his pocket. He could at least spray his arm with burn gel. He reached out to touch the screen.

The kiosk's screen illuminated. The caduceus symbol rotated slowly. But at the touch of Peyton's uninjured fingers, it disappeared. The display turned black.

The image of a gold pocket watch began to dance across the screen.

Worse for Wear

He was several blocks from the Redlight now. The gold watches had brought him this far, but now they were gone. He scanned the traffic screens and weather displays, storefronts and kiosks, hoping for another marker, wishing for a direction. The sirens of an approaching police hovercraft cut through the air and through the ringing in his ears. He turned in time to see the craft cutting between a shuttered stripeasy and a pawn shop.

"Put your hands behind your head!" announced a voice projected from the hovercraft's public address system. "You are under arrest!"

They were private cops, not government employees. He clenched his burned hand, feeling the skin crack, grimacing at the pins-and-needles sensation that accompanied the terrible itching in his skin. The arm was healing quickly. Already, fresh patches of unburned skin were visible through the charred outer layer.

"Go away," said Peyton. "Go away and I won't have to hurt you."

"Put your hands behind your head!" the cop repeated. The nose of the hovercraft closed to within a meter of where he stood. Automatic guns mounted on the nose of the craft swiveled to target him—

He put his fists together, raised his arms, and brought both hands down on the nose of the hovercraft. The blow left a crater in the plastic shell. Peyton scrambled up the front of the machine, between the nose guns, and wrenched open the hatch leading to the cockpit.

A pair of helmeted police officers looked up, eyes wide, only to shout in alarm when he reached in and grabbed them both. He slammed the two men together with bone-jarring force and then dropped them, now unconscious, back in their craft. He paused and, before jumping down from the vehicle, reached inside and smashed the control panel. He had no idea if that would stop them from using their guns, but he hoped it might.

He landed heavily on the pavement, only to come face-to-face with a robot-like figure in a rain slicker.

"Friend Peyton," said Montauk. "You look considerably worse for wear."

Peyton nodded and ran. Montauk followed as if this were the most natural response to its greeting. A similar Og, whom Peyton assumed was Loran, fell in behind them both. Loran carried a pneumatic weapon as it had outside the school. A similar gun was slung over Montauk's metal shoulder.

"May I ask where we're running?" Montauk said, jogging next to Peyton. Its lilting voice was unaffected by the exertion. Montauk could not be winded because Montauk did not breathe. At least, Peyton didn't think the Og did. He realized he wasn't sure.

"Annika," said Peyton. "Look for a gold watch. It will be on one of the traffic screens, or a store display. Anything connected to a network."

"Breadcrumbs," said Montauk. "Brilliant."

"How did you find me?" Peyton asked.

"The same way the police did," said Montauk. "The same way your enemies will, unless we lie low. The interference Annika and the girls have been running only works if you're not actively engaged in bloody fights in the midst of public thoroughfares, Peyton."

Peyton stopped running, taking shelter behind a vacant communications kiosk at the corner of a pay-credit loanery. He turned to the Og. Montauk crouched next to him, while Loran took up a position to guard their backs. "What are you talking about?" Peyton asked.

Montauk shook its head. "Probably it is not my place to tell you this. Forgive me as needed. Annika and the other girls from the school have been manipulating the public surveillance algorithms. It's a combination of something akin to a denial-of-service attack; they've been assaulting the search patterns, disrupting them with random number associations. And they've also made a habit of appearing prominently on camera to foul any spot checks."

"I don't understand anything you just said," Peyton told it.

"Your daughter and her fellow classmates are all geniuses, Peyton," said Montauk. "She's smarter than anyone understands. They all are. Their intelligence is an order of magnitude greater than this Project of VanClef's could have anticipated. It's why he lost control of the school from within."

"So Annika did something to the public drones and cameras?"

"They all did," said Montauk. "Haven't you wondered how it's possible for the two of you to move around Hongkongtown without drawing any police attention? Not since that street doctor, Gorsky, tried to turn you in for the reward. Annika told me she conferred with her classmates through the virts shortly thereafter, to prevent such a problem from happening again. They used their expertise with the networks to confuse the computers processing the images . . . and they further muddied the waters using those of their number who had already escaped the school. Imagine the difficulty that would cause a processing computer: Just when it believes it has isolated Annika, three little blonde girls who look almost exactly like her appear on camera simultaneously in different parts of the city. Of course, none of those little girls can be found in the databases for positive or negative identification, because their identities have *already* been screened out by the very Intelligence agency from which they have escaped. They appear to be ghosts in the machine. The result is utter chaos from a logic-tree perspective. It was a brilliant plan."

"I didn't realize," said Peyton. "I thought we were being careful."

"I've no doubt that you were," said Montauk, "but if not for Annika and her counterparts, the police would have picked you up long ago. The problem we now face is that a region-wide alert has been scrambled in response to your battle with the other . . . whatever that was."

"Big Bill Stillwater," said Peyton.

"Of course," said Montauk. The Og looked up and down the channel between the two buildings, its cameras whirring and moving. "We need to move, Peyton."

"Where have you been?" Peyton asked, suddenly suspicious. "You weren't at home after the school. Annika told me."

"No," said Montauk. "I've had some problems of my own. Human Services raided my flat and occasioned our sudden withdrawal from the premises."

"Human Services?"

"An agency ostensibly charged with managing the sometimes delicate and always complicated relationships between certified humans and Augments," said Montauk.

"I've never heard of that," said Peyton.

"There's no reason you should have," said the Og. "There

is no official Og presence in Hongkongtown; therefore Human Services does not travel in these circles. But my activities have drawn considerable attention from the mainland. It was only a matter of time."

"Activities?"

"I'm a freedom fighter, Peyton," said Montauk. "I'm one of several loosely organized cells fighting for Augment rights. There are many others. Some of them, like the Bhavik groups, I don't trust and won't work with."

"What?"

"Forgive me," said Montauk. "It's not important. But I should admit something to you, Peyton. My assistance to you and your daughter is not entirely altruistic. Annika has outlined for me her vision for how the world should work, a vision shared by her brilliant counterparts. They foresee a world in which humans and Augments live side by side, with no distinction made for what is and is not . . . normal. You can see, I trust, how Annika herself might feel about a given set of human specifications being declared more normal than another?"

Peyton looked down at his enormous hands. Ashes flecked from his burned arm, displaced by the new, glistening skin beneath. "I can," he said. "I can see that."

"I told you that my help was an investment in the future," said Montauk. "I meant it."

"But Annika's a little girl," said Peyton. "She doesn't run the world."

"Not yet, she doesn't," said Montauk. "They grow up faster than you think, Peyton." It looked past Loran, suddenly alert. "Loran," it said. "Do you hear—?"

Loran was already bringing up its own weapon. The pneumatic gun spat projectiles as a ground car bounced up over the curb, crossed the street at the far end of the channel, and then shot up the opening, coming straight for them. Peyton stood and braced himself, like a runner in a marathon, digging in his heels.

Montauk's own weapon began to whine. The Og stood at Peyton's right, heedless of return fire. Peyton looked at the Og for a moment. He wondered if he deserved such friendship, even if Montauk truly did believe it was protecting Annika's vision of the future.

The ground car's engine thrummed loudly. It was picking up speed. Peyton could see two men crouching behind the transparent wind screen. They ducked when Montauk's projectiles stitched a line of smooth holes across that expanse.

Peyton waited. The car came closer. Still he waited. The air-intake of the car was almost on top of him.

Peyton sprang.

A Laudable Shade of Purple

Peyton's feet hit the hood of the car. He lowered his shoulder and put himself into the wind screen, cracking it, causing the driver to swerve. The car's nose crumpled against the wall of the stripeasy. The driver switched off the car's power plant as he and the passenger piled out.

Montauk was already in position, raking the hood and roof of the car with his automatic weapon. Peyton did not see Loran. The two men took cover, one behind the car, another behind the closest garbage bin. Montauk seemed intent on turning the car into plastic shards.

Peyton circled the car. When the taller of the two men realized the vehicle was no shelter, he turned and pointed his service automatic.

"Stop! Don't come any closer, Peyton!"

When Peyton didn't stop, the tall man emptied his weapon into the giant's chest.

The bullets tore into his flesh. Peyton felt them pass; felt them rend his flesh; felt the one that punctured his lung. He dropped to one knee, staggered. The pain caused the ache in his burned arm to flare. His vision doubled, then tripled.

He laughed.

The taller man's face turned pale. Peyton, still stumbling, reached out and grabbed him by the throat. He could already feel his body healing. It felt, in fact, as if it was working faster than it had in the past. That was probably because of the damage to his arm. His glands were working overtime to fix the damage, flooding his body with whatever it was they produced that accomplished these things.

"It's going to take more than you," said Peyton. "I should—"

"STOP!" shouted the second man. Peyton turned. This one was short and balding, with a fat face. He wore a stained trench coat. He was holding Loran by the neck joint. With his other hand, he pressed a small, black box to Loran's head.

"That is low, Detective Moxley," said Montauk, who had stopped firing and now pointed his weapon's barrel to the sky. "That is low even for you."

"What?" asked Peyton. In his fist, the tall man struggled. "What's going on?"

"Stun gun," said Moxley. "Just an electrical transformer. Nothing more complicated than that. Takes its power cell and pumps out a hundred times the volts at low amperage. It hurts to get stuck with one . . . if you're human. If you're an Og, well, let's say your pal here might not walk away from the experience."

"Let's not be hasty, Detective Moxley," said Montauk.

"Shut up and put that 'noomer on the ground," said Moxley. "Everybody just disengage. We aren't here to take you in. Peyton, stop choking Neiring."

"He's referring to his tall friend," said Montauk. The Og laid its weapon carefully on the pavement. "Inspector Neiring, there. I might add that Inspector Neiring has achieved a laudable shade of purple."

Peyton released Neiring. The inspector staggered back against the wrecked ground car, massaging his throat.

"How do you know our names?" Moxley demanded.

"You don't exactly keep a low profile," said Montauk. "You are known to us here in Hongkongtown."

"'Us,'" said Moxley. "By that you mean other Ogs? How many are there?"

"Enough," said Montauk.

"Harry," said Neiring. His voice cracked. "We don't have time to argue like this."

"What does he mean?" Peyton asked. He flexed his fingers. Moxley caught the movement and, if he was smart, understood that only Peyton's regard for Loran kept the big man from wading through him.

"We didn't come for you," said Moxley. "We came for VanClef. Just your bad luck, we found you instead."

"VanClef is mine," said Peyton.

"You're in no position to make demands!" Moxley said. As Neiring retrieved and reloaded his pistol, Moxley gestured with the stun gun. "I mean it. I'll give this creep the whole battery. He *might* live. You never really know, with an Oggy."

"Please do not do that," said Montauk. "And there really is no need to be overtly hateful."

"VanClef has my daughter," said Peyton.

"What do you want me to do?" Moxley demanded. "You think we can just keep this quiet? You're a walking wrecking machine, Peyton. Do you realize the position it puts us in, finding you here? How many people have you killed? Have you even kept count? Do you realize the gleeful holiday the news outlets have been having with you? Some of those murders were *pornographic*, they were so imaginative. You couldn't have *asked* for more attention."

"They were child molesters," said Peyton. "Sexual predators. Garbage living among good people. One of them was going to rape and murder a little boy. None of the people I killed will be missed. The world is better without them."

Moxley stared at Peyton, his expression hard.

"He's right," gasped Neiring. "God help me, he's right."

"He knows I am," said Peyton to Neiring. A green blob of illumination danced across the wall of the stripeasy. It moved left, then right, before finally alighting on Neiring's chest.

Peyton looked at the blob of light quizzically.

"DOWN!" shouted Moxley. He dropped his stun gun, shoved Loran away from his chest, and threw himself over the wrecked hood of the car. His momentum carried him into Neiring. The collision was not gentle. Blood sprayed.

Peyton turned; only then did he hear the shot, echoing through the channel between the buildings. That single sniper's round prompted other gunmen to open up with their own weapons. Peyton, on instinct, dropped low to shield the fallen Moxley and Neiring with his body. He felt several small-arms rounds rip into his back. He grunted.

A familiar pneumatic chatter filled the wide alleyway. That would be Loran and Montauk again. As Peyton looked down at them, Neiring rolled Moxley over. The fat detective had a bloody wound in his flank. Neiring ripped off the sleeve of his uniform and pressed the fabric against Moxley's wound.

"It's all right," said Moxley. "It's in and out. I don't think it went deep enough to hit anything important."

"You saved my life," said Neiring. He looked up at Peyton, looming over them both. "And *he* saved both of us."

"You really owe me lunch now," said Moxley, muttering.

"VanClef is in the warehouse across the street," Neiring told Peyton. "We tracked him thanks to a radiolocator in his bloodstream. We came to arrest him. We . . . we really weren't looking for you anymore, Peyton. Mox wasn't kidding when he said it was bad luck."

"Why?" Peyton asked.

"Because we both know what you're trying to do," said Neiring. "VanClef has been disavowed by the government. Go get him, Peyton. Get your daughter back."

"What will you do?"

"We'll let you go," Neiring promised. "If you're gone, somehow the dust can settle. I'm not sure how yet. But we'll manage it. Leave Hongkongtown. Live your life. Let things get back to their crazy version of normal around here."

"Why would you do this for me?" Peyton asked.

"I believe in the law," said Neiring. "But I believe in what's right, too."

Peyton stood. The shooting was over. Montauk and Loran were scouting the far end of the alley, surrounded by corpses.

"Would you really have killed Montauk's friend?" Peyton asked Moxley.

"Maybe if I had a power cell for the stun gun," said Moxley. Something in his face was . . . off. Peyton looked at him carefully.

"Is it your wound?" Peyton asked. "Are you—?"

"I'll be fine," said Mox. "Just get your little girl. I'll pretend I never heard of you."

"Why?" Peyton asked again.

"I had a family," Moxley said. "Once."

Peyton nodded. He turned and, flanked by Loran and Montauk, left the alley without another word.

Loose Ends

"You think you're very clever, don't you, Annika?" VanClef demanded. On the floor by his boot was a fistful of wiring, which he had ripped from the climate control computer in the back of the cargo truck. "I have to admit, I would not have considered the electronics in a climate control system to be a suitable broadcast exploit. It didn't occur to me that a mechanism so simple could be made to respond that way."

"I could show you how," said Annika.

She sat handcuffed to a chair in the middle of the vast, empty warehouse. The truck was parked nearby. On another chair, positioned opposite her, VanClef sat, rubbing his silver pistol with a polishing cloth, checking the weapon's magazine and the rounds inside it.

"That's not necessary," said VanClef.

The only other object in the warehouse was an enormous crate. To Annika it looked like a coffin. It was big enough that Daddy could have walked inside, if he wanted and the lid was off. She didn't like that thought.

"You do realize that having your father come here is precisely what I wanted?" VanClef told her. "Project Violet must be sanitized. That means purging any evidence of it. Your father, regrettably, is evidence."

"If you want Daddy to come here, why did you smash the

computer so I couldn't make watches appear?"

"Because you're ruining my timing," said VanClef. "My men weren't ready. I hate having to rush them into the field without proper planning."

"It doesn't matter," said Annika. "The people you sent out to kill Daddy won't come back."

"My dear," said VanClef, "these are highly trained government operatives. What's more, they're smart enough to be loyal to *me* before Intelligence. Your father is no match for trained agents with laser-guided smart carbines."'

"My Daddy is the biggest, strongest man there is."

"Your father is a *side effect*," said VanClef. "Haven't you figured that out yet? Project Violet's purpose was to create super-intelligent children. Children like you and the other girls. We were never funded to create bag-job monstrosities like Ian Peyton."

"Daddy is not a side effect!" Annika told him.

"Of course he is," said VanClef. "The process of rebalancing and enhancing the endocrine system, introducing the genetic markers and manipulations we require . . . it is a very complicated science. In order to make the DNA sample viable, it requires an almost super-human donor. The implants we grafted to Peyton's systems made him as he is today, but we didn't do that for him. It was an ancillary effect, a collateral result of the endocrine manipulation itself. We simply wanted his DNA to produce *you*."

"That's why being pregnant killed my mother," said Annika.

"You've guessed that, have you?" said VanClef. "Yes. Regrettably, the mortality rate among surrogate mothers was one hundred percent. Their bodies simply could not withstand the strain."

"You're a very bad man," said Annika.

"That's a meaningless concept," said VanClef. "I'm an

intelligent man, doing what I was trained to do. I'm trying to better all of humanity, Annika. You and your . . . your *siblings*, if you'll allow me to misuse the word for convenience, will be the key to a new class of super-computing soldiers. Imagine what we can accomplish if we are able to operate unfettered by electronic hardware. Thousands, millions of computations carried out within the magnificent human brain alone. The ability to integrate concepts, to see patterns in world events. Why, one day, your genetic descendants could be a master race, an elite ruling class."

"You're not going to find the other girls," said Annika. "We're already smarter than you think we are."

"I found *you*, didn't I?" said VanClef. "To be honest, the only reason you took priority was because of your father's activities. I couldn't risk him bringing undue attention to the Project. As it is, I will be lucky to survive this. It's going to take all of my diplomatic abilities to get back in the good graces of Intelligence. I've strayed a bit far afield . . . but they'll forgive me if I can present them with you, at least a few of your sisters, and a clean slate with no loose ends. That's why we're waiting here now. You're bait. I'm waiting for your father and, when he arrives, I'm going to tie up the loose end he represents."

"How many Daddies are there?" Annika asked.

"There *were* three others," said VanClef. "I used them to take down your father. Unfortunately, they didn't work together as I'd hoped. Big Bill was always a disappointment to me. If he had been successful, I could have used him to move the Project forward. But he was unstable. Narcissistic Personality Disorder, among many other issues."

"So Daddy is the father of all the girls."

"No," said VanClef. "With only a single, viable DNA sample from one donor, I used a DNA sequencer to create unrelated variations. Endless genetic possibilities resulted from a single batch. Your father is, technically, the father of all the girls, but only on paper. In reality, you are his only genetically traceable offspring. At best, the other girls are very distant cousins. I will collect those girls I can. The others I will eliminate."

"Your dead men are 'loose ends,'" said Annika. "Couldn't you hear the shooting outside?"

"No," said VanClef. "Your hearing extends higher in the audible range than an ordinary human being's. It's part of your genetic heritage. Why? Are you claiming you heard a gunfight?"

"I'm not claiming anything," said Annika. "The men you sent are all dead now."

VanClef holstered his gun. He was so angry he didn't even bother snapping the retention strap closed. He wanted a fast draw. He wanted to put a round through Ian Peyton's brain, put a stop to this monster once and for all. Placing two fingers to the transceiver in his ear, he said, "This is VanClef. All units, report."

There was no response.

"I told you," said Annika. "Daddy's coming."

"Shut up!" VanClef told her. "It's a communications error." Again, he said, "This is VanClef. Report! I say again, any available units, report."

"He's going to pull your arms and legs off," said Annika. "He's going to crush your skull."

"Shut up!" shouted VanClef.

The doors to the warehouse, which were locked and bolted, shuddered as something impossibly heavy crashed against them. The very walls of the structure shook under the attack. VanClef's hand fell to his gun belt.

"When you're dead," said Annika, "we're going to go through your pockets."

The doors to the warehouse crashed inward. Metal shrapnel littered the floor. Peyton had shattered the hinges onto which the doors were built.

"*I want my daughter*," he said. His voice was a menacing rumble. "Give her to me and I won't break everything you have."

"Peyton," said VanClef, standing. "I have someone I'd like you to meet. I call him Orrin." He reached out and pulled the lid off the crate. It fell to the floor. The creature that emerged was as big as Peyton.

"Daddy!" Annika called.

The armored, bipedal figure turned to face Peyton. Its head extended on a metal stalk. An array of cameras built into its sloped forehead projected laser targeting lights. Its heavy arms raised. Weapons pods snapped into place, revealing gun barrels and the noses of small missiles. A military designation was spray-painted on the metal monster's flank. The whole thing was a mottled desert brown in color.

"This isn't your fight," said Peyton. "Step aside, whoever you are."

"Orrin is a military Og," said VanClef. "He's not a *who* at all. He's really more of an *it*. And I'm afraid he *does* have to obey every word I speak to him. I am his commanding officer, after all."

"Don't do this," said Peyton to VanClef. "Just give me my daughter."

"Orrin," said VanClef, "kill this man."

The military Og began marching toward him. Peyton lowered his shoulder.

"Well," he said quietly. "Come on, then."

Orrin

Sparks danced across the carapace of the military Og. Loran and Montauk, emerging from behind Peyton, advanced on the weapon, triggering their guns at maximum output, spraying the armored monster with as much firepower as they had. The Og shuddered, settled lower on its hydraulic legs, and spread its arms in a convulsive motion. The act caused its weapons pods to extend fully. Peyton drew in a breath to shout a warning.

The Og pointed its arms and drenched the warehouse in flame.

Peyton was blown backward by the wave of destruction. Micro-missiles, bullets, gouts of fire, and sonic-denial pulses battered him simultaneously, ripping up the floor around him. He saw Loran blown to pieces, its legs and one arm ripped free of its metal torso. Montauk, too, fell under the hail of projectiles.

The sheer power of the attack pushed Peyton across the floor of the warehouse, rolling him, ripping him, puncturing him. He felt countless wounds open on his body, felt shrapnel and bullets and flame cut him and gouge him and scorch him.

Orrin pressed its attack, following him, firing again and again. Peyton watched his body open up. He saw holes blown through his arms, watched furrows dug in his chest. He convulsed with the pain, shook with the attack, felt himself being hammered into the floor. He tasted ash and hot metal.

He realized he could see from only one eye. The other was

swollen shut or gone forever; he did not know which. In the dimming tunnel of his remaining sight, he saw a flash of blonde hair. He saw his daughter. He saw Annika, standing just behind VanClef, clutching her pocket watch in her hand. She was crying. She was calling his name. He couldn't hear her, but he could read her lips.

Daddy. Daddy.

Orrin stood above him now. The racks of its weapons pods were empty. It had expended them all in its sudden blitzkrieg. Its electric guns spun, but no rounds came from their barrels. It had emptied its payload completely. As Peyton watched through his one good eye, the blade of an enormous combat knife snapped into place, attached to Orrin's right forearm. The monster was so close now that Peyton could see flecks of rust on the mottled paint coating the machine's armor plating.

Stand up. Stand up and fight. Stand up for Annika.

He felt his eye start to close. He didn't want to close it. He couldn't help himself. The world, and his pain, began to recede. Stand up. Stand up . . .

"STAND UP!" shouted Montauk in his ear. "STAND UP AND FIGHT!"

Peyton's eye snapped open. He rolled aside just as the blade of Orrin's knife slammed into the floor between his face and Montauk's. The badly damaged Og rolled in one direction while Peyton went the other. Peyton caught a glimpse of his friend: Montauk had both arms, but its legs were gone. It was dragging itself along using only its upper limbs.

Peyton staggered to his feet.

The military Og advanced, thrusting with its knife. Peyton dodged the blade, felt it cut him down to the ribs on his right side, the side he couldn't see. He grabbed the metal arm and, with all his remaining strength, *squeezed.*

The armor was too strong to give . . . but the wrist joint was not. Peyton crushed it, pulled it free, and threw the severed hand far away. Orrin tried to counter by slashing Peyton open, but Peyton still had the limb. He drove it into the floor, so deeply that the blade lodged fast. Then he let himself fall to the floor and rammed both booted feet into Orrin's knee joints, causing the top-heavy Og to lose balance and fall sideways.

The combination of Peyton's weight and the Og's own mass snapped the blade off, ripped it free of the floor, and sent it spinning across the room. The soldier Og simply rolled out of its fall and came up on its feet again, the fingers of its remaining hand held rigid like a spear. It again began to advance on Peyton.

It did not see Montauk crawling behind it. The damaged Og was dragging Loran. As Peyton watched, Montauk peeled back a layer of metal foil over an opening in Loran's chest, reached inside, and pulled out a pair of heavy cables. The Og snapped the cables apart in its pincers. When it drew one severed end against another, sparks flew.

Power. Loran had a power source in its chest.

If you're an Og, well, let's say your pal here might not walk away from the experience.

Montauk beckoned, holding up the spitting, sparking wires.

The distance was too great. Montauk could not reach more than half a meter above the floor in his current state. Peyton knew at once what Montauk was asking of him.

The military Og lunged for him.

Peyton balled his fists and started boxing. He could feel his knuckles breaking under the power of the strikes, could feel the skin flaying from his fingers, could feel the armored carapace giving under his jackhammer advance. Orrin shook left and right as Peyton focused on varying his targets, pushing the Og this way and that, trying to overwhelm whatever governed its equilibrium. It was working. He was pushing it back.

What came next would be bad.

He judged the distance very carefully. This was difficult to do, with his depth perception gone, but the warehouse floor was tiled. Each square was about the size of his foot. He counted tiles, using them as a grid, waiting until Montauk was in position.

Peyton dropped to his knees, feeling something break in his kneecap. He ignored the pain, grabbed Orrin's knee joints, and pulled with all his might.

The military Og toppled to the floor. Montauk struck, jamming the wires from Loran's chest into the junction of Orrin's tiny metal skull and the neck stalk that supported it.

An electric arc traveled across Orrin's chest. The military Og convulsed, smoked, shrieked once in a mechanical death howl. Then it was still. Montauk collapsed next to it, trembling slightly, still holding the wires. The smell of burning insulation and roasted human flesh filled the air.

"Amazing," said VanClef, walking over to inspect the dead Ogs. "I've never seen such loyalty in an Og before. Not to anyone human, at least."

"He was more human than you," said Peyton, swaying on his feet.

VanClef frowned and shot Peyton in the face.

The Best Father

Peyton spat one of his own teeth onto the tiled floor. He reached up with one aching hand and probed the wound in his cheek. The hole in his face would close. The tooth would grow back, although very slowly. He had learned that lesson in prison. He felt himself slump back to the floor.

He tried to get up. He couldn't. He simply didn't have anything more to give. VanClef came to stand over him.

"You poor, deluded bag of flesh," said VanClef. He held his pistol loosely in his hand, as if he had forgotten it. "Did you really believe you could do it? Fight your way past everything I could throw at you, kill me, take your daughter back? I think you did. I don't remember you being so deluded, Peyton. But then, it *has* been a long time."

"I don't know you," said Peyton from the floor. His arms were so heavy. So very heavy.

"No," said VanClef. "I forget that I observed you from behind one-way glass. Believe me, Peyton, I regret not simply ending your life, or placing you immediately in cold storage, once you delivered your sample. But your prison sentence made that quite impossible. As much power as Intelligence has, its power is nothing compared to the almighty bureaucracy. It was easier to let you rot in that place, even after you put yourself on death row. Why couldn't you have just done us all a favor and gone through with it?"

"My daughter," said Peyton. "She wasn't supposed to exist. I wouldn't know. But there was an error."

"You . . . you still haven't figured it out, have you?" VanClef said. "I had to make quite a show of my ignorance for the others on my staff. If any of them had suspected just *how* brilliant your daughter and her cousins are, there might have been a panic. Even your daughter thinks I'm a moron. I've known all along just how brilliant the children have become. If I hadn't, I would hardly be fit to run Project Violet."

"Figured it out . . . ?" Peyton asked. His voice was a whisper.

"The computer 'error,' Peyton," said VanClef. "*She* programmed it. She made it happen. She and the others were digging around our computer system for weeks before we discovered them and tried to shut them out. By then it was too late. Some of them escaped. The others locked themselves in and reprogrammed the defenses. It was all we could do to keep them contained while I kept my staff believing it was a series of malfunctions."

"She's . . . smarter than you," said Peyton.

"Of *course* she's smarter than me," said VanClef. "She's smarter than *everyone*, you fool. I had hoped that through brain analysis, we could learn how their minds work. Selective breeding and the cultivation of a perfect genetic sample through endocrine rebalance will only take us so far. I have to unlock the mystery of *why* their minds operate as they do. For that I need at least one subject. Your daughter will do for a start. If I can show Intelligence real results, they will reinstate Violet and I can stop looking over my shoulder."

"Annika . . . Annika . . . wanted me . . . to find her."

"You don't look well, Peyton," said VanClef. "But yes. That's what I said. Peyton, you don't realize this, but she's been using you from the start. You think targeting child molesters was *your* idea? You think any of the steps you've taken to this point were done on your initiative? Think about that, Peyton. Try very hard. When have you *ever* in your life shown initiative? You're a concrete thinker, Peyton. You aren't creative. You don't *imagine*. It's why you turned to violence as a profession, and why you ended up in prison in the first place."

"No—"

"Yes," said VanClef. "At every turn, she told you what you needed to hear, led you in the directions she needed you to go, in order to accomplish her aims. You completed the plan to free the girls from my 'school.' You targeted a class of criminals that she and her counterparts find particularly upsetting—and specifically a threat to them. You think *you're* protecting *her*? You've been taking your cues from her for weeks. That's what she *does*, Peyton. That's how she's designed. Hers is the kind of mind that will run this world one day. She's the future."

"She's my . . . daughter," said Peyton.

"She doesn't need you anymore, Peyton," said VanClef. "You're nothing but muscle. Or you were. Now what are you? Just so much broken meat."

Peyton managed to look up at VanClef with his good eye. What he saw made him smile. He started to laugh. Each time he laughed it made his ribs grind together. The pain was extraordinary.

"Good-bye, Peyton," said VanClef. He extended his pistol. "I may have to shoot you in the head a few times to kill you. But I think we'll work it out eventually." When Peyton continued to laugh, VanClef scowled. "*What?*" he said. "What is it?"

"She's a genius," said Peyton.

"Yes? And?"

"A genius . . . who knows how . . . to use a watch fob . . . to pick a handcuff lock," he gasped.

Annika, holding the military Og's broken combat knife, slashed VanClef across the back of his thighs. The Intelligence agent screamed and toppled, his hamstrings cut, his legs useless. The chromed pistol flew from his fingers and landed on the floor out of reach.

"Annika," whispered Peyton.

She came to kneel by his side. He felt her blonde hair brush his face.

"What is it, Daddy?" She was crying. Tears fell from her eyes and splashed his cheeks.

"Was . . . Was I a good father?"

"You were the *best* father, Daddy," she said. "You always will be."

"I . . . love you," he said. He closed his eye. He couldn't keep it open anymore. He became very still.

"I love you too, Daddy," she said. She kissed his forehead, stood, and walked to where VanClef's pistol had fallen. Picking this up, she studied it for a moment, made sure the safety was off, and stood before VanClef. The government man was inching across the floor, trying to drag himself, leaving a pair of blood trials from his severed hamstrings.

"You killed him," she said.

VanClef tried to look over his own shoulder as he crawled. "Annika, no," he said. "Don't do this. We need each other. We can help each other. You can be so much more! Do so much more! You just need the right guide."

She aimed the pistol at his forehead, holding it with both hands. "You're mean," she said. "You're the meanest man in the whole world. I hate you. It's wrong to hate. But you killed my daddy and I hate you. And I'm going to fix you."

"Annika!" he said. "Please—"

"You don't have a kind heart," she said. "But I'm going to give you one."

VanClef's eyes grew wide. "No—" he began.

Annika pulled the trigger. She pulled it again. She pulled it a third time.

She kept pulling it until the pistol was empty.

EPILOGUE

Across the Gulf Bridge

The little girl hums softly to herself. She is guiding a powered wheelchair, custom-built, through the busy streets of Hongkongtown. It is a bright, sunny day, with low ozone and a cool breeze coming off the ocean. People are everywhere, coming and going, in cars and pedicabs and hydrogen bikes and ground cars. The city is alive and so is her father.

He is healing, albeit slowly, given the extensive damage done to him. Sight is returning to his bandaged eye. He offers her a gap-toothed smile when she pauses to check on him; she smiles back, proud and happy. She is happy because, for him, the pain and sorrow are over. For once in his life, her father will enjoy the rest, the reward, that he has earned through his blood.

They travel slowly, for there is no rush. Unseen by them both, an army of machine-people is watching: Ogs, disguised as common robots, chart their progress, ready to intervene should any danger befall their champions. They do not know what thc little girl knows: Already, her father's criminal records have been purged forever from every computer network. Any record of her, or him, or the events surrounding the last months, has been permanently deleted. Only in the whispers of the street people of Hongkongtown will their stories be remembered.

The little girl, and those she now calls her sisters, have much work ahead of them. Already, several of their number have gone to different cities throughout the world, positioning themselves for the decades-long strategy they will follow. As they maneuver themselves, they also maneuver in the virtual world. They establish a number of financial accounts, filling them through legal and extralegal means, arranging for the resources they know they will need.

One such account now belongs to the little girl's father, coded to his handprint. It contains more money than he will ever possibly need. Also coded to him is property: He now owns a peaceful island, and a rather extraordinary drinking establishment, in the Keys. There, in the sun, surrounded by pretty girls and a helpful staff that most will believe to be robots, he will convalesce. There, he will live out his natural life, however long that may be. Given his ability to regenerate, it may be forever. He has no way of knowing. The little girl promises to visit him.

He asks her once more if she will not change her mind. Could she come to the island with him? But no, this is not her destiny. He knows it; she believes it. He asks because he *must* ask, because no father could resist. But he also knows that she bears a powerful gift, a remarkable destiny. He tells himself that he will watch the news. That he will look for clues, for signs. That he will smile every time he sees what he thinks is evidence of his little girl and her sisters ruling the world.

She has made a gift to him of the gold pocket watch she carries. Inside the watch, she has placed, very carefully, her own picture. He is too big for wristwatches, she has told him; a pocket watch is appropriate for him. It was for this reason that she chose it. It seems like so long ago that they entered the watch shop together. *Think of me whenever you look at the watch*, she has told him. *It will make me happy, knowing you have something of mine with you all the time*.

He does not know it, but a surprise waits for him on the train that will carry him across the Gulf Bridge and to the Keys. This surprise is his friend, Montauk, an Augment. Montauk has undergone extensive repairs to both mechanical and biological systems. Montauk will enjoy relaxing in the peace and quiet as much as the little girl's father. Montauk, too, needs time to heal, for the Og's loss is great. Their mutual friend Loran was Montauk's son, Samuel, only recently become an Og.

It is Montauk's belief that its son died fighting for Augment rights. This dream of equality, this dream of the future, is one that Montauk shares with the little girl. One day, the people of Northam will let go of class distinctions, will release their insistence on human percentages. Montauk believes the little girl and her sisters can make this dream a reality. From this belief, Montauk draws comfort. In this belief, Montauk may one day find satisfaction. This will take time. Montauk will live out its days feeling the loss of Samuel, of Loran.

Knowing it will help both Og and man, the little girl relishes the thought of her father's reunion with Montauk. She will miss them both. She has a great deal of work to do, however, and if her father remains, they will remain each other's point of vulnerability. Hard choices and difficult politics await the little girl. She cannot have enemies—enemies she has not yet even made—using her father against her or threatening him with her harm. She loves her father. Like all children who love their parents, she wants him to be safe, to live in peace, and to be happy.

She is not sure why she is crying. Her father, too, is crying, but she understands this: He loves her with all his heart, and he will miss her. He will be thinking about her, he says, until she comes to visit him. And he hopes she will come soon and often. She promises him that she will do what she can.

As the wheelchair hums along, she passes a news kiosk. There are ozone warnings. There is talk of the '36 Olympics. There is continuing coverage of what is now called The Hospital Bombing. There is news of a series of recent traffic accidents, officially unexplained. A government employee named Stevens has been killed in a freak accident involving a malfunctioning garbage robot. It has been two weeks since a warehouse in the Redlight burned down mysteriously. In that time, several persons on the public sex offender registry have been found dead, all of them victims of apparent in-home accidents.

Hongkongtown's pedophiles, the little girl suspects, will continue to die mysteriously for years to come.

As they walk to the train station, they pass a block of flats near the freight yards. Children play here. These are the children of the dock workers, playing in the mid-morning sun. There are boys and girls. Many of them skip pairs of rope. The little girl likes seeing them skip rope, likes hearing the rhymes they speak as they weave in and out of the double strands:

Everyone says it can follow you anywhere.
Everyone says that it never gets tired.
Everyone says it won't go in small spaces.
Everyone says it needs darkness to hide.

Everyone says that it crushes your skull.
Everyone says that it follows The List.
Everyone says it may wait in your home.
Everyone says that you'll never be missed.

Everyone says it's already too late for you.
Everyone says that it puts out your eyes.

Everyone says there is no hiding place for you.

Everyone picked by the little girl dies.

The little girl's father is now a street legend. For years, the dregs of Hongkongtown's criminals, the worst men and women in the worst neighborhoods of the city, the Sleepers and the creepers and the thieves and the rapists, will tell a story amongst themselves. They will speak in hushed tones of the monster, the creature that stalks the streets of their city, the creature that knows neither pity nor mercy . . .

. . . and her father.

THE END

AFTERWORD

The book you've just read started with a single short story and originally ran under the title "4104." The novel that resulted, *Monsters*, originally began with a short story that I've since removed (and reprinted at the end of this Afterword). That's because, in preparing the collection of "4104" serials, I decided to remove the short story that inspired the rest of it. I think the resulting novel is more powerful because it simply drops the reader into the reality of Annika and Peyton's world. In so doing it forces you to wonder how and why this pair is the way they are. The hints and the explanations to and of their backstories are all still there. We, the readers, simply don't see what started the adventure. We instead hear about it in passing, as Peyton and Annika get on with the business of living their lives.

Readers of my "Augment" fiction will note that this book takes place in the same world, but far removed from the events of *Augment: Human Services* and the stories that follow it. I like the idea of interlocking fiction, yes, but there is also the practical matter of being able to tell the story without reinventing an entirely different set of conventions for everything from medical care to weaponry.

After writing the short story that started this tale, I wrote a few more episodes without a real plan in mind. I wanted to explore the world in which Peyton and Annika lived. I wanted to know more about them. As I kept going, I realized I was writing what would have to be a loosely connected serial novel. Eventually, I wrote out the plot arc and based it on fifty total episodes, forty-nine of which now make up *Monsters.*

If *Monsters* has a running theme apart from a father's devotion to his child, it is the murdering of child molesters. I did not set out, originally to write a book of this type (unlike, say, Tim Green's *The Fifth Angel*, a novel whose plot explicitly concerns a vigilante who executes sex offenders). As I set up Hongkongtown as a kind of libertarian dystopia, with much less law and control than Central City in *Augment: Human Services*, it made sense to me that this was the type of locale that would attract and concentrate sex offenders.

We already take registries of such creatures for granted, and this gave Peyton and Annika a means of moving around as fugitives—by preying on this plentiful demographic. As I kept writing, though, I realized why the topic struck such a chord: Everyone, on some level, understands that if our children have a natural enemy, it is these mentally sick, incurable monsters who live among us and seek to victimize them. To the molester, harm to a child is a primary good, something that gratifies for its own sake. Already, we tolerate in our presence far too many of these people, who (in my opinion) should either be gathered into camps permanently and kept away from society, or simply killed. Peyton, in fiction, gives us the release we all want but cannot have in real life. We *want* to see these creatures destroyed. We *want* to see them punished, yes, but more than that, we simply want our children to be safe.

That's where the inspiration for the title, *Monsters*, comes from. Peyton is a monster in the most physical sense. The creatures he preys on—the pedophiles and the operatives of the government who become his antagonists—are figurative monsters. Annika herself, we learn, is the greatest monster of them all, because she is directing Peyton's actions with an almost sociopathic detachment. The only time we really see that detachment broken is when she takes up a pistol in the name of vengeance for her father.

My original story, "4104," was inspired by the South Korean movie *The Man from Nowhere*. That film is about a former special forces operative whose pregnant wife is killed during an attempt to assassinate him. Despondent and suicidal, he all but exiles himself from life, taking work in a pawnshop. There, he befriends a little girl, the daughter of a local prostitute. When the prostitute gets mixed up with drug dealers and the girl is kidnapped, our hero moves heaven and earth to rescue her.

I'm going to spoil the movie for you. The film's climax is a bloody gun- and knife-fight in which the protagonist, Cha Tae-sik, battles through a small army of thugs. At this point, he believes the girl is dead. He has nothing now but vengeance, and he proves so effective that the drug dealers' alpha-thug, Ramrowan, wants nothing more in the world than to fight him to see who is better. The two engage in a bloody knife fight and Ramrowan is killed. After dispatching the last of the drug lords, Cha Tae-sik is about to put a bullet in his own brain when the little girl turns up, alive.

Apart from being a very emotionally moving film (rare in an action movie), *The Man from Nowhere* inspired me because I liked the idea of a father figure who would stop at nothing, absolutely nothing, to rescue his daughter. The righteousness of a cause often confers near-superhuman powers on the believer, at least in fiction. Like a woman lifting a car off her baby, a man empowered by his love for his little girl can do almost anything.

The result of pondering this idea was the creature, the man, the *father*, that is Ian Peyton—immensely strong, artificially large, and nearly indestructible. He is a simple man who doesn't understand all of his daughter's complexities, nor even, really, the world in which the two find themselves. He knows only that he loves her and he will do what he can to protect her—even if she is using him as a means to an end. That's fatherhood. That's a father's love.

That's *Monsters*.

Phil Elmore
August, 2014

4104

Richards looked up in horror. "Forty-one oh four," he said. "FORTY-ONE OH FOUR!"

The guards' heads snapped up. At the gallows, Peyton's chin rose from his chest. His eyes bored into the computer kiosk. Richards dove for the switch, the red lever that would release the floor beneath the prisoner and send Peyton to his death. He slammed his palm down.

It was a simple log. It should have showed nothing. Reviewing the observers was standard procedure. Why had the computer flagged it?

Peyton's eyes narrowed. His massive shoulders flexed. The manacles securing his wrists *popped* like a cheap rivet. The enormous man had time to fix Richards with a glare. Then he fell, so slow, hanging and then falling through the square of empty space—

"Seal the gallery!" ordered Richards. "Blast doors. Give me the blast doors!"

Something wriggled at the edge of the empty square. Richards caught it, turned to it, paled. Fingers. Peyton's fingers. They were white with exertion.

The big man pulled himself up from the edge of the opening, landing heavily on prison-issue boots. He was flushed now. That was bad. The surgically implanted hormone sacs in his body would be shunting adrenaline, cortisol, and half a dozen other artificial compounds through his muscles. Painkillers. Stimulants. A chemical cocktail designed to make a mortal man a wrecking machine. Small wonder it was a capital crime.

"Forty-one oh four," said Peyton. "That's impossible."

"It *is* impossible!" Richards lied. "We checked! We checked just as you asked!"

"We had a bargain," said Peyton. Around him, all four guards drew their batons and charged them. On the other side of the gallery, two men with assault rifles waited. Richards dared a look at the window. The blast shield was lowering slowly into place, darkening the mirrored surface inch by inch.

"I looked, I tell you," said Richards. "The computer turned up a random datum at the last possible moment. It can't mean—"

"But it does," said Peyton. "You were going to let me do it. Let me die quietly."

"But that's what you *wanted*!"

"It hurts," said Peyton, flexing his outsized fingers. "It hurts all the time. But it doesn't hurt so much that I would leave without—"

"NOW!" Richards ordered.

The guards struck. Peyton shrugged off the first blow. He endured the second. He suffered the third.

He grabbed the fourth.

Electricity crackled up the length of his arm as he crushed the baton in his fist. The discharge shocked the operator, dropping him to the floor. The guard was dead before he got there; none of them were properly grounded. Peyton's blackened hand was already curling into a fist when the second man got in his way. The blow crushed vertebrae in the guard's neck. He folded.

Fire leapt up the front of Peyton's shirt. He ignored it, grabbed the other two guards, pulled them close. The fire kissed them and enveloped them. Peyton held them, burning, to the coals of his chest until they shrieked for mercy. Then he snapped their necks and dropped them to the floor.

Peyton smoldered. Richards was still clawing at the security compartment of his kiosk. Peyton relieved him of the task. He grabbed Richards' hand, crushed it, folded it beneath the man.

The arm cracked and split. Peyton never blinked.

"We had a bargain," whispered Richards.

"Which you broke, Warden," said the prisoner. He held Richards' skull in his hands until it, too, cracked. The kiosk was harder to break. He broke it. The blast shield lifted. He used Richards one more time, throwing the body through the gallery mirror. The safety glass shattered on the third try.

The body drew the bullets of the men inside. Peyton hurried after it. He smashed the first man with his knee, took the fallen rifle, and beat the second man with the gun. It did not take long. The plastic rifle broke, but not too soon.

There were six people in the gallery. Two of them screamed. Peyton examined them all.

Too old. Too old. Nothing familiar. A reporter. A detective, unarmed.

And a little girl.

"I'm twelve," she said. "I'm Annika." She smiled.

Peyton smiled. He held out his hand. It was bloody. He took it back. He offered his arm.

She took that. He hugged her.

"We're leaving," he said.

"Won't they stop you?" said Annika.

"I won't let them," said Peyton. "I only agreed to today because they said you were dead."

"I'm not," said Annika.

"No," said Peyton. "You're not."

"You smell funny," said Annika. She wrinkled her nose.

"I do," said Peyton. "A little."

They left. On the computer kiosk above the broken body of Warden Richards, the screen still glowed.

"*4104*," it said. "*Next of Kin found (Dependent).*"

About the Author

Phil Elmore is the senior editor of League Entertainment, an intellectual property development firm based in Florida. The author of over two dozen commercially published action and science fiction novels, Elmore lives and works in New York. He can be reached through his website, PhilElmore.com.

www.ingramcontent.com/pod-product-compliance
Lightning Source LLC
Chambersburg PA
CBHW061603170626
46811CB00001B/298